SON
of a gun

Cover design by the incomparable Hang Le:
http://www.byhangle.com

Cover photographed by and copyright owned by: Wander Aguiar Photography
www.wanderbookclub.com

Editing and formatting by: Elaine York, Allusion Publishing
http://www.allusionpublishing.com/

Copy editing by: Bethany Salminen, Bethany Edits
www.bethanyedits.net

JAY CROWNOVER

this one is for my people.

The folks who held my hand this whole year while Jay was on a break and Jen dealt with a lot of shit. I have a very small inner circle I rely on. This extended, very tense, and traumatic hiatus made me love and appreciate them even more. I wouldn't have made it through the year without them. I probably would've never managed to write this book and end my agonizing battle with writer's block without them, as well.

This is a crossover novel between the second generation of the Marked Men and the second generation of The Point. It can be read as a standalone, but for a full reading experience, the author recommends reading the previous Forever Marked books, as well as Avenged and Respect from The Point series.

author's NOTE

Hi!

Long time no read.

I'm so excited you're here.

I'm going to leave a short and sweet author's note at the front of the book and a longer one at the back.

If you're a new reader, I want to reassure you that you can read *Son of a Gun* as a standalone. Even though it's a crossover of the second generations from *The Marked Men* and *The Point* series, you don't have to be familiar with either to enjoy this book.

I worked ridiculously hard to make sure it could stand independently and still feel like a *Forever Marked* novel.

However, I need to drop a warning to those unfamiliar with The Point. *The Point* series is a darker side of my writing, and parts of this story reflect that. The Point is a made-up place. (It's my FAVORITE place!) Think Detroit, Chicago, Oakland, Philadelphia, and New York mixed with Gotham and Frank Miller's *Sin City* all mashed into one location. Since it has shipping docks, a train system, the ocean and mountains, and a big wealth disparity, by default, it must be located somewhere in California. I always pictured the Bay Area for some reason.

I hope you can go in with an open mind and no expectations. I hope you can envision my version of the worst side of the tracks there ever was. In the baddest bad part of town, really, really bad boys thrive.

I've always wanted to mash my two most popular series together. In fact, when I introduced Campbell at the end of *Respect*, it was with the sole intention of bringing him into the second generation of *The Marked Men* series if I ever decided to write about the kids.

I had plans for him all along!

If you've read all my books, this story will be a delight for you.

If you haven't, I will leave a list of all the characters and their books in the end author's note, so you can find them if you're interested.

I had an absolute blast writing this story. It sparked genuine joy and excitement whenever I sat down to work.

I hope you have as much fun with Daire and Campbell as I did. It's beautiful when my worlds collide.

And just as a reminder, while this book is technically set in the future of the *Marked Men* world, I didn't write it to reflect what the world might look like in twenty-plus years. If things feel modern, and references and idioms are current to the time we're in now, that's on purpose. I wanted to focus on the characters and the two series together, not trying to imagine what phones, cars, and clothes might be in the future. That's a creative choice I'll stand behind day and night.

Oh, since so many have asked: Daire's name is pronounced Dare, like take a dare. I know that's not correct if you're Irish or speak Gaelic! So, just use whichever one you prefer while reading.

Love & Ink,
Jay

MARKED MEN SERIES

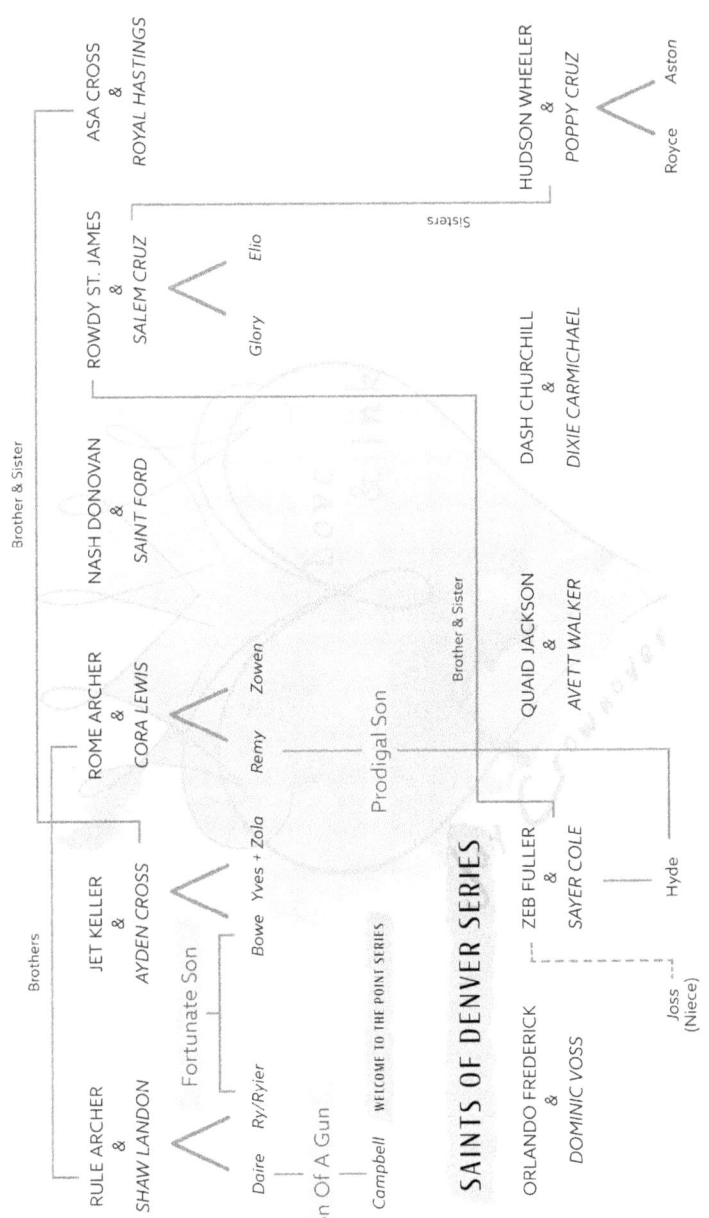

Brothers

Brother & Sister

RULE ARCHER & **SHAW LANDON**
Daire Ry/Ryier

Son Of A Gun

Campbell WELCOME TO THE POINT SERIES

Fortunate Son

JET KELLER & **AYDEN CROSS**
Bowe Yves + Zola

ROME ARCHER & **CORA LEWIS**
Remy Zowen

Prodigal Son

NASH DONOVAN & **SAINT FORD**

ROWDY ST. JAMES & **SALEM CRUZ**
Glory Elio

ASA CROSS & **ROYAL HASTINGS**

Sisters

HUDSON WHEELER & **POPPY CRUZ**
Royce Aston

SAINTS OF DENVER SERIES

ORLANDO FREDERICK & **DOMINIC VOSS**

Joss (Niece)

ZEB FULLER & **SAYER COLE**
Hyde

Brother & Sister

QUAID JACKSON & **AVETT WALKER**

DASH CHURCHILL & **DIXIE CARMICHAEL**

iii

PROLOGUE

"**G**o find the girl and bring her back to her family."

I wasn't a guy who celebrated much of anything, including the holidays. That didn't mean I wanted to spend what was left of Christmas Eve out in the cold, searching for a runaway princess. I sighed and met the unwavering gaze of the effortlessly intimidating man who issued the order.

"She's got a legion of friends and relatives who can brave this blizzard and look for her. They're definitely more concerned about her than I am. Why does it have to be me?"

The man lifted a dark eyebrow and hooked the corners of his mouth up in a grin that sent a jolt of alarm down my spine. Since Benny brought me to Denver and found me a better-than-average-paying job with a place to stay, I pushed the fact that this man was a ruthless killer and reformed criminal to the back of my mind. Benny seemed so domesticated these days; it was easy to forget that he was a very bad man who wasn't used to being questioned or defied. In my world, there was no polished and professional Uncle Benny. Only the version of Benny who had been in and out of jail his entire adult life, and had single-handedly toppled a criminal empire just because he could.

"It has to be you because she's running from the people she loves the most. When she sees you, she's less likely to bolt." His smile shifted from a warning to a hint of pride and affection. "And I know you'll find her faster than anyone else and keep her safe until she's ready to come home." A heavy hand decorated with diamond rings landed on my shoulder and gave it a squeeze. A rough chuckle escaped Benny's scarred throat as he told me, "Besides, when have you ever been able to walk away from the suffering and desperation of others? I haven't met many people in my life who are determined to be heroes. Especially when it's so much more fun to be the villain. You are at the top of the list, Campbell."

Being a bad person was the only way to live a good life when you came from the kind of background Benny and I shared. There was zero time to worry about saving someone else when it took every ounce of will to save yourself over and over again.

However, it wasn't just me who fought daily for survival. My father dragged my five younger siblings into the hell that was my childhood. He forgot all of us around the time we started walking, unless he wanted to use or hurt us. We were nothing more than free labor and government checks to him. Most of us had different mothers who didn't stick around after we were born. The exception was my younger sister with my mom. I had vague recollections of our mother being around when my sister was a baby, and I remembered my father always yelling at her and never hesitating to swing a fist. One day our mom was simply gone. Vanished into nothing. I had nightmares about a rainy night when my father was covered in mud. He stumbled into the tiny shack we called home and tossed a red-stained shovel into the corner. When I was little, I thought the red was rust. Over time, the longer it sat in the corner like a macabre trophy, I understood it was dried blood.

Even if my father didn't kill my mother, and I was simply confused because of the trauma and torture he put me through as a child, I never doubted that he was capable of murder. He only cared about amassing a military-grade arsenal and keeping trespassers off the shithole plot of land that had been in his family for generations. He told me once that the only reason he kept getting women pregnant was so he had plenty of offspring to protect his garbage legacy.

I hated the man to the deepest depths of my soul. But I loved my siblings.

Benny was correct. I'd never been able to walk away when someone seemed to need me. Not that I expected the haughty blonde princess was one of those people. In fact, she'd spent the entirety of our short acquaintance making it known she would like nothing more than for me to drop dead. The dislike was mutual. I worked as a live-in childcare provider for a family friend of Benny's, and I didn't enjoy her constantly looking over my shoulder. She didn't like having a stranger in her kingdom. Especially one who had no intentions of bowing down to her.

I sighed and shook loose from the hold Benny had on my shoulder. I dragged a hand down my face and looked out one of the big windows, decorated with white Christmas lights.

I'd planned to go home for Christmas, but the baby I was brought to Denver to care for had suddenly become very ill. It was hit or miss if she would make it to her first Christmas, and I couldn't disappear on the single dad who had been very good to me and had given me a shot when no one else would hire me.

Now, I was watching a blizzard stack snow outside as the temperature steadily dropped. The little girl was home safe and sound with her daddy, and I was getting dragged into a mess I wanted nothing to do with, by a man I knew I couldn't say 'no' to.

"Fine. I'll find her and bring her home." My tone let it be known that I was not happy with the task.

Benny chuckled again and took a step backward. I instantly felt like a heavy pressure was lifted off me. If he could make someone he considered one of his own feel that type of oppression, I felt a twinge of remorse for his enemies.

"Don't drag her home kicking and screaming. Convince her this is where she belongs. I don't know a soul more loyal to family than you, Campbell. That girl has good people who care about her, and she's going to make a big mistake if she pushes them all away. It might do her a bit of good to see what the world looks like when you turn your back on the people who matter the most."

It was my turn to lift my eyebrows in disbelief. "You want me to put the fear of God into her and scare her back to Denver?"

That sounded easier than using logic on the stubborn, strong-willed young woman. More fun too.

Benny shook his head. "No. I want you to make her *want* to be back home. How you accomplish that is up to you. You might want to keep in mind that you'll cross paths with her whole family in the future, so if you burn that bridge, you better have enough fire to keep you warm when everyone ices you out. I'd think long and hard about how difficult it was for you to find steady work that wasn't tied to your past. This is your shot to start over, if that's really what you want."

If anyone else handed out that advice, I'd blow it off. But Benny got a second chance and practically rose from the dead. He built a life far away from crime and corruption, and now he only did the wrong things for the right people. It was the kind of life I never dared dream I could have.

I blew out a frustrated breath and took out my phone. When Hyde Bishop-Fuller hired me to watch his daughter, he also asked Daire Archer to keep an eye on me. She was the babysitter's babysitter. I thought the pretty blonde was a nuisance—a stuck-up know-it-all who had a knack for getting under my skin. I didn't like being watched and judged. Especially not by someone barely out of their teens who came from the kind of privilege I would never understand.

Daire had secretly dropped Bluetooth-tracking tags in all the baby stuff I hauled around so she could find my location at any given moment, and it took me a minute to find them. I was irritated enough that I pulled one out of the diaper bag, reset it, and stashed it in her purse. I figured she'd already found it since the switch was weeks ago, but when I looked up her location on the corresponding app, I was surprised to see that Daire's little blinking dot was outside Denver. It was also stationary, which was concerning considering the weather over the holidays. Would she be found if she had car trouble this late at night when the roads were mostly deserted?

I didn't want to care, but I had a little sister. If someone left her to fend for herself in the same situation, I would gleefully plot their death and dismemberment.

I waited silently for a few seconds to see if the dot would move, and when it didn't, I looked up at Benny and told him, "I'll do my best."

I got another rough pat on the shoulder as he walked me to the front door of his very normal, nondescript home. The watch on the man's wrist cost as much as the military budget of a small country. There were some trappings from his old persona he could never let go of, and I knew that feeling all too well.

No matter how many opportunities came my way, aboveboard or otherwise, I always felt like that scared, hungry kid, just trying to hold it all together. I never managed to be the hero Benny accused me of wanting to be.

I grabbed my coat and some other winter wear I'd collected during my short stay in Denver. I promised Benny I would keep him updated, then made my way into the frigid Christmas Eve night. The lights from the houses and the cheerful decorations were a stark contrast to my mood, which was so dark it felt like it could swallow all the lights and sound around me.

Daire wasn't the only one who'd run away from home. When I was much younger, I thought my only salvation was to leave the only home I'd ever known. It killed me to leave my brothers and sister behind, but there was no other choice. We were starving. We were sick. We were scared. And I was worried that whatever happened to my mother would happen to one of my siblings next. When I was big enough, my father saw me as a threat; instead of wanting me to take over his homestead, he became paranoid that I was going to take it away from him. But the thought of dying at his hands wasn't what kept me up at night. It was the thought of what would happen to my innocent brothers and sister if I failed to protect them that froze me with fear. My dad was a lunatic, but he wasn't stupid. He quickly figured out the best way to keep me in line was to threaten the kids. I obeyed him to keep them safe. Running away was my only option, before he ripped one of them away as a cruel tool to teach me a lesson.

Fortunately, when I got out from under my father's thumb, I'd run to a place filled with people like Benny. It was a compound and community created to do bad things for the right reasons, and even as a kid, I knew whatever they offered was better than any bleak future my father had planned for me.

I couldn't figure out what sent Daire fleeing into the freezing night when she had such an idyllic life. I couldn't figure out what her deal was. In the time that I'd known her, she was both combative and complacent. She was hard to read.

Daire Archer was very pretty. Almost alarmingly so. It was the kind of pretty that didn't seem like it could be real. No one in the real world looked like that, with white-blonde hair and eyes so vibrantly green they almost glowed. If I hadn't met her mother, who was very much an older, more refined version of Daire, I never would've believed that Daire was naturally that stunning.

She was also smart. I'd heard that she'd skipped out on art school for a year. Daire didn't talk much about her past or future, but when she decided to speak to me, she was always eloquent and thoughtful with her words. I called her a princess and teased her about being a spoiled brat, but she never spoke down to anyone.

She was talented. Daire's whole family was remarkable. There wasn't an Archer who wasn't exemplary in some way. I'd run into most everyone in their entire family at least once since I'd been in Denver, and I had to admit that the Archers were an impressive bunch.

Daire was artistic and creative like her father, while her older brother, Ry, followed in their mother's footsteps and went to medical school.

They were a tight-knit group. From the outside looking in, it was hard to spot any fractures. But what happy home didn't have a flaw or two?

I couldn't imagine what was terrible enough to send a pretty, pampered girl out into the cold and away from her family at Christmas.

Before I attempted to follow the blinking dot while navigating a blizzard, I'd tried to call Daire. It snowed where I was from, but not like this. It took all my concentration to stay in a lane as I crawled along the icy, treacherous roads.

As I got farther away from Denver and higher into the mountains, my tension and irritation rose. Why the hell was Daire trying to cross the Continental Divide in these conditions? If she'd randomly decided to spend Christmas skiing, or in one of the picturesque mountain towns to take cute pictures for social media, I might strangle her when I finally caught up to her. If she made her family worry and forced me to play errand boy for nothing more than aesthetics, I might lose what little cool I'd managed to hang onto since Benny had cornered me.

It took three times as long as it normally would to reach the location of the blinking dot, which hadn't moved for hours. It was officially Christmas morning, but being festive was the last thing on my mind. I pulled into a tiny gas station that was made to look like a building from the Old West. It had a wooden façade and a hand-painted sign, both covered in snow. Christmas lights did their best to shine through the blanket of white, and they reflected dully off the lone car parked in front of the building.

The car was fully immersed in snow, but I could see from the cloud of exhaust that the engine was running. I parked my big, black SUV next to the running car and looked down to see if there was any movement inside. The windows didn't roll down, and a blonde head didn't appear. I had to give Daire credit; she wasn't careless with her safety. I wondered if she'd pulled over to wait out the storm or if she was having car trouble. Either way, it was a good call. Unfortunately, the gas station was closed for the holidays, but the empty parking lot was better than nothing. Someone was bound to drive by eventually.

I rubbed my hands together when I opened the door, and the frigid air hit my skin. I blinked against the cold and watched my breath puff out in a cloud. Before I knocked on the frosty window and scared the shit out of the occupant of the car, I called Daire's number.

The phone rang and rang, shooting me to voicemail after a minute. I frowned as I tucked my phone into my pocket. I stayed on the passenger's side and tapped my knuckles on the window. A thick layer of ice on the glass made the knocking sound sharp.

It took a while for the window to crack down barely an inch. It was just far enough that I could see a pair of wide green eyes staring back at me.

I put my hands in my jacket pockets and lifted my eyebrows as we watched each other silently. Daire looked tired but not particularly alarmed or distraught.

"How did you know where I was?" Her voice was a touch huskier than normal. It could be from crying—she had streaks of makeup on her cheeks that gave her away—or from spending the night in the cold.

I cocked my head to the side and gave her a pointed look. "I returned the tracking tag you so thoughtfully left me."

Her too-pretty face contorted briefly, and her gaze shifted to the designer bag on the seat next to her. It occurred to me that, though she planted the tracker on me, she never must've bothered to look at its location. Otherwise, she would've known I got rid of it weeks ago. It wasn't an outright declaration of trust, but the knowledge made me a smidge less irritated than I was when I left Benny's house.

Daire blinked up at me and rubbed a hand across the tip of her red nose. "I left my phone back at my parents' house. I was pretty sure no one would be able to find me."

That explained why my calls went unanswered. I took a step back and looked at the car. It wasn't cheap. I would bet my last dollar that the car had a built-in GPS tracker in case it got stolen. Daire probably didn't know that, but I'd been around people who boosted cars for a living and never got caught. I'd picked up a thing or two along the way.

Once her family calmed down and realized they had a way to locate Daire, they wouldn't be far behind us.

"Did you break down?" The motor was running, but countless other things could be wrong with her ride.

She shook her head, and her hair, a shade darker than the snow landing on my shoulders, swished around her face.

"I stopped because of the storm. The roads were so bad, and I got a warning on the display that the pass was closed. I decided to wait out the weather until morning."

I looked at the big screen lit up on her dash and saw all sorts of red flags and winter storm warnings. Only us two idiots would be out here chit-chatting instead of at home enjoying a warm beverage and opening some presents.

I sighed heavily and used my now-red, stiff fingers to knock the snow off my shoulders. "Let's get out of here, Princess. I'm not made for this weather."

Daire narrowed her eyes, and a familiar stubborn slant touched her mouth.

"Did you come to take me home?" Her tone let me know the only way that was happening was if I dragged her kicking and screaming off the mountain.

"I did."

She glared at me and started rolling up the window. "I'm not going. Leave me alone, Campbell."

I swore and pulled my fingers back before she could close them in the window. I knocked on the glass again, this time bending down so we could see each other through the ice and glass.

"Open it, or I'll break it." It was a threat made more serious by the abysmal conditions.

Daire weighed her options on the other side of the window before reluctantly rolling it back down.

I scowled at her and told her, "I didn't say I was taking you to *your* home, did I?" She stared at me blankly until I continued, "If your parents bought you this car, I can almost guarantee they're on their way to this gas station as we speak. If you're determined to run away from home, I will help you." I gave her a bored look. "Because you're clearly very bad at it."

I wasn't ever going to be the hero who went out of his way to save the princess. Just like Benny said, while I'd always wanted to be one, I never quite managed to pull it off. I was a pretty terrible guy through and through, and I could corrupt the princess. That was a mission I would never fail.

chapter ONE

Daire

I pulled on the handmade knit beanie and scarf Campbell tossed in my lap as soon as the SUV doors were closed. The heater was going full blast. I sighed as warmth slowly returned to my frozen fingers and toes. I couldn't leave my engine running full time when I'd pulled over to wait out the storm. I was too afraid of draining the last of the gas and running out of power. I was also worried about having a panic attack while I sat in the cold car and cried for hours. I didn't need anything that might make me even loopier and more irrational. My mind was already a mess, and my decision-making skills seemed to have deep-dived into the toilet as of late.

I stroked the soft fabric wrapped around my face and looked sideways at the stern, silent man in the driver's seat. Campbell was the last person on earth I expected to appear in the middle of the blizzard. We weren't friends. We didn't get along. He acted like he hated me. And yet, he was the one who appeared to save me from myself when I needed that the most.

I was secretly relieved to see him. Only because it was him.

I don't know that my conscience would've allowed me to accept help if my older brother or one of my parents had shown up as my savior in the snow. I already felt like garbage because I knew I had ruined everyone's Christmas by disappearing without a word. I was sure my family was in full-on panic mode because I left my phone behind and didn't leave any information about my hurried escape into the blizzard.

An escape it really was.

An escape from the overwhelming amount of love and forgiveness I felt from everyone. An escape from the understanding and kindness I didn't deserve. An escape from the guilt lodged so deep in my heart that felt like it could kill me. I wanted to run away from all the negative feelings that were crushing me under their weight.

My family and loved ones wanted to celebrate, but I didn't feel festive when everyone was cheering on each other's accomplishments and milestones. Being around so many people who looked at me like I had never done wrong felt suffocating. I didn't plan to run away. But as soon as I had my keys in my hand and my feet hit the gathering snow, I finally felt like I could breathe. I kept moving forward and away from everyone...until the nasty weather forced me to stop.

I knew better than to drive into the mountains in a storm. I knew everyone in my life would instantly panic and send out a search party once they realized I was gone. I knew I was being reckless and thoughtless, but none of that mattered in the moment. The farther away

SON *of a gun*

I got from the city lights of Denver, the less it felt like a cinder block was sitting on my chest.

But I didn't know how and why Campbell had suddenly became part of my ill-conceived escape plan.

"This scarf is so soft. It's nice and cozy. Did someone make it for you?" The silence in the SUV was deafening. I felt I had to say something.

It wasn't like the atmosphere between us was ever amicable. And now I'd somehow forced him to track me down in a snow squall. I cringed inwardly when I realized he was missing Christmas, and whatever plans he had were ruined in order to rescue me. Campbell made it no secret that he thought I was spoiled and selfish. This little stunt was not going to improve his opinion of me.

Dark eyes cut in my direction and lingered on my fingers, where they were playing with the end of the scarf.

Campbell sighed and said, "My younger sister gave it to me last year for Christmas. She made a whole set when I told her I was coming to Colorado. She made me promise I would wear it when it got cold."

I tucked my face deeper into the soft fabric and blinked at him in surprise. I didn't know much about Campbell, even though I'd followed him around like a guard dog for several months.

He was the kind of guy who came with a whole arsenal of red flags. He was prickly as a porcupine and probably the most impatient person I'd ever met. He was abrupt and even harsh when he spoke to me. However, the opposite was true when he cared for Hollyn. It never ceased to amaze me that a guy who looked as rough and tough as Campbell could be so soft and gentle with an infant. He was amazing with the little girl. I was sure he was her favorite human next to her father, even though my cousin had recently stepped in to play mom in the little girl's life.

"I didn't know you had a younger sister."

I knew he was responsible for several younger siblings, so Hyde eventually hired him as a live-in childcare provider. And because Hyde's Uncle Benny highly recommended him. Uncle Benny didn't put his weight behind anyone, so praise from him was better than a mile-long list of recommendations in Hyde's eyes.

His sense of brotherly responsibility might explain why he took it upon himself to come and get me. It offered no insight into why he wasn't dragging me back home, though. I knew that option would be easiest for both of us. Fortunately for me, Campbell never struck me as the kind of guy who took the easy way out of a tough situation.

His auburn eyebrows lifted, and his sharp features relaxed into a hint of a grin. "Delta's around your age. She just started college this year. She moved to Boston for school, so I haven't seen her in a while. She's a good kid. Works hard. Doesn't ask for much." He slid me a pointed look from the corner of his eye. He didn't need to tell me he thought I could benefit from being more like her. "I have two younger brothers as well. Delta and I raised them. I planned to go home for Christmas to see everyone before Hollyn got sick. I didn't feel right leaving Hyde and Remy to handle all that alone, since they don't have much experience with infants. A sick baby is one of the scariest things in the world."

Remy was my cousin, and Hyde was her soulmate. She'd been in love with the big, gruff man since he was a quiet, reserved little boy. It took a lot of work for them to get together. I was proud of Remy for conquering her fear about how she might impact Hyde and Hollyn's lives and allowing herself to love them anyway.

"Oh." I didn't know what else to say. I guess I didn't ruin his Christmas after all. But that didn't mean he was happy to be stuck with me. "Is that where you're taking me? When you said 'not my home,' did you mean you'll take me to *your* home?" I belatedly realized I didn't know where his home was.

Campbell dragged a hand over his tired face, and squinted into the unrelenting snow. His Adam's apple bobbed up and down, which sent the tattoo that stretched across his neck rolling.

My father was an infamous tattoo artist. More accurately, as he had gotten older, he became more of an artist who just happened to tattoo. The name Rule Archer was well-known in alternative art circles. His favorite medium was still ink on flesh, but he'd branched out a lot as I grew up. I looked up to my dad more than anyone in the world. He was cool and creative and everything I thought I wanted to be when I was older.

I'd been told I was his mini-me since I was a toddler, which was hilarious since my older brother looked exactly like him. I favored our mother in looks, but my soul and sensibilities were dead-ringers for my dad's. I happily blamed him for the wealth of emotions and intrusive thoughts I was constantly battling.

I'd been around the tattoo profession since before I was born. I was indifferent to most artwork unless I knew the story behind it or the artist who created it. But I'd appreciated the big, aggressive piece on Campbell's throat the minute we met. It was more than a pretty design on a pretty boy. It was technically perfect. It screamed talent and skill. It was a piece of art worn by someone not afraid of showing it off to the rest of the world.

It was a big moth, done in black and gray tones. The line work was delicate and intricate, and the shades and shadows were dark and intense. The white highlights were impressive, and I knew it came from someone with a wealth of experience. It wasn't a tattoo that was supposed to be pretty, but on him, it was.

It was a statement piece.

It was the kind of tattoo that spoke without words.

Why get a moth instead of a butterfly? If you asked me, this was a man who did not think he would evolve into something beautiful. In several old, indigenous cultures, a moth was often tattooed to represent an omen of death. Or it was used as a sign of strength and resilience. Either of those meanings would suit the man sitting next to me.

Campbell rubbed one of his knuckles against the scar that slashed across his chin and bottom lip. Since he was particularly scruffy at the moment, I noticed that his copper facial hair didn't grow in that spot. It was a flaw that should've taken away from the appeal of his face, but it didn't. It just made him look tougher and more untouchable.

"No, not my home. No one deserves what a visit to that place will do to them. I'm going to take you to my brothers' and sister's home. I still want to see them, especially while Delta is on winter break. No one from your search party will think to look for you there."

I let out a tiny sigh of relief as I turned his words over in my mind. I had a lot of questions, but the first was, "Uncle Benny won't tell anyone where we're going?"

I didn't know the mysterious man who popped in and out of family gatherings with no rhyme or reason very well. When I was younger, I'd found him intimidating and a bit scary. He had a big scar that encircled his throat and eyes that didn't seem to hold a single drop of emotion. My sense of self-preservation was strong enough that I always treaded lightly when I was in his company.

Campbell snorted and covered a big yawn before answering me.

"Your *Uncle Benny* might rat us out to your folks, but the Benny *I* grew up with won't say a word. He's the reason I came to find you. He didn't give me much choice. The options were to find you or find a place to hide. There is no way in hell I was sticking around to see what would happen if I didn't do what he asked."

"Oh." Once again, I was at a loss for words as I tried to digest this new information. Why would Uncle Benny care if I was lost in the mountains? And what kind of relationship did Campbell have with him that he would do whatever he asked? Why did he seem genuinely scared of the man with the nasty scar on his throat? "Did you say you and your siblings live in different places?"

He distinctly referred to their home with a softer voice.

He hummed an acknowledgment and yawned again. He blinked and turned to look at me. The dark depths were usually unreadable, but I had no trouble seeing how tired he was right now. The weather made travel take much longer than usual, and he had driven through the night to find that little gas station tucked away in the middle of nowhere.

"We all lived with my dad until I was in my early teens. My family has some property out in the middle of nowhere that my old man guards like it's Buckingham Palace. It's no place for a kid, especially when the only adult around is certifiable. I had a good reason when I ran away from home. I had to find someone to help me get my siblings out of there. I had to save myself, so I could save them. I found a place that took me in and helped me get my brothers and sister away from my father forever. I didn't want them near my old man, so they grew up a few states from where I was based. But the people who took me in ensured I got to see them whenever I wanted. And the family raising them treats me like one of their own." He turned his head and gave me a cold look that caused me to fidget nervously in my seat. "How about you, Princess? What reason do you have for sneaking out on Christmas?"

I blew out a breath and wondered if there was a way to explain my irrational rush away that he wouldn't ridicule. It wasn't like he had gone out of his way to be understanding since I'd met him. That was why I didn't hesitate to abandon my car to go with him. Campbell didn't placate or patronize me. He let it be known he thought the worst of me. His scorn and disdain were the only emotions I'd been able to respond to as of late. His ridicule felt right in a way I knew was very wrong.

"I destroyed my brother's future. I'm jealous because he's dating my best friend, and I feel like they both left me behind. My parents have been too understanding over the fact that I bailed on college at the last minute. I'm tied up in knots because Remy went from being the one everyone was concerned about to being reliable. I'm failing at being an Archer, because Archers stand together and have each other's backs, but right now, I want nothing to do with them. And if I'm not a good Archer, then what in the hell am I?"

The words tumbled out faster and faster. All the dark, ugly secrets I was holding in my heart since the night I caused Ry to get hit by a truck on the interstate spilled out in a tangled mess.

I didn't care if it seemed insignificant and silly to Campbell. Professing the reasons I needed to get away from everyone who loved me made a huge difference in the weight of everything I was struggling to carry. If I sounded like an awful person, so be it.

I was awful. And it was about time someone other than me recognized that.

I waited for a scathing response. I was poised and ready to feel the sting of pointed criticism. I was practically giddy at the thought of being buried under his disgust and loathing. He already called me a princess every chance he got. Of course, he would consider my problems asinine. I desperately needed to know there was someone out there who felt the same way about me as I did. It would make me feel less alone.

To my crushing disappointment, all Campbell did was let out a bored grunt. He yawned again, as if my self-loathing couldn't be more uninteresting.

"If you can't be a good Archer, be a bad one. It seems easy enough to me." He yawned even bigger. "We're going to have to stop soon so I can get some sleep. I don't know how much longer I can keep my eyes open. The kids live halfway between Colorado and the hovel where we grew up. We'll be there sometime early evening if we stop and rest for a few hours." He finally looked at me, dark eyes full of warning. "I don't care why you ran away from home. If all those reasons you just rattled off are good enough for you, then so be it. But if you run away from me..." His deep voice trailed off, and his gaze narrowed, "you will regret it until the day you die, Princess."

I tugged nervously on the beanie and turned to look out the window. The sky was light but still overcast. Everything outside looked as cold and icy as I felt on the inside.

"Do you realize you never give the full details on anything, even when you're talking a lot about something?" I reached out a finger and drew a frowning face in the fog on the window. "We've been talking this whole time, and you've never said where exactly we're going. You never told me where you grew up, or who the people you ended up with after you left your father are. You've alluded to the fact that you know Uncle Benny in a different way than the rest of us, but haven't said how. You don't mention identifiable cities or states. You never said how old your siblings are, or told me what happened to your mother. And even though I've known you for several months, you've never clarified if Campbell is your first or last name. You say so much without saying anything. It's very irritating."

I was surprised to hear him chuckle after a moment of awkward silence. He shifted in his seat, and when I looked back at him, I was taken aback by the slight grin on his face. The scar on his lower lip made the gesture look shades of sinister, but that evil vibe really suited him.

"Pretty and smart. You're worthy of being a princess." His tone made it clear he wouldn't elaborate on anything I just mentioned.

I wanted to sigh, but I swallowed it and muttered, "I won't run away from you."

After all, I was a newbie at this whole escaping-from-my-family thing, just like he said.

He laughed again, and this time his grin reached his eyes. I shivered when his husky voice muttered, "Let's call that a Christmas miracle, shall we?"

It was Christmas morning, and instead of sitting around a massive, decorated tree surrounded by loved ones making joyful memories, I was on my way to God knows where with a man I barely knew.

Probably not the best choice I'd ever made—including running away during a major blizzard—but I had a hard time regretting it.

"Merry Christmas, Campbell. Thanks for coming to find me."

It took a minute for him to respond. When he did, my heart, which was so damn heavy all the time, shook so fiercely I felt it down to my bones.

"Merry Christmas, Princess. You weren't lost. Someone always knew right where you were. It's too bad for you that someone happened to be me."

I didn't tell him the fact he was the one who could home in on me with minimal effort wasn't a bad thing.

Something about him told me he wouldn't appreciate my appreciation.

chapter TWO

Campbell

Even though I was tired and my eyes were watering, I drove for another hour until we crossed the Kansas border. The road conditions lightened up slightly by the time I pulled over and stopped at the same little motel where I'd stayed when I initially packed up and moved to Denver. The place was clean enough, and not too expensive. There was a steady flow of trucker traffic in and out of the building, so it wouldn't raise any eyebrows if Daire and I only stayed for a few hours.

She didn't know how easy it would be to track her if someone knew the right questions to ask. That fair hair of hers and that unforgettable face were easily identifiable. As long as she didn't want to be found, I needed to be more cautious than when I was traveling alone.

I knew one of the reasons Benny dropped this annoying project in my lap was because he understood that if I didn't want Daire to be found, she wouldn't be. I'd spent much of my young adult life making sure my father couldn't locate my siblings, regardless of the underhanded and illegal means I often used. The only way to fight a monster was to become one yourself. You had to become scarier than whatever it was that scared you the most. That's why I never answered Daire's questions about my past or gave more information than necessary. The minute I left home, I stopped being a traumatized kid and became something else. I was a weapon. A threat. A monster. I had to learn to be unafraid and capable of doing anything at any cost to keep the people I cared about safe.

I didn't have much innocence left when I finally found the courage to venture out and ask for help. But whatever shred of it remained was annihilated when I started to learn exactly what it took to be unbreakable in a world that wanted to beat you down.

I had Daire stay in the SUV while I ran in and got a couple of rooms. As I suspected, the guy at the front desk didn't pay much attention to me. I'd put on an old baseball hat I had in the backseat to cover my distinctive red hair, and I looked like any other long-haul trucker in need of a power nap. I kept the collar of my coat pulled up around my face to cover my scar and the tattoo on my neck, and I put on gloves so the ink on the back of my hands wasn't visible. I was pretty good at blending into the background when I wanted to be.

When I returned to the SUV, I tossed the little plastic cards into Daire's lap. She'd nodded off somewhere near the border, so her gaze was sleepy, and her skin was flushed. She was still pale, and had streaks of makeup on her cheeks, but none of that took away from that remarkable face of hers.

"Since you took off in the middle of the night, I assume you don't have much with you?" I asked, even though I knew the answer.

She tugged on the beanie that was still perched on her head. It had gotten knocked sideways during her fitful rest.

"I didn't take anything. Just my purse. I don't want to use my credit cards. My parents will probably be looking to see where I used them."

I handed her my phone and pointed at the open note application. "Make me a list of must-haves. I'll grab what you absolutely need to make it through the next couple of days. Once we get to a bigger city, we can stop at a big box store and get you situated for longer." She opened her mouth to respond, but I held up a hand to stop her. "I'm getting the room and the rations on the condition that you use the prepaid phone I'm going to pick up for you to call someone in your family and let them know you're all right. You don't have to tell them where you are. You don't have to tell them when you'll be back or who you're with, but they need to know you aren't dead. I'm sure they were already very worried, but once they find your car abandoned, that will be a new level of fear. Benny will likely let everyone know he sent me after you, but that is no guarantee that I found you first. We'll change out SIM cards and use VPNs, so it'll be difficult to track. It's not perfect, but it's the best option at the moment."

Her eyes widened, and the green looked glossy as she considered my words. She shifted her eyes to the key cards and appeared to weigh her options.

After a long silence, she relented and started to type out a short list on the phone in her hand.

"I'll call Remy. She's notorious for disappearing on a whim and going wherever the wind takes her. She's most likely to understand why I did what I did even if she doesn't approve of it."

I gave her a nod of encouragement. Calling Remy Archer was a good choice. She was a high-strung and emotional young woman, but I could tell she was good people from the get-go. I liked her quirky and bright personality. She was fun to be around as she learned about caring for an infant. I didn't know being so clueless about kids was possible until I met Remy. I found her lack of pretension and shame charming. And I appreciated that when Hollyn got sick and Hyde needed someone to lean on, Remy held them both up until the baby was out of the woods. She was open about her mistakes and missteps, so I highly doubted she would take Daire to task for exhibiting the same type of behavior when the world seemed overwhelming. She was a good choice to confide in.

She handed me my phone back, and I pulled the SUV around to where the rooms were located. I told her I would be back in a couple minutes, and reminded her that I would be extremely upset if she was missing when I returned.

It was already pure insanity that I was taking her to meet my family. There was no way I would chase her ass all over the Midwest. Not even if Benny tried to make me.

Speaking of Benny, I called him as I drove to the small general store we'd passed a few miles before the motel. I grinned when his sleepy voice came on the line. It sounded like I woke him up.

Served him right for dragging me into the middle of the Archer's drama and not giving me a choice in the matter.

"I got the girl. I'm going to take her with me to see the kids. Hopefully she'll get bored after a short visit and be ready to head home and face the music. I'm not leaving a trail of breadcrumbs to follow, but I can if you want me to."

Benny swore, and I heard a soft female voice mutter something in the background. That was another thing I couldn't believe had changed. Benny had a wife. A very nice woman named Echo who didn't seem like she should be hooked up with one of the most lethal men who ever walked the earth. I wondered if she *really* knew the man she married, but I would never be brave or foolish enough to ask those kinds of questions where Benny might overhear me.

"I already passed along the word that I had someone helping search for Daire. When they found the car, I told them she was more than likely with you. The family is up in arms. Those Archers are not going to be happy when they find out their girl had help running. It's better for you if you remain untraceable until she's ready to come home."

I chuckled as I parked in front of the small store. Unlike the frigid mountain gas station, this shop was bustling with people even though it was Christmas morning.

"You make it sound like I should be scared of the Archers."

Benny snorted, and I heard him shift around. "I think they should be scared that you're alone with their daughter, tough guy." I scoffed, but was cut off when he said, "You should have a healthy respect for the Archers, Campbell. They have unbreakable bonds and love as fierce as you hate."

"Did you get tired of making enemies and decide to pass the torch onto me?" I walked through the aisles and gathered the handful of things Daire had written on her list.

It was more barebones than I thought it would be. There was nothing over the top that screamed *poor-little-rich-girl*.

"Don't act like you need my help in that department. Enemies are easier to find than friends. It's best to know what you're up against and act accordingly. I've got a gut feeling you'll come out of this with the kind of support system you've always wanted. I know Booker took you under his wing and handed you off to me when you got older. And I know that Karsen helped you fix things with your family, but that's not the same as finding a family that accepts you for who you are and has no intentions of asking you to change. You deserve better than you've let yourself have. We're not that different, Campbell. I know exactly what you're missing." He made a sound that let me know he was proud of himself for the string of words, but I refused to let worm their way into my heart. Hope was lethal to a guy like me. Benny knew that better than anyone, and it made me even angrier that he went right for my weak point unprovoked. "My gut never lies. Take care of the girl, and get home safe when you're ready. If you need any help along the way, I'm only a phone call away."

I hung up and gave a middle-aged woman and her kid a hard look when I realized they were watching me closer than I would've liked. I realized I was in the shampoo aisle, staring at the brightly decorated bottles like I wanted to hurt them.

Benny had a knack for bringing out the beast in me. He was simply tied too tightly to my dark history. It had been a couple of months since I had a chance to check in with Noah and Karsen Booker. I owed the couple more than the average person could imagine. They saved my life. They saved my siblings. But they were also why Benny was in my life, and he was right—he and I were more similar than I wanted to admit. One of the first things Booker taught me when he found me shoeless and starving on the side of the road was that there was no salvation without sacrifice.

Once I had collected all of Daire's list along with the burner phone, I headed back to the motel. I was practically a zombie at this point. I was already tired when we'd pulled in, and an extra excursion hadn't helped my situation. After talking to Benny, I was beyond exhausted. My vision was getting blurry, and my steps made it feel like my feet were encased in cement shoes.

I rapped on the door and waited for her to crack it open. It took longer than it should've, which made me impatient. I was tired and cold. Waiting around for Daire was the last thing I wanted to do.

Lime green eyes peered cautiously out of the tiny opening. I watched her heave a sigh of relief when she saw it was me. She reached up to remove the chain, and I belatedly realized her hair was wet and she was wrapped in a towel. Places like this didn't come with plush bathrobes.

I wasn't prepared to be greeted by so much creamy, soft, exposed skin. Her hair might be almost white, but the rest of her had a pretty, rosy glow. In a rush, I remembered it'd been longer than I could recall since I'd been with someone.

My life didn't leave much room for pleasure and attachment to a passing fancy. That, combined with my innate need to keep to myself and protect even the most minute details about my life, didn't make me a prime candidate for dating and relationships. My style was more *here today, gone tomorrow*. Momentary attraction and a hint of distant affection were as close as I ever got to a committed relationship. Since the distance between hookups had grown even greater with my move to Denver, seeing Daire in a state of near undress was enough to short-circuit my sleep-deprived brain.

I thrust the bag of stuff from the store into her free hand, and waved the prepaid phone in front of her startled face.

"Can I trust you to make the call without a babysitter? I'm dead on my feet and might pass out any second." My voice was hoarse, but not because I was tired. I assured myself I was having a perfectly normal reaction to seeing a beautiful girl wet and undressed. I didn't feel this way because it was Daire. I felt that little tingle in places I didn't want to think about since the girl in front of me was this particular problematic princess.

Daire clutched the phone to her chest and nodded. It felt as if she was suddenly aware that she was almost naked and alone in the room with a man she didn't know all that well. Her sense of self-preservation came later than it should've. However, I was proud of her for understanding she shouldn't trust me simply because I showed up when she was at her lowest. I didn't want her to trick herself into thinking I was a good guy. Maybe I would be in the future, but that was a long way off, and the distance seemed to grow each and every day.

"I'll call Remy. You can go to your room and rest. I'm not going anywhere. I swear I'll be here when you're ready to get back on the road." Her eyes darted to the door behind me.

I stepped backward to give her some breathing room and peace of mind. I rubbed a knuckle across my scar, an unconscious habit I had when I was lost in thought or really tired. The scar was the only thing my dad had ever given me that I held onto.

Benny was correct when he called my hatred fierce. There were days when I felt like hate was the only emotion I remembered how to feel. It was a big, heavy anvil nailed in the center of my chest.

"If you change your mind after talking to Remy, I'll take you home. Don't worry about messing up my plans to see the kids. I can get you back to Denver and hop on a plane if need be. They don't care if it's Christmas or New Year's, as long as we're all together."

Daire shook her head, and a few wayward water drops hit me in the face. It was a damp reminder to get my ass away from her and into bed. Alone.

Her head whipped from side to side again. This time I jumped back to avoid the spray.

"No. I don't want to go back yet. I need some time away from everyone. Remy will understand. She won't lay a guilt trip on me. But you're right. I need to check in periodically. It's mean to let them worry that something bad happened to me." She tilted her head to the side and smiled, making my uncomfortable situation even more unpleasant.

I had no right to get chills and goosebumps over this girl.

"Plus, I'm curious about you. I feel like the only way I will know anything is if I keep forcing myself into your life. I'm curious about the cities with no names and the people you protect like they're national treasures."

I turned and walked out the door. I needed to go to sleep. Now. My brain was too tired to keep up with her.

"Curiosity killed the cat." Seriously. How sleepy was I that a lame cliché was all I could come up with?

I heard Daire laugh, but I refused to turn around and look at her in that towel for another second.

"According to you, I'm a princess. Not a cat. I should be fine."

I grunted in response and told her to lock the door behind me. I tripped over my own feet on the way to my room. It took me three tries to get the door open, and once I did, I immediately fell face-first onto the bed. I didn't even bother to take my boots off.

I closed my eyes and groaned when the darkness was instantly flooded with an image of Daire Archer in that damn towel.

I had to keep her safe and return her home better than I found her. There was no chance I was going to get tangled up with her more deeply than I already was. Even if she made my dick hard.

Nothing would be temporary with any kind of entanglement I might have with Daire. And it was likely that her entire family would be after my head when all this was said and done. Truthfully, none of them scared me as much as the girl in the room next door.

The whole situation was messy and rife with pitfalls that might break my neck if I allowed myself to fall into them. I bet Benny was having a huge laugh at my expense right now. Smug bastard.

As I succumbed to sleep, I wondered why I ever let that slick asshole convince me that moving to Colorado to restart my complicated life would be a good idea. I should've known better than to follow a former felon anywhere.

chapter THREE

Daire

I watched Campbell's broad back as he exited the room and clutched the phone and towel in my hands.

He moved well.

Smooth and purposeful. Every step felt powerful and strong. He was tall and on the lean side. But that in no way took away from his impressive aura. He carried himself like the most important person in the world and walked like no one would dare get in his way.

It was attractive in a way I was too naïve to fully understand. It was different from the arrogance of my brother. It was different from the attitude and innate rebellion that oozed effortlessly from my father.

I couldn't explain it, but I knew I liked it.

I wasn't exactly innocent and untouched. But after spending some time with Campbell, it was clear to me that the people I'd thought deserved my time and body were mere boys. Some good. Some bad. But all of them were basic, immature, and uninteresting.

There was nothing childish about Campbell. In fact, it was like he'd never had the chance to be young and dumb at all.

I wasn't shy. Being comfortable in my own skin was something my parents instilled in me since I was a child. I was always more secure in my appearance than in what else I might have to offer. I could secure my future with my face alone, but that was one of my current crises. What was the point of trying when I would always get what I want regardless? My family lived by the motto *if you don't earn it, it's not worth it.* However, everything I had was handed to me on a silver platter. Archers didn't make excuses and took accountability for everything, except when it came to me. I was always an exception to the rules.

Ever since the accident that nearly killed my brother, every Archer went out of their way to excuse the role I'd played in the traumatic scene, to the point of ignorance.

Being around Campbell while I was obsessing about my laundry list of faults gave me an agenda. He already saw the worst in me. There was no need to be nice and polite around him. I wanted to tease him, and maybe see if I could force him to finally show some type of emotion other than irritation. I'd dashed from the shower to open the door. Not because I was worried Campbell would think I left after I promised I wouldn't, but because I wanted to see his reaction when I greeted him provocatively.

His face was always locked in a perpetual scowl. His eyes were always cold and impassive. It was rare to get a rise out of him in any way. When I answered his knock wearing nothing but a towel, I saw Campbell freeze for a second. It was the first time something other than disdain flashed in his dark eyes. I didn't understand him well enough to name the emotion, but I was thrilled there was finally something there aside from disinterest.

Playing those kinds of teasing games had gotten me in trouble in the past. I liked to push people. I liked to get a rise out of them. I liked to be seen as more than a pretty face or the little sister of a future superstar. Some would call my attitude combative and arrogant instead of playful and provoking. They were all correct. I was all of those things on any given day. The truth of the matter was that I'd never been a very good Archer. Only now, I was regretting it.

I was making a conscious effort to do better and be better, but in that process, I'd realized I didn't know who I was.

My identity was tied so closely to those spectacular people around me that all I'd become was a character trying to shine as bright as the rest of the stars in the Archer constellation.

But I wasn't a star. I was an asteroid hurtling toward another planet. And I was breaking into smaller and smaller pieces when the pressure of the atmosphere started to close in on me.

I sighed at the dramatic direction of my thoughts as I climbed back into the jeans and oversized sweater I'd wore for the Christmas Eve family gathering my parents hosted. I could still smell the pine from the Christmas tree and vanilla from the candles scattered around the house. The subtle reminder of home wiped the smile off my face as I looked down at the cheap phone Campbell had gotten for me. It felt like it weighed a ton, but I still punched in Remy's number and lifted it to my ear when it started ringing.

There was no answer.

Not surprising, since Remy was notorious for forgetting to charge her phone, leaving it somewhere, and walking off. Now that she was with Hyde and Hollyn, she was better about keeping it on her. I was calling from an unknown number, though, so she might ignore it because she didn't know I was on the other end.

My heart clenched.

I told Campbell I would talk to my family and wanted to follow through. I was afraid he might ditch me on the side of the road if I didn't comply with his mostly reasonable demand. And while I wanted to get away from everyone I knew and put space between Denver and me, doing it alone was scarier and more complicated than I thought. Sticking with Campbell made more sense. Plus, I got to prick at his stony façade while I did it. Trying to make him crack was more entertaining than anything I'd done in recent memory.

But I needed to figure out who else to call if Remy didn't pick up.

Not my mom and dad; they would come unglued and make me feel worse than I already did. Not my aunt and uncle. While my Aunt Cora would be more understanding than my mom because she was used to this from raising Remy, my Uncle Rome wasn't so chill. He was in the military when he was younger, and even if

Remy didn't know it, he always knew where she was and who she was with. Campbell said the phone was mostly untraceable, but I was scared my uncle had a way around that. I could call my best friend Aston. But she'd left for college, and we didn't stay in touch as often as we used to. She was also my brother's ex-girlfriend. She was loyal to me, but Ry was intimidating and had a way of getting what he wanted no matter what. My other best friend was his *current* girlfriend. While I loved her like a sister, I knew she would put him before me in a hot second. Those two were soul mates, after all. I could call Remy's brother, Zowen, but he was a computer genius. He might be able to find me even faster than his father if I gave him the slightest opening.

No. Remy was the only option. Campbell would have to live with it if she didn't pick up.

I called twice more, and finally, Remy's voice came on the line.

"Hello?" The question in the greeting was clear.

"Hi. It's me." My voice was quiet and apologetic. I wasn't sorry for leaving. I was sorry for putting her in the middle of my choices. It didn't feel very fair. "I'm calling to let you know I'm fine. I'm sure Mom and Dad found my car up on the mountain and are freaked out, but I'm really okay. I just wanted to check in, so you can tell them not to worry."

After a moment of silence, a sharp laugh sounded in my ear. "Tell them not to worry? Have you lost your mind? Of course, they're worried, Daire. Who let you take a page out of the Remy Archer playbook? This shit isn't like you, and it isn't cool. Do you have any idea how frantic Ry and my brother are? They're ready to burn Denver to the ground to find you. You flipped the family upside down, darling."

I blew out a breath and closed my eyes. "I know. I just... couldn't be there anymore. You've been in my shoes, Remy. Don't act like you don't understand."

She sighed, and I could picture the cute, perturbed face she was probably making. Remy was tiny, with bright, curly blonde hair and wild eyes. Her personality was as big as the sky, but so were her heart and compassion. She was annoyed with me, but she wouldn't forsake me.

"I do understand. Since those shoes you're referencing were originally mine, let me remind you that running away from your problems doesn't fix them. They'll always be there. Waiting. Lurking. Lingering. Getting bigger while they wait for you to return. I'm lucky mine didn't eat me alive."

I nodded. "I know that. But my situation is different. I can't run from my problem because the problem is me. I have no idea who I am anymore. I don't know what I want to do with myself. I feel like nothing matters anymore. My family keeps trying to assure me nothing has changed, and if they tell me I'm not responsible for Ry's accident one more time..." I trailed off, unsure I could come up with a threat that wouldn't make me sound worse than I already felt. "I just need a minute alone. I need some distance to determine if I'm the awful person I think I am or if I might be the amazing and unstoppable person you guys keep telling me I am. It's really confusing."

Remy was quiet for a long moment before she sighed softly. "Feeling like a visitor in your own body is the worst." Her sympathy was palpable.

Remy had been diagnosed with Borderline Personality Disorder when she was younger. She'd spent so much time teaching herself how to live a full and productive life with the illness instead of despite it.

"You don't have to tell my parents anything other than I'm really okay, and I'm not alone. Tell them I'm sorry about ditching the car in the mountains. That was selfish and thoughtless. I know my mom probably cried. I'll text them soon."

Remy hummed a sound of agreement. "I'll pass everything along. It's not your mom you need to worry about. It's your brother. I don't think I've ever seen Ry lose his cool the way he did when he heard your car was abandoned up on the mountain in a blizzard. That boy can be scary. And Bowe..." She let her words drift off before coming back with another sigh. "She feels bad. She's blaming herself, saying you wouldn't have taken off if she hadn't come for the holidays as Ry's girlfriend. She thinks you don't approve of the relationship. If they break up because of you, what are you going to do about it?"

I swore into the empty room and shoved my fingers through my wet hair. That wasn't possible. I'd done some sketchy things as of late, but I would not be a part of ruining my brother's relationship. "I'll call Ry when I figure out what to say." I could always tell him the same thing he told me when he disappeared out of nowhere to chase after Bowe. "I'll send Bowe a text too. But you need to text me everyone's numbers since I left my phone behind."

"That's right, I don't know this number. Whose phone are you using?"

I lifted my eyebrows and flopped on the bed. I stared at the ceiling for a beat before laughing at her. "I know you know that Uncle Benny sent Campbell after me. I'm not going to lie to you, Remy. I might be a little muddle-headed at the moment, but I won't fall for the same tricks your mom used on you. He told me I sucked at running away from home, so he's going to teach me the right way to do it. He found me before anyone else did." I don't know why I sounded slightly proud of that fact.

"I've watched the two of you. You aren't exactly friendly. Hyde trusts Benny's judgment more than anyone, so by extension, he told me to trust Campbell. But I don't understand why you would let him help you and push everyone else away."

"Because he has no preconceived notions about me or my last name. He doesn't care that I'm an Archer. He doesn't give a shit that I'm Ry Archer's little sister, or Rule and Shaw Archer's daughter. I mean nothing to him, and that's what I need right now. I need to see myself through the eyes of someone looking at the real me, the Daire who exists without the Archer armor." I smiled, and I was sure Remy could hear it in my voice. "I like that we aren't friendly. It makes the interactions between us feel real. I feel like he doesn't want anything from me."

Remy snorted, and I heard her mutter something to someone in the background. I figured it was Hyde when she turned her attention back to me and dropped a dry warning. "He's a guy, and you're a beautiful young woman. He wants something from you even if he pretends otherwise."

I clicked my tongue at her and fought back a sudden yawn. Since I'd slept in the car, I didn't think I was still tired. But the conversation with Remy was as exhausting as it was entertaining. "Don't be so old-fashioned. Not all guys are wired the same way. When you get right down to it, I'm the one who wants something from him."

Remy heaved one last sigh, and her tone turned serious. "Be careful. That's all I'm saying. None of us know much about Campbell. Benny is being stingy with details when Hyde tries to talk to him. This might feel like a big adventure where you're striking out on your own for the first time, but it could quickly become a tragedy if you don't take care of yourself. Just because Campbell found you doesn't mean he gets to keep you."

It was on the tip of my tongue to assure her that if it was up to the enigmatic redhead, he would've left me buried in snow on the top of the mountain. There were exactly zero scenarios where Campbell was laying claim to ownership where I was concerned.

"He's very different from anyone I know. His world seems so strange and lonely. Trying to get him to talk is like pulling teeth. He doesn't enjoy my company, but he's letting me stick with him for now. And he's not forcing me to go home until I'm ready. I want to see what he sees, and hopefully, I'll come away with a new perspective."

"If he makes you hate yourself, there isn't a hole deep and dark enough for him to hide in." It was always so cute when she got fierce and protective.

"What happens if he makes me love myself?" I threw the words out jokingly, but for some reason, I felt invisible threads tie them to my tortured heart.

"If that happens, I'll be the first to welcome him to the family as an honorary Archer. Remember, Daire, even when you find it hard to love yourself, you have a whole lot of people loving you double to make up for it. You're special. Always have been. And it has nothing to do with your last name."

"I adore you, Remy." I felt myself getting emotional at her words.

"I adore you back. I hope you find what you're looking for out there. I'll do my best to keep the wolves at bay for now."

"Thank you. Reassure the wolves I'm with something with bigger teeth and a nasty bite." It was true. I couldn't picture Campbell being the slightest bit worried about going toe-to-toe with my brother.

"You don't know how men work at all, do you? That will do the opposite of reassuring them. However, watching the fallout after I tell them will be fun. Merry Christmas, Daire." She hung up the phone with a giggle.

I felt a sense of relief flood through me now that Campbell's task was complete. I knew Remy would understand and wouldn't urge me to return home right away. She was the only member of my family who recognized that my depression and anxiety after the accident weren't normal symptoms of stress. She was the one who forced me to take care of myself while everyone else coddled me like I was a baby. She was the one who finally got me to wash my hair and engage with the world around me when I was ready to give up on everything.

My mom and dad voiced their concern several times, but it was easier hearing what Remy had to say. Her words felt more honest, and they hurt when I finally let myself hear them. Pain was a powerful motivator.

I flung out an arm and caught the edge of the comforter. I wrapped the blanket around myself until only the top of my head stuck out, and I closed my eyes and focused on relaxing my muscles one at a time until I felt sleepy.

Before I drifted off to sleep, my final thought was wondering what time I would most likely find Campbell in a towel when I knocked on his door with breakfast in the morning.

There were a lot of things I wanted to find out about him. At the top of that complicated and ever-changing list was whether *all* the hair on his body was that coppery-red color.

I'd never seen a ginger happy trail before, which felt like a life experience I needed to have before I died. Especially since the target of my quest would be absolutely displeased if he knew I was undressing him in my mind and decorating his pale skin with unlimited tattoo ideas. There was no ignoring a beautiful canvas when inspiration struck.

It seemed I really was my father's daughter, even when I desperately tried to inch out from underneath the long shadow cast by his legacy.

I was desperate to stand in my own light and figure out who in the hell Daire Archer really was.

FOUR

Campbell

I usually only needed a couple hours of sleep to re-charge. But the last day must've taken more out of me than I realized, because it was after noon when I groggily opened my eyes. It was plenty of time for Daire to regret her impulsive decision and decide she wanted to go back to Denver. But it was also adequate time for her to pull a disappearing act if she hadn't kept her word to stay put. If she'd bounced, she would have one hell of a head start on me. I doubted running her down would be as easy now that she knew about the GPS tracker.

Deciding to give her the benefit of the doubt for the time being, I jumped in the shower and let the cold water jolt my sluggish body back to life. I was hungry and could use a strong cup of coffee, but first, I needed to see if my travel companion was where I had left her.

Just as I was about to open the door, there was a knock. I frowned and looked through the peephole before pulling it open. Daire was on the other side with a brown paper bag from a nearby fast-food chain was in her hand. She had all her fair hair tucked up in the beanie she'd commandeered from my SUV, and a pair of over-sized sunglasses covered half of her face. She was draped in a big sweatshirt that dwarfed her slender frame. She looked like a little kid. If you didn't look closely, it was hard to tell if the person in the large garment was male or female. I was reluctantly impressed she knew enough not to go out without disguising her most distinctive features. She had to work hard not to leave an impression.

I opened the door and stepped aside to let her enter the dark room. I frowned when she took off the sunglasses and let her gaze rove over me from head to toe. The provocative look felt like a physical touch when it lingered at the base of my throat and some invisible point below my belly button. I was fully clothed, but her laser-like once-over made me feel naked.

"Dammit. I was too late." She held out the fragrant paper bag and shook it in front of me with a cheeky grin. "Belated breakfast. I thought you might be hungry."

"Late for what?" Her first statement confused me, but she shook her head and kept smiling. I was hungry, so I let it drop. I hadn't eaten anything since long before I set out to find her. I took the bag with a mumbled thanks and motioned to her outfit with my free hand. "Where did the hoodie and sunglasses come from?" They weren't in my car, and she hadn't taken anything from hers when we left the mountain.

"I went to the office and asked to go through the lost and found. There was a nice older woman at the desk. I told her my luggage was stolen at a rest stop when I went to use the bathroom, so I didn't have anything warm to wear other than what I had on. She let me pick through what was left behind. I also snagged a pair of sweatpants and a long-sleeved shirt with an In-N-Out Burger logo."

She seemed amused by the situation rather than frantic and scared like she'd been last night. I wondered what she and Remy talked about to cause the transformation.

I grunted and sat at the small table near the entrance to chow down the burger and fries she brought as a peace offering. I would've rather had a breakfast sandwich, but since I slept so late, I couldn't complain.

"It's smart to keep your hair and eyes covered when we're in public. They stand out too much."

Daire wrinkled her nose, sat on the end of the unmade bed, and swung her feet back and forth. The image was oddly innocent, yet enticing.

"My uncle was in the military, and my cousin is practically a computer hacker. My parents have a couple very good friends in law enforcement. If my family wants to find me, they will. I don't have to make it easier for them, though."

I looked at her over the greasy burger and asked, "Do you think you're playing a giant game of hide-and-seek?"

She stopped swinging her feet and gave me a serious look. "No. I'm playing a giant game of Where's Waldo, and I'm Waldo. My family is trying to find me...but so am I." Her voice dropped lower. "Before you came to Denver, my brother and I were in a terrible accident. He nearly died because I called him to help me get out of a situation I never should've been in. He's fortunate that he pulled through, but his injuries ruined his chance to play football in the future. He was good. Really, really good. People always said he was going to make it all the way to the NFL. Now he's in med school. He still has a promising future ahead of him, and my mom is overjoyed he's following in her footsteps, but I can't stop thinking about how I destroyed his life."

She paused for a second and sucked in a breath. I could hear how much pain she was in, both after the accident and now.

"I'm a terrible sister. An ungrateful daughter. And a bad Archer. Even after the accident, no one in my family treats me like I'm any of those things. Which has led me to a total identity crisis. I thought I knew who I was and what my strengths were before I fucked up my brother's life. Now, I'm not so sure. I left thinking I could take the saying 'New-Year-New-Me' literally. When I go home, I want to return as someone *I* can be proud of. I need to figure out who I am without them. I need to try and become a better Archer."

I finished off the burger and shoved the wrapper into the bag. I wiped my face with a thin napkin and leaned back in my chair.

We watched each other silently for a long moment before I told her, "Believe it or not, when I decided to come to Denver, I was also looking for Waldo. When I was a little kid, I had no idea who I was apart from my father's unwanted kid and the caretaker of my siblings. When I got older, the people I found to help me change my circumstances always wanted to mold me into the version of myself that was most beneficial to them. They wanted to make me strong. Instead of fearing a man like my father, they wanted men like him to fear me. They wanted to ensure I knew right from wrong but understood the line between the two changed depending on who drew it."

Memories of my time on the compound started to scroll through my mind. I was already a screwed-up kid. It wasn't like Karsen and Booker took me in and straightened me out. It was more like they bent me in another direction, made me sharper and more deadly. Karsen turned me into a weapon she used to keep her own kids safe from the parts of the world that made my father look like a PTA parent.

"Benny told me that coming to work for Hyde would allow me to figure out if I wanted to be someone different than the person I'd been taught to be. He wanted me to know there was a way out of the life that was going to kill me or make me a killer."

It was the most I'd ever told her about myself. The most I'd shared with a stranger in a long time. But there was something about the yearning look in her eye and her desire to understand herself that spoke to the scared, confused, unloved little boy I still had deep within me.

She was a princess trapped in an ivory tower, but she didn't want to be.

Daire tilted her head to the side and watched me with intent eyes. "So, did you find Waldo?"

I pushed away from the table and stood up. "Still looking. If it were that easy, there wouldn't be endless versions of those books." I quickly changed the subject.

"Let's hit the road. I need to call ahead and let them know I'm coming and bringing a friend."

She hopped to her feet and smirked at me. This version of Daire was a far cry from the one I found alone on the mountain last night. Her moods swung faster than a pendulum.

"Are we friends now?" I could hear the laughter in her voice.

I shrugged into my jacket and ushered her out the door. I touched her lower back and felt her skin's warmth despite her oversized clothes. It made my fingertips tingle and my palm sweaty. I jerked back involuntarily, annoyed that I kept reacting to this girl. Even if it was on a purely physical level, I wanted her to be inconsequential to me, like everyone else.

"That's a good point. I don't have friends. They won't believe me if I tell them I'm bringing a friend. I guess I'll have to tell them we're co-workers, and the boss ordered me to bring you along."

She scowled at me and followed behind to the SUV. Some of the bitter cold had burned off as it got later in the day, and the sun was making a valiant effort to break through the cloud cover.

"Do I get to know where we're going today? Or does it remain a mystery until we get there?" Daire fiddled with her seat belt and peeked at me over the rim of her dark sunglasses.

Figuring she would find out soon enough anyway, I told her, "Kansas City."

We still had to drive through most of Kansas, but it would be faster to get to the border than it had been getting out of the mountains in Colorado because of the weather. It was going to be a flat, straight, white, boring drive from here on out. The scenery was nothing to write home about, but I was used to it. The landscape around where I grew up was also agricultural and desolate. I meant it when I said it was in the middle of nowhere. There were vast properties separated by acres and acres of farm and ranch land. It took hours to see another person, and the ramshackle collection of old buildings and legacy businesses could barely even be called a town.

I found it difficult to believe Booker grew up near the place I called home, and I struggled to understand why Karsen wanted to return to the wretched place once they married and had kids. It wasn't until she effectively took over the town and the local government, with her ties all the way to Washington, DC, that I started to see why she was content as a massive fish in a minuscule pond. As for Booker, there wasn't anything that man wouldn't do for his wife and kids. Even if it meant returning to the last place he wanted to be.

The town wasn't known for much, but anyone who came was there to do business with, or as a favor to, the Bookers. The town wasn't famous, but the family was.

"Kansas City? Interesting. I've never been. How did your siblings end up there?" Daire sounded genuinely curious; not like she was making asinine conversation.

"They ended up there because of football." It was weirdly coincidental that football played such a major part in Daire's past and my siblings' future. "The couple I found to help my brothers and sister was based in Kansas City. One of the husbands played professional football and stayed there when he retired from the team. His husband, Vernon, is in tech, so he can work from anywhere. He helped kids who had deplorable home lives. He organized an underground network to help runaways and endangered kids when he was just a kid himself. I'm forever grateful they took in my siblings as their own. The kids couldn't be in better hands, and it's because of them that Delta got the chance to go to college."

Daire blew out a low whistle as she tapped her fingers against her thigh.

"The more I find out about you and your life, the less weird it seems that I don't know your full name. I'm starting to think you weren't exaggerating when you said you might have become a killer if you hadn't left your hometown."

I blinked and opened my mouth to tell her I was deadly serious, but I stopped the impulse at the last second. I don't know why I suddenly wanted to spill my guts to her, but the feeling was disconcerting. I hadn't talked about myself this much since the day Booker took me home and put me in front of his wife. Karsen wouldn't let me skim the truth about how bad it was at home. She wanted me to be honest with myself about my dire situation, even if I was too young to fully understand it.

Something about Daire gave me a similar feeling. She wanted honesty, no matter how ugly it might be.

"With a mentor like Benny, I'm fortunate I didn't end up as a serial killer." I was also dead serious about that.

Daire turned her head and gave me a curious look. "That's the second time you've made a comment like that about Uncle Benny. And come to think of it, if he's your mentor and the two of you were so close, why didn't anyone in Denver know about you until you came to work for Hyde? You make it seem like he has a double life. It's hard to imagine that. He's very devoted to Echo and Hyde. He's the one who convinced Hollyn's grandparents on her mother's side to leave Hyde alone after she passed away. They were going to fight him for custody and were terrible to him until Uncle Benny got involved."

I snorted, not surprised to hear that at all. It wouldn't end well if you messed with someone important to Benny. The man made sure it was known far and wide that his people were not to be messed with.

"He doesn't have a double life, just had a different one before he found Echo and settled down. He was involved in some pretty sketchy stuff when I was a kid, but left that all behind. Not by choice, but he fell in love and wanted a different future. He offered to pull me out back then, but I wasn't ready to go. I guess I was trying to prove that I was worth the effort people put into saving me." And I wanted to be close enough to my dad that I could intervene if he conned another woman into his lair. I wasn't about to let another woman end up like my mom. I mentally and physically couldn't care for any more brothers and sisters. I already gave my life away. There was nothing else left to barter.

"This information is fascinating. I regret not making you talk to me about your past sooner. I shouldn't have wasted so much effort annoying you." Daire sighed. "I like it when you get flustered and your ears turn red. The curse of being a ginger is cute. Your face might be made of stone, but your skin gives you away every time."

"Fuck you." The words barely had any bite, and I could feel my ears heating.

To divert her attention from how I blushed, I told her to keep quiet for a second while I called Vernon and Harlen, the couple raising my siblings. A moment later, a mellow voice filled the SUV.

"Hello."

"Hey, Vernon, it's Campbell. Sorry for the last-minute call, but my plans changed, and I'm on my way to Kansas City after all. I wanted to give you a warning before I get there this evening. I have a tagalong, so I won't stay long, and you and Harlen don't have to put me up for the night."

"Oh, Campbell! The kids will be so excited to see you. They were disappointed when you said you wouldn't make it until New Year's." Vernon was the more mellow, and delicate of the two men. He was a literal genius and one of the nicest men I'd ever met. He and Harlen were a good match, because the Hall of Fame football player was a bruiser. They embodied brains vs brawn. They both came from a rough background, which is why they were so protective of my siblings. I appreciated the way they tried to include me in everything that involved the kids when they didn't have to.

"Did you say someone is with you? Is it Delta? She called and said she was going to visit you in Denver for Christmas since you couldn't make it here. She didn't want you to spend the holidays alone. She checked in yesterday and told us not to worry because you were coming to pick her up."

I jerked the wheel and swore and Daire gasped as the SUV swerved. "What!? She's not in Denver. I haven't seen her or heard from her in a week. The last time I talked to her, she said she planned to stay with you guys through her winter break."

Vernon swore, and the sound echoed through the SUV. I let the vehicle drift to the shoulder of the road and pulled to a stop so I could focus on the conversation and not kill me and Daire in the process.

"Are you sure she said she was coming to see me?" It was a dumb question, but I had to say something so I didn't scream.

"I'm positive. Harlen is calling her right now. He said it's going right to voicemail. Her phone must be off."

I swore again and caught sight of the way Daire flinched. She was seeing what happened up close and personal when a loved one went missing out of the blue. The fear and panic coursing through me were probably what her brother felt when he realized she was gone.

"Campbell, where would she go if she wasn't coming to see you? Harlen is going to try to get in touch with her roommate from school. Delta isn't the type to disappear and make us worry. This isn't like her."

I punched the steering wheel and shoved a shaking hand through my hair.

"She might not have had a choice. Has my dad tried to contact her?"

Vernon got quiet, and I heard him asking Harlen about my father. My brothers were still young and easy to stash away. Delta was a different story. She was a young woman living independently for the first time in her life. She was making friends and getting the whole college freshman experience, so she was online and doing little to keep her whereabouts secret. I didn't want to stifle her and keep her under wraps forever, but I hated how easy it would be for my dad to find her if he wanted to.

"She hasn't said anything to us. If it's your father, she would tell you before she would tell us, son." Vernon understood my sister all too well. "We'll call Booker and ask him to go out to your dad's property to check."

"Don't." I barked the word so harshly it made Daire jump. She was pale, and I could see her fingers shake as she listened to the tense conversation. "If Booker goes out there, it'll make my dad mad. When he's angry, he's more dangerous. Have him ask around to see if anyone in the area noticed Delta, but remind him not to set foot on the property. It might get my sister killed. I'll go see if she's there. Let me know if you guys hear from her."

"If you need anything, let us know. Bring her home, Campbell." It was an order eerily similar to the one Benny issued about the girl in my passenger seat.

"I will."

There was no other option. And God forbid my old man did anything to hurt her; I was finally going to put him where he belonged.

Buried on that fucking plot of land he loved more than any of his damn kids.

chapter FIVE

Daire

I couldn't sit next to Campbell—his panic and anger felt hot.

All I could picture was Ry in the same situation. I knew he would've been scared and hurt, but being confronted with another big brother who was worried sick over his sister made that knowledge feel cruel and unnecessary. There had to be a way for me to leave that wouldn't bring Ry to his knees. I owed him everything. He was my hero. If Campbell's little sister could see what she was doing to him by disappearing, I bet she would regret her decision the same way I did.

I fished out the prepaid phone and typed out a message to my older brother.

~ Hey, it's Daire. I'm sorry I left without saying anything to you. I'm sorry I ruined your first Christmas with Bowe. Contrary to how it may seem, I'm happy you're happy. I left because of my own issues. It has nothing to do with the two of you or the fact things are changing. I'm not alone. Uncle Benny sent Campbell to find

me. I'm going to stick with him until I'm ready to come home. I know you don't know him and will worry regardless of what I say, but I have a few things to figure out. I can only come back once I do. I know you keep saying you're fine with the new direction of your life, but I'm not. I know in my heart when you say you've forgiven me, you mean it. But that doesn't mean I've forgiven myself. I'll check in periodically and call Mom and Dad soon. I went about it wrong, but this is the right choice for me.

There wasn't a response for a long time. Did I send it to the wrong number? I didn't have the right to get anxious since this was a situation of my own making. However, when I finally realized I might've crossed a line with Ry that I couldn't come back from, my blood went icy cold. I kept telling myself I wanted him to be mad at me. I wanted him to resent me and blame me for taking away his future, but now that I might've pushed his tolerance to the breaking point, I feared the outcome.

"If your sister has a good reason for lying to you, will you forgive her for taking off like this?" My voice was quiet but sounded unnaturally loud in the silent SUV. Campbell was always intense, but at the moment, his aura was so dark and deep it felt like I was standing on the edge of an abyss.

"Whatever she's up to, I'm sure she thinks her reasons are good." He rubbed the scar on his chin with his knuckle and clenched his teeth. A muscle in his jaw flexed, and his dark eyes narrowed. "But knowingly putting herself in danger? I have a hard time getting past that. All I've ever cared about is keeping her and my brothers safe. If Delta took herself to his doorstep, knowing how dangerous and unhinged the man is..." He trailed off, and the hand holding the steering wheel tightened to the point his knuckles turned white. "I can't easily forgive her decision to do that."

"Isn't it her choice to put herself in danger, though?" I sighed and looked at my unanswered message on the phone. "You can't always be there to protect her. At some point, she has to learn how to save herself. Doesn't she?"

That was a resolution I made as soon as Ry was released from the hospital. I was going to be my own hero from now on. If I needed rescuing, I was going to save myself. Only, the first time my resolve was put to the test, Campbell came to my rescue before I had a chance to do that. The truth was, I didn't know what I would've done if he hadn't appeared like a fiery demon breaking through the snowy white landscape. The learning curve to being self-sufficient was steep.

"You're right. She needs to learn how to take care of herself in a dangerous situation. However, there are some things no one should have to face alone. My father is one of them." His tone was sharp, and I could hear his worry in every word.

I leaned my head against the passenger window, the cold immediately sinking into my temple. It felt good. I didn't realize I had the start of a headache until the chill soothed some of the ache building in my pounding skull.

"Didn't you have to deal with your father alone? You found help for your brothers and sister, but stayed behind to ensure he was out of their lives for good. You faced off with him all by yourself when you were just a kid. I'm sure your sister remembers that. And I'm sure she feels like she owes you everything. Every opportunity she's received. Every happy moment she's made. Every step forward from the past. Every improvement she's found within herself. All of that is because you sacrificed yourself, Campbell. Whatever she's up to, I'm sure Delta sees it as something long overdue. It's something she probably felt compelled to do."

The same way I *had* to run away before I dragged my whole family down to my current rock-bottom level.

Campbell huffed out an annoyed breath and tried to call Delta again. Her phone was still off, and with each unanswered ring, I watched his tension rise and his body stiffen. I always thought he had an intimidating presence, but I never picked up on how dangerous he could be until I felt the killing intent pulsing off him.

"She's my little sister. She doesn't owe me anything. There isn't a system of checks and balances between us. It's never been about what is owed and what was taken. It doesn't matter if we have everything under the sun or nothing at all. At the end of the day, if we still have each other, that's enough. She has to be okay. There isn't any other option." I sighed and closed my eyes when I felt them tear up. A brick of emotion lodged in my throat, and I squeezed the phone in my hand so tightly it was a miracle it didn't crack. He sounded so certain when he spoke about his siblings. I wondered if Ry sounded the same way when he talked about me.

We were very close. He was my confidant and my protector. He was the brightest star in our family constellation. He was the best of us. I always knew where to go and how to find home because I could follow his light. The night he almost died, I felt like I was also on the cusp of death. I couldn't see a path forward without him. I had no future if he wasn't there to watch me chase my dreams. I knew I would stay down if he weren't around to pick me up.

I was pushing my brother away because I didn't know how to live without him. I didn't know how to adjust to not being as important to him as he was to me.

He had moved away for school and to be closer to Bowe. For a while, it felt like he was leaving me behind. I even convinced myself he wanted to get away from me since I was the reason he had to change the direction of his whole life. I wanted him to hate me the way I hated myself. I hurt myself because I knew Ry never would. It was all so fucked up.

I knew my mind wasn't right after the accident. I couldn't see exactly how skewed my perspective was until I witnessed what the other side through Campbell's eyes.

I was keeping a running tally in my mind of what was given and owed between me and Ry.

The scale was dramatically tilted in my older brother's direction. It made me feel like a terrible sister and an overall shitty person.

I sighed and knocked my head against the glass. "You're lucky to have each other. I'm sure she'll reach out with an explanation when she has a chance. If she's like me, the guilt won't sit well for very long."

I looked at Campbell from the corner of my eye when he snorted in response.

"You and she are nothing alike, Princess. You've had everything handed to you your whole life. You were pampered. You were loved. You had the freedom to try things and fail. You have parents who love you, and a whole extended army of individuals willing to go to hell and back to make sure not a single hair on your pretty head is harmed. You've got a good life, Daire. I hope by the time you're ready to return to it, you've learned to appreciate it a bit more. There are a lot of people who would kill to have a fraction of what you're currently running away from."

What he said was condescending and judgmental. He made me sound immature and ungrateful, which was exactly how I'd felt lately. Surprisingly, having someone else point out those weaknesses and faults I was obsessed with didn't feel as good as I had imagined. Despite that, I was thrilled that Campbell finally used my name. And even though his words were scathing, they showed he was paying attention to me even though he pretended he was oblivious.

I didn't care that he called me *princess* with a sneer every chance he got. It was much nicer than some things I'd been calling myself recently. However, the way he said 'Daire,' all soft and smooth with his rough voice, did something to my insides. It made my tummy feel warm and had my heart trembling uncontrollably. I was used to being unsteady in my thoughts and feelings as of late, but it was nothing compared to the earthquake of emotions set off by my name on his lips. It was like he finally understood I was a person, not some character in a child's fairytale.

"I never denied that I have a good life. The problem is, I'm not sure if I deserve any of it. Like you said, it was handed to me. I've done nothing to earn it."

He was quiet for a long moment. I could see him turning over my response, dissecting it.

"Nothing's stopping you from earning it now that you realize how easy you've had it. You're still young. You have your entire life ahead of you. It's up to you if you want to be someone worthy of all you've been blessed with, someone willing to work to keep it, or if you want to throw it all away. Don't get me wrong, the good life doesn't suit everyone. Walking away from the path of least resistance isn't the end of the world."

I hummed in agreement.

Even though I was almost twenty, it often felt like I hadn't started to live my life yet. Everything had been so smooth, easy, and unchallenging up to the point that I nearly got Ry killed. I didn't know strife. I didn't know how to navigate sorrow and regret that went deep to the bone. I never had a mountain to climb until I decided to drive up one in the middle of a winter storm like a lunatic. I didn't have to break a sweat to survive, and that didn't sit right with me the more I learned about Campbell's past.

"Does a good life suit you, Campbell?" I was honestly curious if he thought he would eventually find what he was looking for in Denver.

He turned his head to look at me, and I felt like he was seeing me for the first time.

"I don't know. I'll have to experience it before I can tell if it suits me or not. I know how to survive a hard life.

It's exhausting. It feels endless. It turns you into some-one who can't recognize a good thing even when it's right in front of them. I honestly hope you don't choose to live a hard life in the future, Daire. Because it just might break you."

Just then, the phone I was clutching like a lifeline pinged with an incoming message.

My heart stumbled over a beat, and I sucked in a breath so sharply it hurt my chest.

Ry replied.

His message was short and sweet.

It was exactly what I needed to hear from him at the moment.

> *~ I love you, Daire. I trust you. I'll be waiting for you to come home. If you need anything, let me know.*

I burst into tears.

I didn't know how badly I needed to hear Ry tell me that he would love me no matter what I did. Love with-out pressure was easy enough. Love under duress, when things were hard, was something else. It was raw. It was real. It was rough. It was important.

Campbell reached across me and pulled open the glove box. He shoved a handful of napkins that smelled like a fast-food restaurant in my hand, and met my wa-tery gaze with a confused look.

"Are you okay?"

I could tell he was a good big brother by the effort-less way he handled my tears. He didn't get awkward or annoyed. He let me cry it out and made sure I was all right, even if the napkins smelled like French fries.

"I'm fine. I messaged Ry. I didn't realize how much I needed to hear back from him. We were always close, but things got distant and weird after the accident. He was only on the side of the road that night because I had a situation I couldn't handle alone. I was being a brat, and I knew he would come if I called him. Neither one of us should've been out that night. It should've been me to get hurt. I hate that he suffered from my foolishness."

Campbell sighed and lifted a hand to push back his hair. "I can tell you from the perspective of a protective older brother, if you'd been hurt instead of him, he wouldn't have been able to live with himself. I'm sure your brother went out of his way to be the one in danger instead of you. Instead of resenting him for acting on an instinct he's had since the moment he became a big brother, you should consider thanking him."

I went completely still, his words swirling inside my brain like buzzing bees because of the brutal honesty.

Had I thanked Ry once since he got out of the hospital? Had I given him an ounce of gratitude when I owed him my life? Did I tell him I appreciated his sacrifice and was grateful we were both still alive? Was I so caught up in my own misery that I let something as simple as a 'thank you' slip through the cracks?

If that was the case, the fact he could tell me he loved me and trusted me meant even more.

My fingers rapidly typed out a hurried thanks to my brother and hit send. He might think I was only thanking him for responding so nicely to my frantic message from earlier, but I knew I was expressing my overwhelming thankfulness for so much more. I was so lucky he was my brother. I'd truly been blessed that the best Archer had always been there to keep an eye on me.

When I lifted my head, I saw a big sign announcing that we were leaving one state and entering the next. Campbell already told me he planned to drive through the night to find his sister, and we should reach his hometown early the next morning. I offered to drive part way so we could switch off sleeping for a few hours, but he rejected the idea before I finished speaking. He told me he needed to concentrate on the road. If he had nothing else to occupy his mind, he would go crazy thinking about the worst-case scenario his sister might be walking into.

"Since Kansas City is no longer the final destination, can you tell me where we're headed now?" He was being slightly more forthcoming with information now that we were on this forced road trip together. I figured I should pry as much as possible while I had the chance.

"The middle of nowhere." His voice was dry, and the corners of his mouth twitched in amusement. "It's a small town on the border between Kentucky and Ohio. Neither state wants to claim it because it's such a shithole. No one knows whose jurisdiction it falls in, so there's practically no law and order for miles. All the services and infrastructure are lacking. At one point when I was young, the town had an actual name, but somewhere along the line, everyone just started calling it Nowhere. No one wanted to admit they were from there. So whenever someone would ask where we lived, we'd say Nowhere. The nickname stuck, and now that's what everyone calls it."

I frowned and contemplated this new information. No wonder he didn't tell anyone much about himself; it sounded unbelievable when he did.

"Places like that exist?" It was so far from the world I was familiar with. How were there towns that no one wanted to claim?

Campbell chuckled, and his dark eyes glimmered with a trace of humor. "They do. The people who came to Nowhere and helped me get my siblings out came from a place called The Point. It's a suburb in a big city. People don't talk about it much, and very few folks manage to leave." He shook his head, and the mirth drifted out of his gaze. "You should stick to places people can find on a map. There's something reassuring about being able to say, 'I'm from Denver,' and not having to explain anything more. No one asks questions. It's just a fun fact about yourself, not a defining feature or badge of honor."

I hummed a soft agreement. "I love being from Denver. I couldn't imagine living anywhere else until recently. I've always wanted to see more of the world. I was jealous every time Remy would find her way home with wild stories from whatever new city she lived in for the last six months. I always thought my entire family would stay in Denver. I took it pretty hard when Ry decided to move to Texas for school and to be closer to his girlfriend."

It felt like the earth shifted under my feet when it registered that my brother would no longer be in the bedroom down the hall. He would no longer be able to get to me in under twenty minutes if I had an emergency. He wouldn't be there to watch scary movies with me when I had a bad day. It felt like I was losing a limb, which might've brought the depression on even harder in the aftermath of the accident.

I didn't know how to be alone. I was scared shitless of the prospect. It seemed counterintuitive that my instinct was to run away when Ry finally came back. I knew the reason I needed space was because I wasn't sure I could let him go again and keep my sanity.

I needed better coping mechanisms, but until I developed them, settling into the distance between us was the only solace I had.

Campbell sighed and quietly told me, "It's nice to have the choice to go as far as you want but always have a home to return to. That's better than being stuck in one spot your entire life, or aimlessly trying to find your place because nothing ever feels like it's where you belong." He rolled his head like he had a stiff neck and huffed out a breath. "You've got endless options in front of you, Princess. Don't overlook how powerful that is."

Options tended to overwhelm me. I never saw them as something that made me special. There were a lot of things I was blind to before Campbell forced me to open my eyes with his quiet words of wisdom.

It was a lot harder for Waldo to hide with the broody redhead by my side.

chapter SIX

Campbell

"We're almost there."

Instead of a statement, the words sounded like a warning.

Daire turned sleepy eyes in my direction and gave a slight nod. She'd been quiet the last several hours of the drive. She offered to get behind the wheel more than once so I could sleep, but I knew the minute I closed my eyes, I would see that shovel covered in blood and the triumphant look on my father's face. I couldn't stomach the thought of Delta ending up like our mother. I couldn't understand why she would lie about her whereabouts or what could possibly possess her to return to that hellscape we called home. She was a smart girl. There was no way she could've forgotten what kind of monster our old man was.

"Are you taking me to your childhood home?" Daire rubbed her eyes and sat up straight in the passenger seat. She sounded confused and curious. "The way you talk about it, it doesn't sound like we'd get a very warm welcome."

I snorted and glanced at my silent phone. Each hour that crawled by while Delta didn't respond to any of my messages made my skin feel tighter. Anxiety was eating me up from the inside out. I couldn't remember the last time I was this nervous.

"No. I'm taking you to the compound. It's the safest place I can think of in this area for you to stay while I deal with my family stuff. Benny told me to get you back home in one piece, and that's what I'm going to do." I rolled my stiff neck and tried to loosen the knot between my shoulders. It had been a long drive. I felt like I was sitting on a bed of nails the entire way. I missed yesterday when I thought I was just indulging a pretty princess. Now, not only did I have to rescue Daire, but I also had to save my sister from Lord only knows what. Everything felt a lot more complicated than it had when I left Denver, including my perception of Daire Archer.

When I started to work for Hyde, he told me Daire wasn't a princess. He warned me that she was strong-willed and stubborn. He told me point-blank that her defiant attitude and difficult personality were new developments, but I thought he was just trying to paint her in a good light so we would get along.

Now, I understood she was difficult, but in a different way than he probably meant. Her personality was layered. Her heart was conflicted. She felt unworthy and lacking in the eyes of those who loved her. She was naïve in many ways, but also savvier and more self-aware than I'd previously given her credit for. I started to wonder if I'd been too hard on her and unfair because I'd been conditioned to believe the worst of everyone.

"The compound? Why does that sound so scary?" She shifted nervously in her seat and looked ahead at the long, winding dirt road that stretched on for miles.

I remembered walking this road and wondering if I would die before I reached the end. Fortunately, Booker picked me up before I keeled over from exposure and malnutrition.

"It's called a compound because there are a lot of buildings on the property, as well as the main house and farm. The security is practically impenetrable and as high-tech as you can get. There are always a bunch of people in and out of the place besides the family, so calling it a farm or a family home isn't quite right. The couple who owns the land have a couple of kids. I grew up watching over them. Their daughter, Charley, is around the same age as you and Delta. She's probably home for the holidays, so you won't be alone at the compound when I go to my dad's place. The son, Nolan, is still in high school. This should be his final year."

When I was at a crossroads, Karsen had asked me if I wanted to stay on as part of the family's personal security detail until her youngest was ready to leave for college. The Booker's have a lot of enemies, and their biggest weakness is their children. Being their personal security detail was no easy task, and the reward was as high as the risks. I was tempted by the offer, but then Benny popped up out of the blue and offered me a way out. It was hard for me to turn him down. I'd spent my entire life caring for others, and I couldn't walk away from the opportunity to finally put myself first. It felt indulgent, but necessary.

Too bad my freedom was short-lived.

Before Daire could respond, a bright yellow sports car flew up the dirt road in our direction. A cloud of dust kicked up by the wheels obscured my view. I frowned as I let the SUV drop to zero miles per hour. The low-slung import coasted to a stop next to the driver's side, and the dark tinted window rolled down.

Daire leaned forward so she could peek around me, and the two girls stared at each other while I sat stiffly between them.

The dark-haired girl in the yellow car lowered her sunglasses and flashed me a grin. Her gun-metal gaze was just as sharp as her father's. Charley Booker was a very pretty girl in a totally different way than Daire. She was edgier, tougher, and more lethally sexy than Daire. She used her looks as her primary weapon. Daire saw hers as a burden that was constantly getting in her way.

Charley was her father's daughter down to her marrow, so even though she was young and generally easy-going, I never made the mistake of underestimating her. I knew firsthand that she knew more ways to kill a man than I could count using both hands. She was not someone to be taken lightly.

"Are you the welcoming committee?" I kept my voice light and tried to soften the tense expression I'd had on my face since the phone call with Vernon.

She shook her head, which sent her dark hair flying around her face. "No. Dad asked me to run an errand in town for him, and I have to pick up Nolan from a friend's house. You look like shit, Campbell. You aren't going to do Delta any good if you push yourself so hard you break." Her gaze shifted to Daire, and her brows furrowed. "Who is she?"

I lifted my eyebrows and looked between Charley and Daire. They appeared to be equally curious about one another.

I was currently in a super-hot-girl-who-cannot-be-fucked-with sandwich. I knew it would be a dream come true for many guys, but I was so uncomfortable.

"A co-worker. We've been taking care of the baby together in Denver. She was brought in to keep an eye on me for the first month or so. The dad is new to fatherhood and wanted to be extra cautious. This is Daire. Daire, this is Charley."

A hint of visible relief flashed across Charley's face as she asked even more directly, "She's not your girlfriend?"

Daire scoffed and rolled her eyes as she told the other young woman, "We're not even friends."

I grunted and gave Daire a hard look. If she wasn't my friend, Charley might interpret that as meaning she was my enemy. And none of the Bookers went easy on an enemy. "It doesn't matter who she is. I'm entrusting her safety to you guys while I figure out what's going on with Delta and my dad. Daire's important, Charley, so play nice."

Gray-blue eyes narrowed, and her mouth turned down into a frown. I knew she was upset that I called Daire important. I never classified anyone I wasn't related to that way.

I was aware that Charley had a longstanding crush on me. She never made it much of a secret. Her unrequited feelings were another reason I jumped at Benny's offer to move to Denver.

I liked Charley. We had a lot in common. We grew up together. But that was the problem. We were too similar. We had seen and done too many questionable things. The version of me Charley liked for so long was the version I constantly questioned. Charley thrived in her hard life, while I was lucky to barely survive mine. Any future she was part of was bound to be bloody and violent.

"She's important in general, or she's important to you, Campbell?" Charley's voice was as sharp as the point of a knife.

I heard Daire gasp at the pointed question. Charley wasn't one to beat around the bush or play games. I had a gut feeling Daire would be hurt if I answered the question wrong.

I sighed. "Both." Charley wouldn't like the truth. However, she could sniff out a lie a mile away. It was better to be honest with her, even if it meant Daire learned how I viewed her was changing in difficult and dangerous ways.

Charley huffed an annoyed breath and rolled up her window. The sports car zoomed off, fishtailing on the dirt road before it disappeared.

I put my foot on the gas and headed the rest of the way to the compound. Daire was quiet. She was tapping her fingers on her knee, and her eyes were focused on a point a million miles away. Occasionally, she would wrinkle her nose like she was deep in thought.

"Charley's bark is worse than her bite. She'll keep an eye on you while you're at the compound. She's spent most of her life trying to emulate her dad, so she's got a hard shell that doesn't want to crack."

Daire turned her head and tucked a wayward piece of white blonde hair behind her ear.

"I didn't say anything about her." She was right. She didn't mention Charley at all. It was my assumption that she was worrying over the other young woman. "I'm a stranger you're dropping on her doorstep unexpectedly. You told me you don't have any friends, so it makes sense that the people who know you are concerned about my motives." She lifted a pale eyebrow and said, "I think it's nice she's looking out for you. She kind of reminds me of Bowe. She doesn't take shit from anyone, either. She's my brother's girlfriend. We've known each other since we were in diapers. She and my brother have had this hate-to-love thing going on since they were kids. Even when they weren't together, even when Ry was involved with someone else, Bowe still looked at him like he was the beginning and end of everything." She pointed the finger at the end of my nose. "That's exactly how that girl looks at you."

"You're exaggerating." I kept my voice dry and bored. Charley had a crush. It wasn't as intense as Daire made it out to be.

"I'm not. The biggest difference is that my brother looks at Bowe the same way." She shrugged. "You look at that girl like she's family. It's the same way my cousin, Zowen, looks at me. With fondness, a bit of pride, and a touch of exasperation. You care about her, but you definitely don't plan on sleeping with her."

The gravel road curved, and the massive gates that were the first hint the Booker farm wasn't like any of the others came into view. Before I pulled up to the entrance, two men armed to the teeth appeared from the other side.

Daire made a startled sound, and her eyes popped wide.

I motioned for her to sit still and keep quiet. Booker had to have told security I was coming to visit, but the guys who worked for him never slacked off. A bad day while working for the Bookers might lead to your funeral.

After I was cleared and the gates were open, I replied to Daire's statement.

"I don't plan on sleeping with anyone. Sex isn't even on my radar at the moment. I will get my sister out of whatever mess she's in. Then I will convince you to go home, and hopefully, all will return to normal. Once things settle down and I decide if Denver is where I want to be, maybe then I can focus on fucking."

Daire laughed and turned to look out the window as the main part of the compound came into view.

"Or maybe you take care of everything else and let someone else focus on the fucking. Some things don't appear on the radar, even when they are very much there. Doesn't a surprise attack sound kind of fun?" She pointed out the window and changed the subject so fast that I felt like I got whiplash. "Look how cool all this stuff is!"

There was a big red barn with every kind of cute farm animal you could imagine, like something out of a kid's book, on one side of the land, and a massive steel and glass house that was nothing but modern lines and sharp angles on the other. Old and new. Traditional and

79

futuristic. Family-friendly and starkly inhospitable at the same time. It was a juxtaposition that perfectly fit everything about the Bookers and their lifestyle.

Daire whistled and leaned forward until her nose was practically touching the windshield.

"This place is unbelievable. I've never been to a real farm before. Do you think they'll let me play with the goats?" She sounded like a little kid on Christmas morning.

"Yeah. They'll let you pet the goats." I was a little baffled that we were greeted by an armed guard, had passed by an endless number of security cameras, were followed to the house by more than one drone, parked next to an armored SUV that looked like it was stolen from the Secret Service, and yet all Daire seemed to care about were the goats.

This girl was either completely unflappable or had a screw loose.

"This is where you grew up after you left your dad's place?" She turned to look at me with excited eyes. "It doesn't seem so bad. Between the guns and the goats, it had to be interesting at the very least."

I was taken aback by the humor in her voice.

"It was eventful. I had to learn a lot. My dad never sent any of us to school, so when Karsen set me up to watch her kids, I had to learn a lot about protection and self-defense, but even more about basic education. I was so far behind any other kid my age, it felt like I would never catch up. When other people my age were thinking about which college to attend and looking at what they wanted to do in the future, I was still struggling with freshman English and math comprehension."

Typically, talking about my lack of formal education was off limits. I didn't like to highlight my weaknesses or open the door to places where I might be lacking.

A flash of sympathy crossed Daire's face. She quickly hid it and returned to the playful personality who asked about the goats.

"They always say it's not what you know; it's who you know. From where I'm sitting, you know some very interesting and powerful people, Campbell. Don't focus so much on what you think is your weakness; keep your eyes on what you know is your strength."

I pushed open the door and looked at her over my shoulder when a very large man stepped out of the front of the house. His gaze hit us, and I felt the weight of it like a physical touch. Daire stopped rambling, and I heard her swallow nervously.

"Oh, wow. Isn't he impressive?" There was a touch of wonder in her soft voice.

I made a faint sound of agreement and told her, "That's Booker."

We met at the front of the vehicle, and I paused when her small hand hooked my elbow. She tugged until I lowered my head so that she could whisper in my ear, "Is he like you? No first or last name, just Booker?"

The tiny hairs on the back of my neck lifted when her warm breath caressed the shell of my ear. That damn tingle was back, and I still had no idea what to do with it. I gritted my teeth and practically growled, "Booker is his last name. Everyone calls him Booker except for Karsen, his wife. She calls him Noah."

She didn't drop her hand as we approached the big man. Her fingers dug into the fabric of my coat. She held me tighter the closer we got.

Booker took a couple of steps down from the entryway and reached out a big, scarred hand to shake mine. His gaze was unreadable as always, but I could tell by the slight uplifting of the corners of his mouth, and the way the long scar that slashed across one side of his face twitched, that he was happy to see me.

"Glad you remembered the way back, kiddo. We missed you around here." One of his dark eyebrows lifted. "Some of us more than others. I'm sure you ran into Charley on your way in."

I nodded. "I did."

His steely gaze drifted over to Daire. "I didn't tell her you had someone with you. Thought it would be easier to defuse that bomb once you were here."

"She handled meeting Daire better than I expected. There was no bloodshed. She let me bring her up to the house without a fight." I hoped Daire thought I was joking around, but I was serious.

I offered a quick introduction. Booker couldn't hold back a grin when Daire referred to him as Mr. Booker. He quickly corrected her that it was simply Booker and offered to take her inside to meet his wife and get us settled.

I was ready to hand Daire off to someone else so I could race out to my father's property and get Delta out of there as quickly as possible.

Before stepping away from Daire, Booker put a hand on my shoulder and kept me in place.

"I have some guys keeping watch up at your dad's place. There is no sign of him or Delta yet. Come inside, get something to eat, and take a minute to rest. I know you drove through the night. I'm not letting you face off with that lunatic when you're so tired you can't see straight. That's a guaranteed way to lose you and your sister. If something happens to you, Benny will be so far up my ass, you'll be able to see that ugly watch he always wears whenever I open my mouth."

I wanted to resist.

My dad could have stashed my sister anywhere on his property. There were old mine shafts out in the woods and lots of caves and hidey-holes. Just because the shack was empty didn't mean he wasn't somewhere on the land watching Booker's people right back.

However, it was ingrained in me that Booker was the boss. I'd followed his orders for years. I owed him and Karsen for saving my family, and for offering me a way to keep my father in check all these years. Defying him wasn't something I knew how to do.

Sensing my discomfort, Daire jumped in to ease some of the tension.

"Come on, Campbell. You said I could pet the goats. Let's go in and get some rest, pet some farm animals, and then you can go and be a hero. Who knows, maybe Delta will call you back in the meantime and tell you all of this has been a big misunderstanding. Little sisters screw up sometimes but don't mean any harm. I know that better than anyone at the moment."

I followed Booker out of habit.

But I listened to Daire because I wanted to. I wanted her to be to be right.

chapter SEVEN

Daire

"You seem to be taking this in stride. There aren't many new people who make it up to the house and very few make it past my husband. You probably have a lot of questions."

I looked at the woman sitting across from me and tried to pinpoint who she reminded me of. She was a stunning woman with curly blonde hair almost as light as mine and hyper-intelligent eyes. She was very tall and dressed like she was about to step onto a runway, not do farm chores. Everything about her was fascinating and oddly familiar. She resembled someone famous, but I couldn't put my finger on who it might be.

I wrapped my hands around the cup of tea she'd placed in front of me and tilted my head to one side. "I do have questions. Has anyone told you that you look like someone famous? And what was Campbell like as a kid? Did he ever smile? Has he ever let himself have any fun?" There was a laundry list of them to assuage my curiosity about the man.

The older woman smiled, and the massive wedding ring on her finger glinted even though the light filtering into the room was dim.

"When I was younger, I often heard I looked like a certain pop star." Karsen smiled at me. "I never saw the resemblance, though." She picked up her mug of tea and looked at me over the top. "No questions about the men with guns or why this property is harder to access than the Pentagon?"

I shrugged. "The guys with guns don't have anything to do with me. Neither does this place. My dad always told me to know when to make something my business and when to keep my curiosity to myself. Campbell is different. He's in my life, and I've decided to make him my business. He's interesting."

"I don't think anyone has ever been more interested in Campbell than in what goes on around here. Going to Denver was a good choice for him. Initially, I was worried about him venturing out on his own. Campbell is a lot more fragile than anyone knows. That outer armor of his is bulletproof, but it's not seamless. There are cracks that allow him to be wounded by the right weapon—or the right adversary. He reminds me of my husband in that way. I knew I could keep protecting him if he stayed here."

There was obvious fondness in her voice when she spoke of Campbell. It wasn't quite like a parent talking about a beloved child, more like a teacher with a prized student accomplishing great things.

"He seems to think *here* is too close to his father. He needs some space to figure out who he is without the threat of that man hanging over his head. I understand the need to know who you are when you step out of the shadow of your parents. That's one of the reasons I'm curious about him. We shouldn't have anything in common, but the more time I spend with him, the more similarities I find. It's fascinating, and it makes me feel less alone while struggling with some personal stuff."

The other corners of Karsen's eyes crinkled as her smile widened. "It took me a lifetime to convince my husband that we were more alike than different. He never wanted to admit it, but I wore him down. I feel like I should warn you that Campbell doesn't need someone like him. If he did, I would encourage my daughter's blind infatuation with him. He needs is someone the opposite of him. He needs someone who can balance all the bad things he has been through since he was a child."

I gave a hum of agreement and looked down at the warm liquid in my mug.

"Maybe he just needs someone who understands him. Someone who gets the old parts and the new parts of him." I shrugged again. "I'm not saying that person is me, but I do know how far having someone like that in your life can take you."

Karsen Booker, who looked like she should be famous and not infamous, stared at me like she could see all the way to the center of my soul. Everyone kept alluding that her husband was the scary one. However, this woman was terrifying. She gave me chills. Between the two of them, she was clearly the bigger threat.

"You could be right. After all, I never knew that Campbell wanted to call somewhere other than Nowhere home." She put her mug down and braced a hand on the ornate dining table to lean closer to me. "To answer your earlier questions, he was a quiet kid. Shy. Reserved. He was scared of everything and worried sick about his brothers and sister. He was obedient and willing to learn. I don't think he ever walked away from a difficult task. He smiled at his siblings, and occasionally when he mastered something new, but his smiles were few and far between. He was excellent with my kids. I never treated him like one of my own because he made it clear that he wanted to remember where he came from. Those experiences made him who he is and gave him a direction. He was a *good* kid, but he's grown into a *great* man. I won't allow anyone to say anything different. He always has a place here in my home and within my organization."

I refused to push back in my seat. I had a gut feeling I was in the middle of some kind of test, and if I showed any fear or weakness in front of this woman, I would fail.

"When he decides to talk about himself, which isn't often, he always speaks highly of his time spent here with you and your family. Campbell has nothing but respect for the opportunities you gave him. I don't even know him very well, but I can tell you that with confidence. He makes it sound like you saved his entire family. I know he's really the one who saved everyone when he decided to escape his father and come find you and ask for help. He's always been brave, but it seems like he can't see that side of himself very clearly."

One of her golden eyebrows lifted, and her smile softened slightly. "You've got him figured out."

I laughed. "Not even close. But paying attention to what makes him tick is a nice distraction."

"He's not used to being the center of attention. He's used to being in the background, caring for everyone else. The focus you have on him might make him uncomfortable at first, but keep it up. He deserves your curiosity." She pushed away from the table and rose elegantly to her feet. She really was statuesque and oozed authority.

My mother had a similar way of carrying herself. As a surgeon, she had the power of life and death in her hands daily. She made big decisions that could alter someone's entire existence all the time. My mom was an impressive woman who wanted to heal others. Karsen Booker was an equally impressive woman, but I got the distinct impression that her goal was the opposite. It felt like she could destroy whatever and whomever she wanted with nothing more than a word.

"Those mistakes you keep mentioning..." Karsen trailed off after motioning for me to follow her down a hallway where Campbell had disappeared earlier. "Acknowledging them is a good first step. Work to fix them and learn from them instead of using Campbell to distract yourself."

The advice was given in a friendly manner, but the underlying threat wasn't lost on me. If I made Campbell another one of my mistakes, the transgression would not be forgotten by this woman and the people who cared about him.

Before I could think of a witty or reassuring retort, I was led to a spacious, airy bedroom. Karsen waved her hand at the entrance and told me to make myself at home. She mentioned that she'd had Charley toss something for me to wear into the attached bathroom before my arrival and told me if I needed anything to simply ask.

I thanked her profusely and watched with wide eyes as she walked away.

Few people had a leg up on me when it came to *who* they knew. The Archers were not to be taken lightly, and were more powerful as a unit than they were as individuals. But after meeting the people in Campbell's corner, I was starting to grasp that there were different levels of powerful and untouchable connections.

I tossed the borrowed hoodie onto the pristine white bedspread and shoved my hands through my hair. I'd slept on and off in the car, and with the excitement surrounding this property and the peek into Campbell's past, I was too keyed up to sleep. I sat down on the edge of the bed to text Remy an update and to send that message to Bowe I promised. I got the first one typed out and ready to go when there was a knock on the bedroom door. Before I could get up to answer it, Campbell walked into the room like he owned the place.

"Rude." I sniffed at his entrance and looked up as he loomed over me.

He crossed his arms over his chest and squinted his dark eyes in my direction.

"Why are you so calm about all of this, Daire? Any normal person would be losing their shit over everything they've seen since we hit the outskirts of Nowhere. How can the goats be the only things you're interested in?" He sounded mad that I wasn't a hysterical mess.

I shrugged a shoulder. "You called this place a compound. It's in a town without a name. You guard information about your past like it's the Crown jewels. If I asked questions about this place, you'd tell me it's none of my concern, or you'd lie to me. The phrase 'ignorance is bliss' was made for this trip and for being around you. Understanding this situation isn't about me. Keeping my curiosity in check is personal growth. If I was this enlightened the night I called Ry to help me with my car, neither of us would've been in the line of fire of that truck."

I pushed to my feet and was momentarily surprised by how close the movement put us. I was eye-level with the base of his throat, and watched in fascination as his Adam's apple bobbed. I put a hand on the center of his chest to balance myself. I felt his heart thud erratically under my palm.

"I want to tell you something, Campbell."

He caught my hand and moved to step back, but I didn't let him put any distance between us. I lifted my free hand and wrapped it around the back of his neck. I needed to stand on my tippy-toes to be at eye level with him. His dark gaze was full of conflict.

"Whatever you have to do to keep your sister safe is fine with me. No matter how extreme your actions are, if you think they're justified, that's all that matters to me. Who you were in the past and who you are now deserve better than you've been given. My support probably doesn't mean anything to you, but I want you to know that you have it, nonetheless. It's the least I can offer after you came up a mountain in a blizzard to save me."

I couldn't explain the gnawing need to be close to him. I didn't understand the pull he had on me. There were no words to describe how alluring I found his warmth and how badly I wanted to bring some light into his dark eyes.

Trying to get under his skin may have started as a game, but at the moment, all I could see, smell, hear, and feel was him. Now it felt much more serious than some innocent teasing to get his attention.

Did I plan to kiss Campbell? No.

Did I have any right to kiss Campbell? Also no.

Did I think he would welcome the press of my lips against his? Fuck no.

But none of that stopped me.

We were already so close, and I breathed in with every breath he exhaled. Like we were giving each other life. My circumstances were a mess of my own making, but that didn't stop me from wanting to drag him into the turbulent current of my emotions and the rushing flood of desire that suddenly overtook my whole body.

When I touched my lips to his, I felt his entire body jolt. His hands grabbed my waist reflexively, and his head started to pull back, but he couldn't go anywhere because I had a solid hold on him. I pressed closer to his chest, letting the heat from his body sink into my skin.

It was far from my first kiss and, honestly, way down on the list of the best kisses I'd ever had, but none of that stopped it from feeling like my very first adult kiss.

It was the first kiss that struck me as important. It was a kiss that felt weighted by more than simple lust and unchecked passion. There were things caught between our lips, like longing and acceptance.

I dug my fingernails into the back of his neck and plastered my chest to his. I flicked the tip of my tongue against the slightly parted seam of his lips and breathed a sigh when I felt him react to the shy caresses.

One of his hands resting on my waist stopped being polite the second I tried to deepen the kiss. His palm slid enticingly around the curve of my ass and squeezed the handful of flesh playfully.

I gasped in surprise, and Campbell took the opportunity to take control of the previously innocent advance.

Unlike me, he wasn't hesitant. He used the hand that wasn't holding me against all the hot, hard parts of his body to press on the center of my chin. He applied a hint of pressure, and my mouth opened obediently.

In the back of my mind, an alarm bell started to ring.

This behavior was reckless and couldn't lead anywhere.

We came from different worlds.

But not right now.

We couldn't be any closer at the moment unless our bodies were joined.

His tongue forced its way past my parted lips with no delicacy or flirtation. It swept against mine, leaving behind the taste of coffee and a rush of desire. Campbell's kiss was bold and brazen. It pulled the air from my lungs and made my heart beat frantically.

I wanted him. Desperately. Uncontrollably. Viscerally in a way that would've frightened me if I was thinking clearly.

I could feel it from the way my scalp tingled to the way my insides clenched. I couldn't remember any other kiss turning me inside out, making me forget every bit of sense I possessed.

His teeth tugged on my lower lip, and his tongue twisted around mine. He left no corner of my mouth untouched. He let me return the favor, my teeth and tongue as hungry as his. If his kiss was an attack, mine was a heady exploration. I was amazed at how soft parts of him were. It was a nice break from the hardness, making the spot between my legs throb in time to my heartbeat. I felt my lips sting and my breath catch. My hands couldn't pull him closer, even though they tried. His hands were hard where he held onto me, and I could feel his body tighten the longer the kiss went on. It might not have been the best kiss under the sun, but it was the hottest.

It was wet and sexy. It was hot and frenzied. It was the kind of kiss that led to naked bodies, multiple orgasms, and regret the morning after.

It was a kiss that could consume me if I let it. I wanted it to go on forever and pretend it never happened.

It was unbelievable that average sex up to this point in my life was wholly forgettable, but this kiss...I knew it would be ingrained in my memory and linger on my lips for eternity.

It wasn't clear who woke up from the intoxicating haze first. We pulled away from each other like we'd both been struck by lightning.

Campbell practically pushed me away, and I landed on the edge of the bed with a grunt. I pushed my messy hair out of my face and looked at him guardedly.

"Sneak attack." Joking was a defense mechanism to make light of what happened, even though I was shaken to my very core. If I pretended it wasn't serious, I wouldn't be wounded when Campbell did the same. I cleared my throat and lifted my fingers to touch my swollen lips. "Consider it a kiss for luck. It sounds like you need all you can get to deal with your father."

Campbell touched the scar on his chin and his eyebrows twitched. The expression on his face wasn't one I'd ever seen before, but he didn't look like he wanted to argue with me, so I decided to consider my strategy of laughing off our sudden intimacy as a winner.

"I don't need luck to deal with my father. I need weapons and the element of surprise. Don't make trouble while I'm gone, Princess. I'll make sure someone takes you down to see the goats."

I nodded and grabbed his hand when he tried to leave. "Be careful." I couldn't explain why, but I suddenly felt my well-being was tied directly to his.

Campbell gave a brisk nod and shut the door with a quiet click.

I threw myself back on the bed and covered my hands with my face. I had no clue what I was doing where this man with only one name was concerned. I did know to the center of my bones that I unequivocally wanted to kiss him again.

I wanted to do so much more than kiss him.

EIGHT

Campbell

"Keep an eye out for anything that looks like it doesn't belong. My dad is a big fan of homemade booby traps, and he got his hands on some legit landmines at one point. He would be thrilled if we blew ourselves up while trespassing on his land."

I looked over my shoulder at Booker, who nodded silently and passed the message on to the rest of his men surrounding the property behind us. There was still no sign of Delta, but my father had returned to the shack before dark, a wild boar carcass in tow. It appeared he was out hunting and had no idea hell was about to descend on his beloved plot of land.

I was still anxious that there was no sign of Delta. I didn't want to believe the worst, but there was no forgetting that blood-covered shovel from my childhood.

"Can I ask you a question, kid?"

Booker's voice was a low grumble that practically disappeared with the breeze.

"You can ask, but can't promise I'll answer." Especially if it had to do with Daire Archer. I was too turned around in my head and upside down under my skin where my not-so-royal princess was concerned.

"I've known you for a long time, Campbell. I watched you grow up. I watched you become a young man I'm proud to have stand by my side and protect my family. I understand you better than most. After all, I know what being from Nowhere does to someone. But one thing has always bugged me about you." Our eyes met, and I could see the genuine puzzlement on his scarred face. "All these years, why haven't you done anything about your old man? Why do you let him stay on this land he loves and live his life in relative peace after what he put you through? You're more than capable of making him disappear. Even if you have some misplaced sentimentality because he shares your blood and you didn't want to get your hands dirty, all you had to do is mention wanting him gone to Benny or me. We would fix the problem for you. Are you more sympathetic than I think? Or stupider?"

I stumbled over a rock and swore under my breath as the sudden motion and sound sent a couple of birds squawking into the air. If we had the element of surprise before, it was gone now. I gave Booker a dirty look and steadied myself, physically and mentally.

"If I took my dad out, I would be no better than him." I sighed and shook my head. "I would end up stuck in Nowhere, tied to that kind of secret and his fucking land forever. And if anyone ever found out what I did, my brothers and sister would be devastated. They need me to be better than he was."

I gave him a pointed look. The truth is, I often imagined what my life would be like if I killed my father.

Wondered what it would mean for me and if it would change who I was. He deserved every bad thing coming his way, but I didn't want to be tied to it. I didn't want anything from the man now that he was out of my life, including his suffering. My opinion might change if he hurt Delta. I couldn't be as objective if he was messing with my siblings again after all this time.

"I would never ask you or Benny to get involved more than you already have. You saved my life, Booker. You saved my siblings. You made sure they were safe and gave them a chance to have a loving family. I could never give them anything like that. Benny offered me a chance at a new life, even if I'm not sure that's what I want. None of that can be repaid. Do you think I want to add to my debt?"

A dry twig snapped underfoot as we cleared the tree line surrounding my dad's homestead. Booker and I paused and listened for any sound. Booker touched his ear while one of his men relayed information over their communication device.

"Your dad went inside the house. He wasn't acting suspicious, but the guys watching the front think it's odd that he left the hog unattended. Still no sign of Delta on the premises." He narrowed his eyes and patted my shoulder. "I kept your siblings safe. You kept my kids safe. None of the bad parts of what their mother and I do ever touched them because of you, Campbell. I can't speak for Benny because he's a lunatic, but there is no debt as far as the Bookers are concerned. We're on equal footing, kid. You're part of my family. Don't forget it."

It was a nice sentiment, one that maybe I had needed to hear for a long time, but the moment was broken when a shotgun blast rang out. Buckshot hit the ground near the tip of my boot, sending dirt and debris flying.

Another shot rang out as Booker put a broad hand on the top of my head and shoved me to the ground.

Return fire echoed in the valley from the shack.

"Tell your guys he has an arsenal in the root cellar under the house. Our side will run out of ammo before the old man does."

Booker relayed the message as another shotgun blast hit the ground in front of me. A rock ricocheted from the impact and sliced across my cheek. I felt the cut start to bleed and swore as Booker fired a shot back over my head.

I wiped the blood away with the back of my hand and pushed to my feet. I yelled at my father even though it would give our exact location away.

"Put the gun down, Dad. I came for Delta. Let me see her, and I'll have everyone hold their fire." Booker tried to pull me back down, but I stepped farther into the clearing so my dad could see exactly who he was firing at.

"You're trespassing. I told you not to step foot on this property ever again, you ungrateful bastard. You're no son of mine! Never were."

My father's words were slightly slurred as if he'd been drinking. However, even inebriated, he was still one hell of a shot. The next blast sent buckshot whizzing past my arm close enough to rip my jacket.

"I want to see my sister. If you don't tell me what you did with Delta, I will burn that shack to the ground with you in it, old man. Don't forget, you still get to call this garbage pile 'home' because I allow it. Put the gun down, asshole."

Karsen bought all the acreage surrounding Nowhere. All the local farms and ranches were offered the chance to repurchase their property through her versus owing outrageous sums to the local banks. She ensured legacies were kept intact and not lost to unpaid mortgage payments. She made sure she was the only debt collector in the area and offered terms that reflected they barrowers loyalty. She offered to buy out the loan on my dad's land once my siblings were far away and safe. I knew there was no way he could ever buy it back from her or the bank, and that the Bookers would never cut him a deal. She wanted to put the property in my name so I would have something to hold over the bastard's head. I asked her to leave him alone on the land, and told her I would work off the mortgage. She refused, but reminded my father regularly she could take everything he held dear if he misstepped in the slightest. I believe he hated being controlled by a woman, even more than he hated me.

I didn't do it because he loved it more than me. I didn't do it because my mother was buried somewhere I'd never been able to locate.

Nor because I wanted to take it from him on his deathbed.

I wanted my father to keep the land so none of his kids would ever be tempted to return to Nowhere. I wanted more for my siblings. I wanted more for myself.

As long as my dad stuck around to protect this property, there wasn't the slightest chance the kids would call Nowhere home. Or so I thought, until Delta disappeared.

"If you don't tell me where Delta is right now, I'll make sure every last corner of this property goes up in flames, and I'll make sure any legal claim you have goes away."

"You always had a big mouth, boy."

I heard him cock the shotgun to reload, and a moment later, something flew into one of the cracked windows of the hovel. Smoke immediately started filling the house, creeping through all the gaps in the siding and billowing out of the holes in the roof.

My father started coughing. I heard him gag as he called me every bad name under the sun.

Booker and I moved closer. The blood from the gash on my face started to trickle down my neck and seep into my shirt collar.

"Those smoke bombs won't hurt Delta if he has her in there, will they?" I was worried about my sister, but we had to get closer to the house and this was the only way.

Booker shook his head and frowned when he caught sight of my bloody face. "Her eyes are gonna burn and she's gonna puke. She'll probably be very uncomfortable, but she'll be fine. Guys are about to breach the house through a busted back window since you distracted your dad. They'll pull her out if they locate her."

My dad was groping on the ground for his shotgun shells. He was swearing up a storm but refused to move off the dilapidated porch.

I took a running leap and barreled into him, taking in a mouthful of the teargas as we tumbled through the rotten wood of the decking.

I gagged, and my eyes immediately clouded over as the toxic gas hit me in the face.

I waved Booker back so we weren't both incapacitated as I struggled with my father. For a drunk old man, he was still scrappy. I caught a fist to my temple and an elbow in my ribs before I smashed his nose in and knocked out a couple of his remaining teeth. There would've been more damage on both sides if the teargas hadn't done its job and knocked us out of commission.

A long time after I'd been doused from head to toe and had the teargas flushed from my eyes for a solid hour, I finally found out my sister was nowhere to be found in my father's home. Booker's guys practically took the building down to the studs looking for her, and to my surprise, there was no sign of Delta, but they stumbled across another young woman locked up in the root cellar.

She barely looked legal, was strung out on something, and could hardly string together a coherent sentence. She couldn't tell Booker how long she'd been down there or where my dad had picked her up. She didn't seem particularly grateful to be rescued either.

I wanted to beat on my father until he told me where Delta was, but he didn't regain consciousness before I had to leave.

"Campbell." We were headed back to the compound. Booker hadn't said much since his men pulled the girl out of the cellar. He didn't get the teargas as directly as I did, so he was behind the wheel while I tried to figure out where else my sister could be.

"What?" I couldn't go back and forth with him anymore. Getting shot by one of your parents tended to take a lot out of you.

"Karsen isn't going to let the fact slide that your dad had a woman locked in his basement. It doesn't matter if the girl is a junkie or was there willingly. Her bottom line, where your old man is concerned, is that he stayed out on the property alone. He's not allowed to do what he did to you and your mom to anyone else. I need you to understand what's going to happen next."

I rubbed my irritated eyes and slumped down in my seat. "I understand."

I truly did.

Karsen had been lenient and let me call the shots with the old man up until now. A line was crossed today, and there was no going back.

I was about to tell Booker I had no issue with doing what had to be done when my phone rang. I wasn't in the mood to talk to anyone, but when I saw Vernon's number on the screen, I bolted upright and swiped to answer the call. "Vernon, did you hear from Delta?" I couldn't keep the quiver out of my voice.

"Campbell, it's me."

I froze when I heard my sister's voice. I jolted upright and reached out a hand to brace myself against the dash.

"Delta. Where in the fuck have you been? Why aren't you answering your phone? Do you know how worried I am about you? I can't believe you lied to Harlen and Vernon about spending Christmas with me."

For someone who didn't talk much, it was a lot of words at once for me. I wanted to crawl through the phone and hug her. I also wanted to throttle her. I wondered if this was an identical conversation to the one

Daire had with her brother when she finally gave in and sent him a text message.

"I'm so sorry. I left my phone in Boston. I didn't know everyone thought I was missing until I got ahold of my roommate, and she told me everyone was launching a nationwide search and rescue. When I found out, I got on the first flight to Kansas City."

I gritted my teeth and shoved a frustrated hand through my hair.

"Your phone is in Boston, but where were you?" Delta went quiet on the other end of the phone, and I could picture her nervously twirling her hair around her fingers. It took a lot for me to scold or pressure her, but her disappearance was unforgivable, and not only because it led to a showdown with my dad.

"I was going to tell you, Campbell." She sniffed like she was crying, and I felt my heart squeeze in response. "I met a really nice girl in one of my classes. We live in the same dorm. She invited me to come home for Christmas with her, and I really wanted to go. I didn't want to hurt Vernon and Harlen's feelings because they're great, but when you said you weren't going to make it, I saw an opportunity. I just wanted a normal holiday, surrounded by a normal family that doesn't have to unwrap trauma alongside gifts." She sniffed again. "I messed up. I know it. I should've been honest, but I didn't want to hurt anyone. I was just excited and forgetful. If I had my phone, I would've cleared everything up in a heartbeat if I knew I had caused such a mess with everyone. I'm really, really sorry, Campbell."

Delta was sobbing full out by this point. I knew anything I said would only make the situation worse, and it all required a more in-depth, face-to-face conversation.

I swore under my breath and rubbed at my eyes. They were burning again, but not because of the teargas.

"I'm glad you're okay. You need to sincerely reflect on lying to the people who love you and apologize to Harlen and Vernon. You're old enough to make your own choices, including where you spend the holidays. But they've always done their best to be the family you needed. The truth is the least you can give them."

She sobbed even louder and continued to apologize repeatedly.

I sighed and gave Booker a helpless look. "I'm coming back that way shortly. Don't go anywhere until I get there. We can have a family meeting. I love you, Delta. The thought of something bad happening to you makes me a version of myself I'm trying to leave behind. I want to be a *normal* big brother, not an unhinged and vengeful one." I was starting to wonder if that was even possible. Even if I wanted a quiet and uneventful life, it felt like bad things were going to find me.

She sniffed and then blew her nose. I had to hold the phone away from my ear as she honked into the speaker.

"Did you have to see Dad?" She was a bright girl. She knew my first thought would be that our father had something to do with her sudden disappearance.

It was a question I dreaded, but I answered honestly. "I only saw him for a moment."

There was no need to tell her he shot me.

"Are you okay?" She started crying even harder because if anyone knew how hard facing my father after finally escaping him was for me, it was Delta.

"Honestly, I've been better." Everything was still burning from the teargas, and the shot I thought missed my arm had actually grazed it. Karsen was going to have to pick buckshot out of the wound for me. All in all, it was a shit show. "Don't worry about me. Everything on my end is under control. Now that I know you're safe, nothing else matters."

"You don't sound like everything is under control. And what's this I hear about you traveling across the country with someone? Between canceling on Christmas and suddenly being social, you aren't acting like yourself, Campbell."

I snorted and closed my irritated eyes. "That was kind of the point when I left for Denver, Delta. I don't want to act like myself anymore. I want to try and be someone better."

I didn't want to be the guy who could talk about murder without blinking. I didn't want to be the guy who wasn't surprised his father greeted him with a firearm.

I wanted to be the guy Daire Archer fought like hell with and then turned around and kissed as if her life depended on it. That guy didn't seem like he had much to complain about. I wanted to know what she saw in that guy, and if it was possible keep him around a bit longer.

"Don't totally get rid of the guy who raised me and the boys. You might not like him very much, but he means the world to us." She sounded slightly panicked at the thought of me evolving.

Which was ironic, considering her reasoning for dropping out of contact the last several days.

"I'll see you soon. Give the boys a kiss for me, and make things right with Harlen and Vernon. Next time you need a minute to experience normal, just let me know with a text at least. I gotta go, Delta."

I hung up and smacked the corner of my phone against my forehead. "Booker, I need you to pull over. I think I'm going to be sick."

The SUV swerved to a stop, and I threw open the door. I practically fell to the ground, landing on my hands and knees as my entire body heaved. Every place on my body where the blood had stopped running across my skin started flowing again.

I was a wretched mess, and it didn't have anything to do with being shot or inhaling teargas.

chapter NINE

Daire

I was feeding a black-and-white goat when a caravan of dark SUVs rolled to a stop in front of the eccentric farmhouse. I watched as a passenger door opened, and Campbell stumbled out. His face was bloody, and he held an arm protectively against his chest. He staggered when he took a step, and stumbled when he closed the SUV door. I immediately dropped the handful of grapes Karsen had given me to lure the animals closer and dashed across the distance separating us. The line of dark, intimidating cars drove off in a cloud of dust as Campbell hunched over and dry-heaved while steadily dripping blood onto the dirt.

I reached for his uninjured arm and bent down to see his face. He was abnormally pale and looked like he was in a lot of pain.

I didn't bother to ask if he was okay. The answer was obvious. "Let me help you inside and get you cleaned up. Do you need medical attention? God. How far away is the closest hospital from a place like this?"

At first, I thought the little town with no name was quirky and cute, but now I understood that being isolated from everything was risky business.

Campbell grunted and allowed me to help him walk toward the house. His steps were slow and measured, and his breathing was labored. "Don't worry about the blood. It's nothing. I got gassed. That's what's fucking me up. Karsen can take care of wounds for me. Just help me inside."

I gasped, holding onto him more tightly when he staggered, and almost pulled us both to the ground.

"You got gassed? Should I call my mom and ask her what to do? She's a doctor. What the heck happened out there? Did you find your sister? Did you see your father?" I sounded as bewildered as I felt. Why did it sound like he was returning from a riot, not a visit with an estranged parent?

Campbell groaned and shook his head, sending tiny drops of blood flinging in all directions. "Delta is fine. She decided to spend the holidays with a friend and forgot her phone. She didn't want to hurt anyone's feelings, so she lied about where she was. The whole thing was a giant misunderstanding just like you suspected. She's in Kansas City with my brothers right now." He made a face and coughed extra hard, hacking up a lungful of something nasty. "As for my father, he's on his way to the other farm. I won't have to worry about him from this point on."

I frowned and pushed open the door to the house. "The other farm? Aren't we on the farm?"

"This is the family farm." Karsen's voice came from the kitchen as she motioned for me to drag Campbell closer. She didn't seem to mind the blood, mud, and whatever else he dragged across her pristine floors. In fact, she seemed used to surfaces marked by unmentionable things. "There's a working farm located farther back on the property. It's not nearly as welcoming as this one." She winked at Campbell and pushed him into a sitting position at her fancy marble island. "There aren't any cute goats and fluffy chickens on that part of the land. Only hogs and a processing plant. Do you know that hogs can make a human body almost completely disappear?" She gave me a slight smile, but the flash of her teeth sent chills down my spine.

I felt like Karsen often said a lot without saying much of anything. It appeared to be a common trait among those who called Nowhere home.

"No. I didn't know that. I guess I can consider my high school education somewhat lacking." I tried to smile back at her but knew my expression had fallen short. "You make a good case for me to figure out my college situation sooner rather than later." I didn't want to tell her I couldn't imagine a point in my life where I would need that information, and I felt a bit uneasy now that I knew it.

Karsen's smile softened as she helped Campbell wipe the blood off his face. She grabbed his chin, moved his head back and forth, and looked at the gash across his temple.

"I didn't realize you were quite so young, Ms. Archer. You have a lot of life left ahead of you. You never know when all the little things you pick up along the way will be useful." She seemed to pause and think about something. "I actually went to college in Colorado. I lived in Boulder all four years of my undergrad, and my roommate was a Denver native. We were very close, but something bad happened, and we drifted apart. Losing touch with her is one of the few regrets I allow myself to have." I gasped, shocked at the revelation that this fierce, frightening woman had a connection so close to home. My brother had recently left the massive college in Boulder for one closer to Bowe in Texas. She patted Campbell's shoulder and changed the subject. "As for you, it looks like you were just grazed. This one doesn't need stitches. Let me look at your arm. You know the drill; you need to ditch what you wore when you were exposed to the gas as soon as possible. Strip."

Campbell obediently started pulling his clothes off as she fussed over him, no one seeming to care that he had a bullet wound on his arm. I bit the tip of my tongue to keep my worry in check. If no one else was going to make a big deal out of his injury, I could play along with them. However, that didn't stop concern from clawing at the back of my throat.

I wanted to avert my gaze. Seeing Campbell all ruffled and bloody seemed more intimate than trying to shove my tongue down his throat. This was a vulnerable moment, and he deserved to keep some dignity. However, with each piece of clothing he lost, another part of his arresting figure was revealed.

The broad shoulders were a ten out of ten.

The strong back dotted with different tattoo designs was also top tier.

The long, lean arms, far more defined than I thought they would be, were praiseworthy. My favorite part was the ink that scrolled from his shoulder to his fingers. I always liked it when someone was confident to go big and bold with their artwork.

My dad always said it was a person's right to claim their skin. It was a declaration of independence and individuality.

I also liked the hint of abs he flashed and the cut definition in his torso. I knew Campbell was lean and fit, but seeing him without most of his clothes on revealed his strength.

Both literally and metaphorically.

I didn't miss the plethora of healed scars that were scattered across his pale skin. They were vibrant slashes of color that didn't belong among the black and gray tattoos that decorated so much of his flesh.

"Help Campbell clean up a little so I can patch him up. See how much blood you can get off his arm. There are latex gloves under the kitchen sink."

Karsen issued orders as if it were second nature. I stepped closer to the island and silently took the handful of damp towels she thrust in my direction.

I turned to Campbell, but he simply took the towels out of my slack grip and swiped at his bloody arm on his own.

"The worst thing you can do is show fear around someone like Karsen. Don't let her intimidate you." He frowned as he poked his wound a bit too forcefully. "She likes to push people the same way you do."

I blinked in surprise and involuntarily moved closer when he flinched again. I took a second to wash my hands because my mom had taught me that touching someone without clean hands was a no-no.

"Was she joking about the pigs?" I practically whispered. "I feel like she's been testing me since we got here. I can't tell if I'm failing or not."

He sighed and dragged his free hand down his face.

"She was not joking about the pigs. Don't ask questions about the working farm. That's in your own best interest." He hissed a breath through his teeth when my fingers grazed the inflamed skin around his wound. "She is testing you. She tests everyone. Does that remind you of someone?"

I lifted my eyebrows and tried to lighten my touch as he flinched again. "You think I'm like her?"

No way. That was delusional.

I was scared and sad. I ran away when I didn't want to deal with my life and family. I was the furthest thing from frightening as one could get.

"Maybe not who Karsen is now, but who she was once upon a time. You're both smart and pretty. You both come from a position of privilege and know what it's like to be protected by a big family. Karsen didn't want to live in a gilded cage anymore, either. So instead, she broke free and became a bird of prey."

I scoffed and dabbed at the blood that was still dripping. The gash on his arm seemed deeper and more serious than the one on his face.

"First, I was a princess in a castle. Now I'm a bird in a cage. Have you ever seen me as a normal person?" I couldn't deny that I was desperate to spread my wings. That analogy fit me better than the royal one, because I was not fit to rule over anything at the moment, even my own life. The problem was, if I was a bird, I needed to figure out how to fly.

Campbell reached up and caught my hand. He gently squeezed it, and the blood-soaked towel dropped to the countertop with a plop.

"When you kissed me, I saw you as nothing more than Daire. It was hard not to." He let his gaze roll from the top of my head to the tip of my toes. "And when I saw you in the towel a few days ago, it was impossible not to see you as anything but a desirable young woman. Which I'm sure was your plan all along." His mouth quirked up on one side in a playful smirk. "When you're cunning, it especially reminds me of a younger Karsen. I couldn't see it until you were out of your comfort zone and dropped some of your civility."

"I'm not sure cunning is a compliment." My voice dropped to a whisper as I leaned closer to Campbell...or maybe I was pulled. It was hard to tell which one of us moved toward the other, but we always seemed to end up closer than we started.

It was magnetic.

Campbell turned his head, and my breath paused as our lips hovered millimeters apart. He was colder than when I kissed him earlier, and the element of surprise was gone. None of that decreased the tension or my desire to press my mouth to his.

"Cunning is a compliment. Especially when it comes to a woman. Anything that men get lauded for, a woman should too." Karsen's voice held a hint of laughter in it as she walked back into the room carrying a big, red box. I jerked away from Campbell and nervously cleared my throat, not sure why I felt like a kid with my hand caught in a candy jar. "Anything can be a compliment. It all depends on how you interpret it. When I was your age, people told me all the things that most young women want to hear. That I was pretty. That I had a bright future. That I was intelligent. That I was a good sister and loyal friend. None of that mattered to me. I wanted to be powerful. Fearless. Feared. It took a long time before I got the kind of compliments that mattered to me." She smiled at me and started to disinfect Campbell's wounds with practiced movements. She was almost as efficient and smooth as my mom when patching up a battered boy. "And my husband tells me I'm beautiful every day. When he says the words, they mean something. You learn to listen for the difference as you get older."

When I set out to find myself, I had no idea I would find a woman who was like the blade of a sword, cutting right into the heart of everything that confused me.

I was playful and flirty. I liked to be the center of attention. I had a big group of friends, many of whom were boys. But the night of my brother's accident, I overheard several of those so-called friends talking about me behind my back. They called me all kinds of names. They attacked my virtue and decided, without my input, that all my actions and motivations were questionable. I thought I was the life of the party. As it turned out, I was the only one who viewed myself that way. And with Aston, my closest confidant, gone, and Bowe, my second bestie, entangled with my brother, I didn't have anyone to talk to about the sudden shift in my self-perception. I knew I wasn't using my face and body to lead boys on and build worthless popularity. I thought it was fun. I thought it made me different and memorable. I didn't realize I was leaving an impression in all the wrong ways. Still, for some unexplained reason, I let the words of others carry a weight they absolutely shouldn't. As a result, I got myself and my brother into a bad situation that made me feel even worse about myself.

The lightbulb moment brought on by Karsen's words felt monumental. I was listening to all the wrong words but not hearing the ones that should matter most. I told myself I needed to see myself through other's eyes, but I never let anyone see me clearly. I was the only one who could do that. My gratitude at her tough love was swept away in a flurry as Charley and an equally dark-haired teen boy rushed into the kitchen.

"I saw the blood outside. I knew you shouldn't have tried to confront your father. Are you okay?" Charley's voice was frantic, and she none too subtly elbowed me out of the way so she could inspect Campbell. Her reaction was the one I'd battled to keep locked down, and I was jealous she was so free to fret over him. Her worry didn't make her weak in anyone's eyes. Would it have been the same for me if I'd given my concern room to wrap around and comfort him?

The teenager rolled his eyes at his sister's back and turned to give me a cheeky grin.

"Hi. I'm Nolan. I didn't believe Charley when she said Campbell brought someone to the farm. He hates new people. I can't believe you're real."

I shook his outstretched hand and couldn't help but grin back at him. He came across as a baby bunny raised in a nest of vipers. I liked him instantly.

"He hated me a few days ago, but I think I've worked my way up to strongly dislike." I laughed and gave Campbell a pointed look. "I'm wearing him down."

Charley whipped her head around, and her slate eyes pinned me in place. She was fierce, but I didn't find her nearly as terrifying as her mother. Maybe it was a false sense of safety because she so strongly resembled her father, and I didn't find him as scary as his wife.

"Campbell doesn't need to be worn down. Can you not see what his asshole of a father did to him? Do you not comprehend that he was basically tortured his entire childhood? He needs to be built up. How could someone like you understand that?"

Her words were biting, and I could tell she was incensed at my little joke. Her feelings for Campbell were big and vibrant. If I were him, I would've been moved by her ages ago. She was a force of nature.

I didn't want an enemy like Charley Booker. But I wasn't about to let her steamroll over me now that I was paying attention to whose opinions I let carry weight in my world.

"What is *someone like me* exactly? You don't know enough about me to make any assumptions. I don't even know who I am yet, so there is no way you can tell what kind of person I am based on our short interactions.

Campbell is a big boy. He can decide what he needs, and who he needs it from, all on his own." I shrugged a shoulder and turned to the teenager who was watching me with wide eyes. It seemed like it was unexpected that I'd snapped back at his older sister. I probably needed to sleep with one eye open until I left her home.

"I was playing with the goats earlier and got interrupted. Campbell and I have to head back to Denver soon. Can you show me around the rest of the farm?" I looked at Charley, who gritted her teeth and shot flames out of her eyes in my direction. "The family farm I mean. I want to see the rest of the family farm." I didn't want to see the other one on the property.

Karsen slapped Campbell on the back and told him to go get dressed. He gave me a hard look I assumed meant he wanted me to behave. I wiggled my fingers in a little wave as he reluctantly disappeared down a hallway. Charley clearly intended to follow, but Karsen stopped her and instead sent the dark-haired beauty to put the first-aid kit away and get rid of Campbell's ruined clothes.

As I was getting ready to follow Nolan back to the big red barn, Karsen suddenly mentioned, "My friend from college was studying nursing. She's the one who taught me how to fix up basic battle wounds. Her name is Arabella Voss. She goes by Ari. I bet it's a long shot, but I'm curious if her name sounds familiar? I know she still has family in Denver."

I balked and bumped into Nolan as I turned with a bewildered expression. "I know the Vosses. Ari's older brother is married to my Uncle Orlando." I gave my head a bewildered shake. "He's not my biological uncle, but he was involved with my father's twin brother for a long time before he passed away. Uncle Dom, his partner, is a police officer."

Karsen gave me another sharp smile that made my sweat icy cold.

"I know. I met him several times when Ari and I lived together. Dom's profession is another reason I didn't try and reach out to her after we drifted apart. When you see her next, tell her I never forgot about her and hope she's doing well. Tell her I got the guy, and he gave me everything I ever wanted. I'm very happy with how my life turned out."

I nodded like a broken bobblehead doll and followed Nolan into the yard.

"I can't believe the world is so small." The disbelief was deep in my tone.

Nolan hummed a sound of agreement. "My mom always says everything is connected. She says you never know when something you did, or someone you met, might come back to haunt you. She tells us to remember everyone we've ever wronged, no matter how slight it might be. There are always debts to pay and debts to collect."

I quietly agreed even though Campbell had tried to convince me that love was the opposite of that not too long ago.

Maybe love was a touch of both debt and credit. A mix of what you owed one another and the unwavering belief that the other person would keep all their promises no matter what.

chapter TEN

Campbell

"You like her."

I told Benny I would call him back and hung up the phone. I looked at Charley as she brazenly walked into the guest room. When I stayed with the Bookers previously, I never lived in the main house. The compound had its own staff quarters built closer to the working farm, and even though Karsen wanted me to stay under the same roof as her kids, I was never comfortable with that setup. I wanted a clear line between being family and the hired help. However, there was no amount of distance or closed door that stopped Charley from acting like she owned the place.

I tossed the phone onto the bed and climbed to my feet. I needed the height advantage when dealing with a worthy adversary, and it was never a good idea to be in a room with a big bed and Charley.

"I don't like her. But I don't dislike her." I wanted to say I was ambivalent about Daire, and while that might've been the case not too long ago, I could feel how my ideas about her had shifted. I couldn't deny I very much liked how she kissed me.

"Don't you think it's weird? What kind of normal person comes to Nowhere, sees how my parents run things, learns about the *real* farm, and barely bats an eyelash? Does she even realize what it means that your old man is getting taken to the pigs?" Charley was clearly frustrated. Her voice rose with each question. "What is wrong with her? Your dad shot you, yet she only cares about the fluffy farm animals. I don't get it, Campbell."

I shrugged and met her steely blue gaze. "Daire didn't ask to come here with me. She has never pried into my past or asked questions I can't answer. She is curious but knows when to keep to herself. I think you forget that while your father was always in this brutal world, your mom grew up in a normal family environment. Just like Daire. And let's not even mention your uncle. You underestimate people all the time, Charley."

She scowled at me, but we both knew my point was on the nose.

Karsen Booker started life like any other middle-class kid. Then, the trajectory of her life changed forever when her father broke the law and her older sister hooked up with a man even more dangerous than either Booker or Benny. But no one would ever look at Karsen's brother-in-law, Race Hartman, and think he was a cold-blooded killer. The man looked like an executive on Wall Street. His background was more like a Kennedy, not a Gotti. Charley should know better than most not to be fooled by what someone showed on the outside. Pretty masks often covered very ugly truths.

Charley sighed and moved to sit on the edge of the bed. She crossed her legs and bounced her foot up and down. I could tell she was irritated, but I didn't have it left in me to soothe her. Plus, keeping her happy was no longer my job.

"How do you feel about everything that went down with your dad? You haven't made a move on him in all these years, and now it ends... just like that. It has to be a relief."

I absently lifted my fingers to touch the stinging wound on my temple.

Was I relieved?

I honestly couldn't tell. I was mostly numb when I thought about my father's gruesome fate.

"He had a young girl up at the property. She was messed up, so she couldn't tell us how long she'd been there. And who knows if she's the only one he's had trapped out there with him. He's just as deranged and dangerous as he always was. He knew what would happen if he didn't abide by Karsen's rules when she let him stay on the property. I always knew if I ever had to see him again, it was going to end with one of us dead."

"What are you going to tell Delta and the boys? I know you didn't come all this way with no plans to stop and see them on your way home."

"Nothing," I grunted. "They don't need to know." Especially Delta. She already felt terrible about how her irresponsible actions affected me. She would inevitably take the blame for my father's demise if she knew what happened today.

"You're taking that girl to meet your family." It wasn't a question, and I could hear the raw pain in Charley's voice.

I softened my tone when I replied. "It's not like I have a choice. I'm going to see them, and she goes where I go for the time being."

Charley snorted. "I can force her to get on a plane and go home. I can have someone tie her up, throw her in the back of a van, and forcibly deliver her back to her family. You don't have to stick to her like glue."

I sighed and gave her a pointed look. "I told Benny I would bring her home. So that's what I'm going to do."

Only, now it didn't feel like as much of a burden now. It was crazy what a little close contact and some high stakes could do to bring people closer together.

"You'll introduce her to your family, but will she introduce you to hers? I'm not talking about brief encounters or as a casual friend. Do you think you're someone she could ever take home to her parents? And if she does, what happens when they ask questions about where you're from and what your family is like? You can talk about my mom and Uncle Race all you want, but look how they ended up. Instead of conforming to a normal life, they embraced this as their new normal. They purposely walked away from everything that girl you're holding onto represents."

"He's not holding onto me."

Daire's amused voice came from behind me. I looked over my shoulder and noticed her leaning on the door frame. I had no idea how long she'd been there, but the look in her eye told me she had heard enough to have questions.

"I'm holding onto him for dear life because I'm adrift at the moment. I'm lost, but Campbell still managed to find me. As for what a normal life should look like," Daire stepped into the room and met Charley's gaze unflinchingly. "That's different for everyone. I left home because I wanted to experience someone else's normal. Did I anticipate it involving guys with guns and feral hogs? Absolutely not. But I'm not here to judge anyone's normal. I know I'm just a blip in your world, Charley, but I'm more than that in Campbell's. And if I have to defend him from my family in the future, I will."

Charley scoffed. She got to her feet, her hostile gaze skipping between me and Daire. "You're both delusional. Maybe you deserve the pain you're going to bring each other."

She paused when she walked past me and gave me a final look. With a shake of her head, she pushed past Daire and left the room.

I blew out a breath and looked at the pretty blonde in the doorway. "I think she might finally get over her crush after that encounter."

Daire snorted and flipped her long, pale hair over her shoulder. "I think she might murder you in your sleep."

I agreed.

"She's fully capable of doing that." I watched Daire as she walked in and took over the spot that Charley had just vacated. "She does have a point. Several, actually. You are taking this detour far better than most would in the situation. You were on the verge of breaking apart when I found you up on that mountain. What changed between now and then?"

Daire lifted her eyebrows and made a broad gesture with her hands. "Anxiety and depression don't have any rhyme or reason. My boring, basic life still seems overwhelming and scary, but whatever happens here feels surreal; it's not real life. It feels like I stepped into a wild book and I'm just flipping pages to find out what happens next. I'm not worried about making amends and figuring out my place in this power ranking. I'm already an Archer, so being a Booker means absolutely nothing to me."

"Your ability to compartmentalize and rationalize is parallel to none." I couldn't help the amusement that found its way into my voice. "Do you want to stay here for another night, or are you ready to get back on the road? The next stop is Kansas City. After I see the kids and talk to Delta, you'll have to decide our next move. I'm not chasing you all over the country."

She rolled her eyes and tilted back on her hands. All I would have to do was lean over her and she would fall back on the bed, trapped under my body. The invasive thought was followed by the vision of her in nothing but a towel and the faint memory of how she tasted when we kissed.

A girl like Daire looked like she should taste sweet. She didn't. She tasted minty and fresh, with a hint of spice. That kind of flavor awakened your senses and made all your sensitive places wake up and take notice.

"We can leave now since I know you're anxious to see your sister. But you have to agree to switch off some of the driving. I can't sit in the passenger seat and look at barren corn fields for hours again." She tilted her head back, and our gazes locked. "I'm going home after Kansas City. Watching you worry about Delta and seeing how things ended with your father," She sighed as her words drifted off. "It's given me some of the perspective I was searching for. I don't want Ry to worry about me. I don't want him to put himself in danger or reopen old wounds because of me. I don't want my family to blame you for keeping me away from home for so long. The Archers can be a bit irrational when it comes to protecting family."

I battled down the urge to scoff, but a bit of disbelief still slipped through when I asked, "Even after seeing the compound and learning about where I come from, you still think I need someone to defend me?"

It didn't matter that her brother was a former all-star athlete. Or that her uncle was former military. Or her father was a notorious badass who took no shit from anyone. None of them stood a chance if I decided to push back.

Benny was the only person in Denver who could give me a run for my money when it came to violence and vengeance. And that bastard was supposed to be on my side.

Supposed to be.

Benny really only cared about himself and his wife. I wasn't delusional enough to think he would have my back if I rocked the boat too hard in his shiny, new, rehabilitated life.

Daire laughed and pushed up off the bed. "You don't *need* someone to defend you. But I think you might *want* someone willing to do it anyway." She moved toward the door. "I don't have much to pack up. Karsen gave me a bag of clothes I'm sure came from Charley's room. Other than that, I'm ready to go whenever you are. I want to say goodbye to the Bookers and thank them for their unusual version of hospitality. I doubt I'll ever see any of them again." She stilled and made a quizzical face. "But then again, Karsen knows my Uncle Dom. The world is more connected than I imagined, so who knows. I'm going to message my brother and parents to let them know I'm on the way home after a quick stop to see your family. Don't think I didn't notice you never agreed to share driving duties with me. That is non-negotiable." She gave me a stern look to emphasize her words.

I grunted a vague agreement.

I didn't like the idea of letting her be in charge. Part of me was worried she still might run off for parts unknown, this time with me as a hostage. But a bigger part of me, the part that trusted no one, knew that relinquishing control of the car meant I had more faith in Daire than anyone else on the planet. That was too much to swallow at the moment.

I cleaned up the guest room and gathered the few things I'd brought with me. I took the pistol Booker had given me when I went to face my father and placed it into a lock box, then stashed it on the top shelf at the very back of the closet. He told me to keep the weapon, but the Campbell who carried a loaded gun everywhere was on hiatus. I wanted to feel what it was like to spend my days like I wasn't under a constant threat of attack.

The Campbell escorting the Mile High Princess back to Denver didn't need to be armed to the teeth.

I heard voices coming from the open living area of the big house. When I came around the corner, Daire was thanking Booker profusely and gushing about the home and the family farm. She thanked Karsen with more reserve, and even reached out to hug Nolan. The kid blushed a fire engine red and awkwardly patted her on the back. I don't think I'd ever seen him so bashful.

Charley didn't blink or move a muscle when Daire told her it was a delight to meet her and thanked her for sharing her clothes. She was being deliberately rude, but it only amused Daire, which irritated the sassy brunette even more. I had to give Daire credit. She was a master button pusher.

"It's been a long day, and it'll be dark soon. You've been through a lot, and Campbell is injured. Don't feel like you have to rush off." Booker extended the invitation to stay longer, and when our eyes met, his flickered in the slightest way that let me know without words my father was no longer going to be a problem.

"We're gonna take turns driving. We'll be fine. I need to see Delta as soon as possible and clear things up with her. I want to talk to Vernon and Harlen as well. If the boys ever have questions about Nowhere or our dad, they need to be ready with an answer that keeps them from digging into the past." I kept my reply to the point so there was no room to be persuaded. Booker pulled me into a tight hug and pounded on my back with a heavy hand. I bit down a sound of discomfort and pulled back, only to be hugged fiercely by Karsen and Charley. "You guys don't have to act like you'll never see me again. I'll come to visit when I get time." I needed to burn every acre of my father's beloved property to ash so that all my ties to Nowhere were severed. "Next time, I'll bring Benny."

"Don't you fucking dare." Booker was not joking when he growled back at me.

I chuckled and absent-mindedly took Daire's elbow to lead her outside. "It was good to be back. Thanks for everything."

Karsen dipped her chin down in a slight nod. "Anytime. You're one of us, Campbell. Even if you don't see it that way. Stay safe on the road. Give me a call when you get back to Colorado."

I agreed and ushered Daire to the SUV. Once we were settled inside, I left the compound in a flurry of dust, the same way I had arrived.

Daire turned on some music, and I watched Nowhere get smaller in the rearview mirror until it disappeared. I'd been trying to make that happen for years. I didn't know if it was because my father no longer lingered in the back of my mind like a specter, but I finally felt like I was escaping the little town that always seemed more like a prison than a home.

We drove in companionable silence for a long while. Daire was on the prepaid phone, messaging back and forth with her family. I could tell by her expression she was excited to go home but was still apprehensive about seeing everyone after her grand disappearing act. Occasionally she would lift her head and look at me with conflicted eyes, but whatever she was dealing with, she clearly didn't want to share.

We stopped once for gas and loaded up on snacks and enough caffeine to keep us going. Daire asked if I wanted to switch drivers. It was dark, and we were making pretty good time, so I asked her to hold off for a bit. I coaxed her to go to sleep for the next few hours, and I told her we would stop and switch when she woke up.

I couldn't tell if she really went to sleep or if she was faking. She turned the burner phone off and shut her eyes, but I felt a bunch of tension coiled around her. I decided to let her be and concentrated on driving.

I kept up a steady pace for two more hours, but my eyelids started to get heavy, and so did my thoughts.

I wanted to think I was immune to anything concerning my father. However, the longer the silence dragged on, the more I thought about the fact he shot at me. I shouldn't be surprised; after all, my childhood was haunted by that bloodstained shovel. It did something to your soul when you realized how little value you held in some people's eyes.

Daire was worried about being worthy of her family name. I was starting to wonder if I would live up to mine. Since I didn't have a real first or last name, was I going to be different from my old man? Was my existence necessary? What value would I bring to the world by being my father's son? Would I have to carry the repercussions and karma for his sins since I was the reason he was no longer around to atone?

Feeling my thoughts spiral downward in a dark direction, I pulled over at a rest stop and parked the SUV.

I looked at Daire to see if I should wake her, but her green eyes were fixed on me as if she'd been watching me for a while.

"How long have you been up?" I dragged a hand down my face and tried to shake off my morose mood.

"Are you ready to take over?" I needed to get out and stretch my legs. The grind of everything since Christmas Eve was starting to take its toll.

Daire unbuckled her seatbelt and suddenly launched herself over the seat divider. I caught her out of reflex and let her land on my lap. I hissed as her knee grazed the sensitive bulge between my legs and watched warily as her hands skimmed over my shoulders and across my chest.

Her eyes seemed unnaturally bright in the darkness, and her hair felt like silk where it brushed against the side of my face when she bent her head so our foreheads touched.

"What are you doing?" My voice was husky, and my hands tightened on her hips as she wiggled and aligned our bodies into an even more suggestive position.

She flashed a smile at me, and her lips lowered closer to mine. "Taking over."

Her hand dipped lower and brushed over the front of my jeans. Everything behind the zipper gave an appreciative throb, and my heart rate kicked into high gear.

It was dark inside the car, but every so often, a vehicle would pass on the interstate and cast shadows over us.

A decent man would stop her and remind her we were both emotionally vulnerable at the moment. He would tell her that neither of us were thinking straight. He might mention that he didn't need to be added to her list of mistakes, and she didn't need to be dragged into his darkness. Good thing for me, I'd never been very decent.

At times like these, I appreciated that being a bad version of myself meant I often got much further in life than a better version ever could.

ELEVEN

Daire

I felt Campbell getting further away from me, even though he hadn't moved from the driver's seat. I could feel how he went from being confident and in control when we were at the farm to being scared and hesitant about whatever awaited him in the unknown.

And I was irritated after messaging my mother. She was overjoyed I was on my way home, but she was finally pissed off about my erratic and selfish behavior. I promised I would explain everything when I was back in Denver, and she immediately set up an appointment so I could talk to a therapist. I wasn't opposed to seeking professional help with my current unstable mental state. I was annoyed that it took my freaking out and ruining a major holiday for my family to finally see how imperfect I was and to acknowledge how much work I probably needed. If my mom and dad had just held me accountable for what happened to Ry, I never would've doubted myself to such a huge degree. Which started a guilt trip for not taking accountability for my own issues. It wasn't fair to blame my parents for not punishing me after the accident. There was no need. I was punishing myself far more harshly and irrationally than they ever would.

It was all so messy in my head. Staring at Campbell and fantasizing about touching and tasting him all over was far more enjoyable. I liked having my focus on him instead of all my broken pieces.

When he stopped the SUV, my first instinct was to throw myself at him to keep him from slipping through my fingers. I don't know why, but I felt like he also wanted to run away. When we touched, I felt his body harden underneath me. I suddenly wanted him to know that even if he was more comfortable living in the sticky shadows from his past, I wasn't afraid of the dark. I wanted to hold onto him, even when I wasn't lost and alone.

"This isn't exactly a private place." Campbell caught my hand as I tugged on the hem of his dark t-shirt. I wanted a closer look at his abs and the ginger happy trail I'd been daydreaming about. I really wanted to lick it. His hold was hard to break.

"I don't care. It's the middle of the night. You have tinted windows. I'll never see this rest stop again in my life. I would've never pegged you as the shy type, Campbell." I wiggled my fingers in his grasp and tickled the center of his palm with my thumb. "Let's live a little."

His dark eyebrows lifted, and I could see the indecision on his handsome face. "I've done a lot of bad things in my time, Daire. But I've never been to jail. That's an experience I can live without."

I snaked my other hand between our bodies and pressed it against the bulge between his legs. He was hot and hard. When I touched him through his clothes, he sucked a sharp breath between his teeth.

"What about this? Is this an experience you can live without?" He let my hand drop and I used a fingertip to trace the outline of his mouth. His facial hair was bristly against my fingers, and his breath was warm and damp when he exhaled.

His hand slid around my waist, and his fingers crept under the bottom of my borrowed shirt. He touched the base of my spine, and tingles shot out from the faint caress. My whole body felt electrified.

I tilted my head and touched my lips to his ear. The slight contact made his body shudder underneath me. I deftly popped open the fastening on his jeans and squeezed my hand between flesh and fabric. His hard cock filled my hand and then some. He was intoxicatingly hard and soft at the same time. It was heady and addicting to feel how his body throbbed and stiffened with my gentle touch.

"I used to play with boys before my brother got hurt." I tightened my hand around his cock and gave it a squeeze. "I liked to lead them on. It was fun to let them think they would get more than I was willing to give. When I touched them, they melted and would do whatever I wanted. And when I put it all to a stop, they would either get so mad I thought I might get hurt, or they would be so pathetic, begging for more. I knew I could destroy them if I wanted to."

"Sounds like a very dangerous game, Princess." Campbell shifted when I leaned in closer to him and the tip of my tongue touched the curved shell of his ear.

"It was dangerous. And mean." I rubbed the rigid flesh in my grasp, and with my other hand brushed my fingertips over his furrowed eyebrows and the blades of his cheeks. I wanted to trace the moth on his throat, but I didn't want him to perceive the movement as a threat. Campbell wasn't a guy I wanted to play games with anymore. Because I knew I would lose. He was not some kid who hadn't experienced the highs and lows of life. He was intimately acquainted with the good and bad sides of hard choices. "Making someone else mad, or causing desperation, was so I could feel something vicariously through them. Things have always been easy for me. You said it yourself; anyone would kill for my life. I was making bad situations for myself because I knew they would never happen organically. And if they did, my family would fix everything before I could feel anything painful." The callous and careless way I carried myself worked just fine until the night I almost got my brother killed.

At that moment, I realized how little empathy and compassion I'd shown others. I was so wrapped up in my own pity party and diminished sense of self that I couldn't see what my actions were doing to anyone else. I was not a good person. I was not a good Archer.

The truth is, I probably needed help for my mental state long before the accident. I was just too good at masking all the ugly and unhappy parts of myself. I knew the people who loved me wouldn't understand my internal conflict. I didn't even understand it.

"Are you trying to make me feel good so you can feel good vicariously through me?" Campbell's voice was rough and uneven. I used the pad of my thumb to circle the tapered head of his stiff cock in my hand. A tiny drop of moisture pearled at the tip, and I used the liquid to make my movements smoother.

I wanted to grind myself against it. I wanted all of our clothing gone. I wanted to feel his hands all over my body. I wanted to trace his tattoos with my tongue. I wanted to kiss him until I couldn't breathe.

I didn't want to steal his emotions and responses because I had none of my own. Campbell made me feel plenty. I was overwhelmed with sensation.

I used my teeth to bite his earlobe and whimpered softly when his big hands slid enticingly along either side of my spine. One of his hands tickled across my ribcage and then softly guided along the fabric of my bra. He shifted underneath me, pushing his hardness more fully into my hand. It was reminiscent of the first time I ever let a guy feel me up, kind of clumsy and rushed and a little bit forbidden. But this was infinitely better because the guy was Campbell, and I wasn't trying to get any specific reaction from him.

I just wanted us to make each other feel good. I wanted us to help each other forget our troubles and move forward together. We were both pretty bad humans, but we were trying to do better. Only, being bad with him felt far better than it probably should.

His fingers skimmed over my nipple under the sheer fabric. I leaned into his touch and moved my hand faster on his thick erection. More liquid pooled at the tip, and his breathing became shallow and uneven.

I dragged my lips across his face until they landed on his mouth.

Immediately, the kiss was hot and wet. Teeth and tongues collided. It was leaps and bounds better than our first kiss, but I knew we could still improve. It would take practice. So much delicious, arousing practice. I felt the stroke of his tongue against mine directly between my legs. If I wasn't straddling him and didn't have my hand shoved down his pants, I would've happily rubbed my achy and eager center against his cock. He made me alarmingly greedy. I was vaguely aware of why those boys I tossed to the side became desperate when they couldn't fulfill their body's demands. Desire pulsed so strongly between my legs that it bordered on pain. If he pulled back, if he decided to play with me the same way I played with others, I would lose my mind. I would be both furious and miserable.

Campbell made a growling sound in the back of his throat, and his teeth clamped down on my lower lip. I hissed at the sting, and the tip of his tongue immediately darted out to soothe the tiny wound.

"I'm going to come." Campbell bit out the warning and pinched my nipple for emphasis. I could feel the hot member in my hand pulse enticingly.

"If we weren't in your car, I'd let you finish in my mouth instead of my hand." I was dead serious. I wanted him in my mouth and inside my body. I wanted to absorb him.

He took control of the kiss, lips gliding lightly over mine as our breath mingled. I liked how his facial hair scraped across my skin, and the way his rust-colored eyelashes dipped when I touched him in a way he particularly enjoyed.

I gasped as pleasure sparked under my skin and reflexively tightened my hold on him. Our eyes met. His were hooded and full of questions behind the desire. I'm sure mine were bright and full of nothing but delight. This was the most fun I'd ever had with a boy I was attracted to. I knew that could be attributed to the fact Campbell wasn't a *boy* at all. He had never been allowed to be young and immature. Everything with him was serious because there was obviously no room in his life for foolish affection and childish games.

I rolled my thumb under the arrowed tip and pressed lightly. "I'm good at making a mess of things." I giggled and touched the tip of my nose against his while gently running my fingers around the edge of the bandage on his temple. He had freckles. I had never noticed before, but this close, I could see the slight dusting across the high bridge of his nose. "The difference with you is I'll stick around and help you clean up. I usually make a mess and it's someone else's problem. In this instance, I won't let anyone else take credit for my hard work."

A car drove past on the interstate, and the light illuminated our compromising position. Campbell slammed his eyes closed and made a rough sound low in his throat. My hand was awash in a warm, sticky fluid a moment later.

Campbell's hand squeezed my breast almost painfully when he opened his eyes and stared at me. I gave him a soft peck on the lips and wiggled off his lap so he could situate himself. I handed him some napkins from our last fast-food stop, and found a disinfectant wipe in the glove box to take care of my messy hands.

The SUV was full of the sounds of rustling clothing and ragged breathing. Another car drove past and lit up our faces as we looked at each other.

There was a lot to say, but neither of us started talking. Fortunately, depending on how you looked at it, the car that interrupted our moment pulled into the rest stop and parked ridiculously close, considering the place was deserted.

I cleared my throat and told Campbell I needed to use the restroom before we got back on the road. I reminded him it was my turn to drive and asked him to put the directions into the GPS.

When I got out of the SUV and went to the bathroom, a guy got out of the car parked next to us and followed me up to the building. I didn't turn around and acknowledge him in any way, but I was keenly aware of how isolated and dark this spot was..

"Daire, hold up a minute." I stopped and moved quickly to the side so the stranger behind me didn't bump into me. Campbell jogged up next to me and kept his eyes on the stranger as he grabbed my elbow and escorted me all the way to the door of the bathroom. "I'll wait here for you."

I nodded gratefully and hurried through my bathroom routine. I was sure that person wasn't a threat. They were probably just another tired traveler who had to pee, but I was glad I didn't have to risk finding out I was wrong.

The other car was gone when I came out, leaving me and Campbell alone in the dark.

We walked back to the SUV in silence. I was pleasantly surprised when he walked to the passenger side after clicking the fob to unlock the doors. Once I was settled behind the wheel and the display showed where I needed to go, we were off.

It was quiet for a solid twenty minutes before Campbell spoke. "It takes more than someone changing their mind during sex to make me mad, Daire. When I'm angry, it doesn't end well for anyone. And when you've been desperate to eat because you can't remember the last time you've had any food, being desperate for something you can live without, like sex and companionship, is ridiculous. Whatever you need to feel, you have to get there on your own when you're with me. I can promise you that Waldo is not located in my pants." He cleared his throat, and I could hear a hint of amusement in his voice when he told me, "It was an experience I can't seem to live without. You were right."

A zing of pride shot up my spine at his words. He made no secret of the fact he had a lot of experiences he'd rather forget about. I was happy to be one he would hold onto and one that might linger when he thought about his minimal good memories. I don't think I'd ever been a significant positive memory for someone other than my family.

It wasn't long before Campbell crashed out. He leaned the seat back, closed his eyes, crossed his arms over his chest, and breathed quietly and steadily within minutes.

Campbell wasn't the type who looked younger and more innocent when his defenses were down. In fact, he didn't look peaceful or rested at all. Even in sleep, there was a tiny furrow between his eyebrows and tension around his mouth.

He was quiet for the first hour, but as the drive stretched into the second, he started to mutter incoherently, and when I looked over at him, the front of his hair was damp with sweat, and the frown was deeper and more furrowed across his forehead. He whimpered as if in pain, and curled in on himself like a wounded animal.

I kept glancing at him with concern, but I didn't want to stop on the side of the road. I was worried about waking him up in the middle of a nightmare in case his reaction was to lash out. He was still unpredictable enough that I knew when to keep my guard up around him.

All of a sudden, he jolted awake. He slammed his injured arm into the door by

accident, and a string of swear words filled the SUV.

"Fuck me." He rubbed his arm and poked at it as the faint scent of blood circulated around us. "That hurt."

I hummed and looked at him out of the corner of my eye. "It seemed like you had a bad dream. Do you want me to stop next time we pass a gas station so you can stretch your legs?" I wanted to ask him if he was okay, but he clearly wasn't.

"I wish it was just a dream. I'm fine. I don't need to stop unless you do."

I shook my head and focused back on the road. "I'm good to go for at least another few hours. But you should probably try to sleep a little bit longer if you want to keep driving straight through."

He rubbed his eyes and dug through the stash of goodies we got at our first stop. He found a bottle of water and swallowed half of it down.

"It takes a while to shake off the residue of those memories. It's black and gooey like tar. No matter how hard I scrub my mind, the gunk will always be there."

I knew that feeling. Right after the accident, every time I closed my eyes, all I could see was the truck barreling toward my brother, and the scent of blood and rain mixed together as I called desperately for help. I often woke up with tears on my face and a pain in my heart so sharp it felt like it might kill me.

"You were dreaming about your father?" That was my best guess. His dad seemed to be the source of all his angst and issues.

"I was dreaming about my mother. I can't remember her without thinking about how I know that my father killed her, and there was nothing I could do to stop him." His voice was quiet and strained. "I hate that I don't remember much about her aside from what my father did to her. I'd like to have a memory of her he hasn't tainted. The man ruined everything he ever put his hands on."

I sighed and turned to give him a sympathetic look. "You're wrong. He *tried* to ruin everything he put his hands on. But he didn't destroy you. He didn't get the chance to do any real damage to your siblings. As for what happened to your mother, she was an adult. She was stuck in a shitty situation because of her own choices. She was supposed to protect you, not the other way around. Whatever happened to her was undoubtedly a tragedy, but none of that falls on you, Campbell. You were just a child."

He made a noise that didn't sound like he agreed with me. He leaned back in the seat and closed his eyes again.

"You don't seem overly concerned about the amount of death and destruction that follows wherever I go. Why is that?" He asked the question quietly, but I could tell he was nervous about how I would answer.

"I am concerned. I know all that death and destruction stays with you no matter what. Those things will always be part of you. But there is a difference between someone who is dangerous and someone who is only dangerous when a situation calls for it. And from the start, I've never felt that you were a danger to me, Campbell."

I was raised around men who were many different types of dangerous. Men who would do anything to protect the ones they loved. I understood Campbell was a different color on that bloodstained rainbow, but he was still there when the sun came out after the rain.

He huffed an aggrieved sound and crossed his arms over his chest again. "I wish I could say the same thing about you, Princess. You feel like a spectacular danger to me."

I snickered because that was an even better compliment than the one he gave me after he came all over my hand.

chapter
TWELVE

Campbell

We kept a brutal pace, trading off driving after a few hours of sleep and only stopping a couple of times to grab food and use the restroom. I thought Daire would complain because the drive was both boring and stressful. She had to be uncomfortable. I knew, because I was. I would be happy never to see the inside of my SUV again after this trip. My lower back was throbbing, and my knees were sore. My neck was so stiff it hurt to turn my head in either direction. I was ready to stretch my legs and not be in motion.

Daire either played DJ, switching through music via Bluetooth on my phone, or armchair detective, listening to true crime podcasts and working through the crime with me while I drove. She spent a lot of time texting on the throwaway phone. It didn't take a genius to realize she was talking to her family. The longer she messaged, the worse her mood got. I didn't ask who she was talking to. I figured she would tell me if she wanted me to know. Whatever was going on with her family, only the surface of the issue was scratched after her disappearing act.

We both heaved a sigh of relief when the SUV finally rolled to a stop in front of a very large house in an affluent suburb. The house sat on a body of water surrounded by beautiful, mature landscaping. It was really nice. It was safe. It was the perfect place for my younger siblings to grow up.

It was more than I could have ever given them on my own.

"Wow. This place is fancy." Daire released a low whistle before she bent over and touched the palms of her hands on the driveway like she was doing yoga.

I didn't know she was so flexible.

"Vernon likes the finer things in life. The last time I was here, my brothers were wearing Prada and Gucci. They go to a private school where the tuition per semester costs more than my SUV. Wait until you see the inside of this place. Fancy doesn't cover it."

As we started toward the front of the house, the big French doors swung open, and a well-dressed Asian man burst through them.

Vernon was a unique character. The man was a literal genius, but he dressed like a fashion icon and looked like an anime character. His hair was black, but there was a stark silver streak in the front. His features were fierce and delicate. These days he and Harlen lived well and had more than enough money to do whatever they wanted, but I knew he was a man who came from nothing. Vernon wasn't a millionaire because he was born into it. He earned every dollar through blood, sweat, and tears. And some slightly shady activities I did my best not to think about.

His husband, Harlen, shared a similar story. The man was a beast, born with a gift for athletics. He came from a piss-poor backcountry town and had zero support from anyone. He made it to the NFL, became a big shot, and watched his career nosedive when he was publicly outed by a sports gossip social media account. His stellar career became nothing but fodder, and all his achievements were ridiculed. Harlen's team made it to the Super Bowl that year. They won the ring, and Harlen retired. He could have played for a few more years and won another championship, but he wanted to get married and live quietly with his long-time partner. And because Vernon allowed Harlen to keep him hidden for so long, now the former athlete indulged the other man with no limits.

"Handsome boy, it's been too long since I've seen you." Vernon's voice was silky and smooth. He was naturally charming and entertaining. He was pretty but deadly, like a poisonous flower. "You're hurt. Not a fan of that."

I absently touched the bandage on my temple. "It's not bad. It definitely could've been worse. How are the kids doing?"

Vernon switched his gaze over to Daire and lifted a dark eyebrow. "The kids are good. Delta is doing some self-reflection, which is needed. We all want you to stay through the new year. Try and make that happen, Handsome. Introduce me to your girl."

I didn't correct his assumption that she was mine. I also didn't think too much about *why* I didn't immediately jump to deny Daire was my girl. I turned to Daire and watched as she gave the other man a bright smile. She was also charming and enigmatic. They would get along well.

In fact, she seemed to fit herself seamlessly into all the complicated corners of my life on this trip.

"I'm Daire Archer. Nice to meet you."

Vernon sighed and shook her hand. "Vernon Danvers. Aren't you a stunner? Hard to look this good after the trip you two have had. Impressive. Come inside, get cleaned up, and have something to eat."

When we got to the front door, we were greeted by another man who was even bigger than Booker and no less than intimidating.

Harlen was the opposite of Vernon. He wore old jeans and a faded black T-shirt. He was taller than me by a lot and was built like a tank.

I was surprised when Daire stopped beside me and pointed at the big man in surprise.

"I know you!" Her eyes widened. "I mean, I've seen you before. My older brother is a big fan. I'm pretty sure he had your picture on the wall at one point. He played football too."

Harlen gave her a soft grin which in no way made him look soft and cuddly. "Tell him I appreciate the support."

She nodded and pushed her hair behind her ears. "He got hurt not too long ago, so he can't play anymore." Her voice caught, and her smile dropped.

"It's a tough sport. It takes its toll on your body and mind. You have to give up so much of yourself when you make the move to play professionally. He may not see it now, but it might be a blessing in disguise that he has to go another way."

Daire made a non-committal sound and followed the two men inside.

A moment later, we were ambushed by my little brothers.

Both boys were dark-haired and tall for their ages. They had different mothers; one had blue eyes, and the other had green. You could only tell we were related by the similar arch in our eyebrows and the nearly identical face shape. Delta and I shared more features and coloring, but her face looked like our mother's. I was always glad she didn't have to see our old man when she looked in the mirror like I did.

They tugged at my clothes, clamored for me to pick them up, and rattled off stories about school and their friends so fast I couldn't keep up.

I kissed them on top of their heads and gave them a tight squeeze.

"Who is she?" I looked over my shoulder at Daire and noticed she was watching the reunion with her heart in her eyes.

"She's my friend from Denver. Her name is Daire."

The older of the boys stuck his chubby hand in her direction in a mirror image of Vernon's greeting. "Hi. I'm Lucas. My brother doesn't have friends. You must be special."

Not to be outdone, the younger brother elbowed his way to Daire and introduced himself in a rush. "I'm Eddie. You look like a princess."

Daire laughed. "Your brother tells me the same thing, but it doesn't sound as nice as when you do. It's nice to meet you both. I hope you had a great Christmas. I know your big brother was very sad he couldn't be here with you."

"Delta is up in her room. I think you need to take care of her first." Vernon ushered everyone out of the entrance and toward the living room. "You go up and chat with her. When you're done, come down, and we'll all eat together. I'll take care of your girl for now. Don't worry about her."

I looked at Daire to see if she was uncomfortable being left in a room full of strangers, but she was preoccupied with talking to my brothers about some comic book movie, so she didn't even notice I left.

I stopped by a bathroom on the way up to Delta's room. I needed to splash cold water on my face and wipe the dried blood off my arm so she wouldn't worry.

When I knocked on the door, it flung open, and I was pushed back a full step as my sister launched herself into my arms. She was tall and excited. It took all my strength and coordination to keep us both upright. When she finally met my gaze, I could see her eyes were all red and puffy. The tip of her nose was also pink and irritated. It would be cute if she wasn't so upset. It was obvious she'd been crying.

I guided her back into her room and shut the door behind us.

Her room was decorated in chic black and white. There was hardly any color in the stark space. I always thought the kids would be maximalists once they escaped poverty. However, they all leaned toward simplicity. If it weren't for Vernon, they would all be happy with white walls and single beds with sheets from a big box store.

I pulled out a white leather chair that was pushed under her computer desk while she sat nervously on the edge of the bed.

Delta was a good-looking girl. She was not classically pretty, her features were too bold for that, and her hair was too fiery red. She was aggressively attractive in a way that I knew would be problematic as she got older. However, to my surprise, it wasn't boys I had to warn away from her; it was other pretty girls. Delta was a late bloomer.

We all were.

I think it took being out from under my father's thumb and seeing how devoted Vernon and Harlen were to one another to realize that when looking for a good match, she might want to look at the same sex. I had my suspicions that one of the main reasons she lied about her holiday plans was because the 'really nice girl' from her class was more than just a friend.

"Tell me how we got here, Delta. I can forgive almost anything, but when you lie, that's a dealbreaker. We've always been honest with each other."

Her dark gaze clashed with mine. "Did Dad do that to your face?"

I nodded. "He did. It was my fault. I wasn't careful enough when I went out to see him."

"I bet Karsen was pissed."

"She was. For more than one reason. Dad hasn't been careful, and those risks caught up to him." It was as close as I was going to get to telling her what happened out in the holler. She was smart enough to put the pieces together.

"I didn't mean to screw up everything. I had no idea I had left my phone behind. I was so excited to be included in something so normal, to be seen as an average college student; I lost my mind a little bit." She sniffed and dragged the back of her hand across her nose. "College is hard, Campbell. Not the classes, but trying to integrate with a bunch of people who would be horrified if they knew my real story. I feel like I'm hiding in plain sight. Cleo makes me feel seen and accepted. When she asked me to go home with her for the holidays, I said yes before my brain could catch up. I kept thinking about how ungrateful I seemed and how disappointed you would be."

I sighed and stroked a finger over my scar. "I'm disappointed you lied, not that you wanted to make your own plans. As you get older, you'll make new friends, fall in love, start your own family, and have your own life and traditions. And even if you don't do any of those things, as you get older, you're going to find your own way of doing things and might want to spend holidays your way. That's how I know I raised you right. It's not your responsibility to hold the family together, Delta. It's mine."

She scowled at me and fisted her hand on the comforter. "And when I have my own life, and the boys have theirs, where does that leave you? Alone?" She sounded so sad when she asked that question.

I shrugged and tried not to flinch when it pulled on the wound on my arm.

"I don't know. But that is my problem, not yours. I want you to make good choices for yourself, Delta. I want you and the boys to be happy. I want you to be normal. Let me carry the burdens of the past."

She gave me an annoyed look. "No. It's not only your past. We all share it. We should carry it equally. It makes me feel terrible when I realize how much you sheltered us. If anyone deserves a break, it's you." She scooted closer to me and grabbed my hand. "Don't you want that?"

I didn't know what I wanted.

I knew I was ready to experience a different kind of life than the one I'd been living up until Benny pulled me out of Nowhere. But I had yet to figure out what made that life happy and fulfilling. It was similar to learning how to walk or write my name all over again.

"We're getting away from the point. I understand you're worried about me and want me to be happy, but that doesn't justify lying about where you were. What if something happened? What if there was an emergency? It would kill me, Delta." I exhaled and ensured she could see the worry I'd been drowning in since I heard she was missing. "You can't do that to me."

She lowered her head and gnawed on her lower lip. "I'm sorry."

"Make sure it doesn't happen again. Vernon and Harlen deserve better. And if you're struggling at school, talk to them. They both went to college and found a way to fit in even though they had things they didn't want the other kids to know. Especially Vernon. He started school when he was younger than most freshmen. It probably wasn't easy. You have resources at your disposal; use them." She was smarter than she'd been acting since this whole mess started.

She got teary again and launched herself into my arms for a hug. I gave her a squeeze and ran a hand over her hair. When we parted, she pulled herself together and gave me a probing look.

"Tell me about the girl you've been dragging all over the country with you. I peeked out the window when you pulled up. She's very pretty."

I grunted and looked over her head to hide some of my confused feelings about Daire. "She is pretty. She kind of hates that's what people immediately associate with her. Her looks hide the fact that she's a touch ruthless. She's like a wolf dressed up as a cute little lamb."

Delta let out a snorting laugh. "Sounds like Karsen."

I nodded. "That's what I told her. There are things about them that are weirdly similar. I imagine Karsen would've ended up like Daire if she stayed out of The Point and away from Booker."

"She sounds interesting. Do you like her?"

"No." The denial was immediate. "I feel some sort of way about her, but I wouldn't call it like. She's frustrating. She's irritating. She's stubborn. But she's also tough and smart. She's goofy and flirty. I think about her when I don't want to." I finally met Delta's gaze. "She's seen Nowhere and didn't run screaming back home. I told her a little about Dad and our childhood, and she was unfazed. I don't know why she's so cool about everything I throw at her, but she is. I can't say I've been the same regarding her."

"You always keep everyone a safe distance away. You don't trust anyone. You think everyone approaching you has some kind of agenda because even though the Bookers took you in, you still had to do terrible things for them. You don't think anyone can be interested in you just for you. You don't see your inherent value as a man. It's so sad because you have *so much* to offer the right person, Campbell. Look how amazing you have always been toward me and the boys."

I didn't want to tell her I was terrified that part of my father lingered within me, since she had part of him within her too.

"Don't spin fairy tales in your mind. I helped her run away from home over Christmas. She's got a big, protective family. They'll be good and pissed when I finally get her back home. I might end up fighting for my life. And I wasn't exactly nice to her when I first got to Denver. We're getting along much better than we were. I think that's as good as it will get for now."

She reached out and punched me playfully in the arm. Thankfully, she missed the one with the wound.

"You getting along with anyone, in any capacity, is a big deal. In case you missed the memo, you are challenging to get close to, big brother. I can't wait to meet the woman who finally moved you. You've been stuck in one place way too long."

"She wants to meet you too."

We hugged one more time and headed downstairs. I assured Delta that Daire wouldn't say anything about her red eyes and irritated nose.

As we walked toward the living room, we heard laughter. My brothers were giggling at the top of their lungs, and Daire's laugh was loud over the top of them.

Delta said Daire moved me, and she was right. The more time I spent with her, the more I felt my heart shift. It'd been dormant for so long that it took me longer than it should've to realize she'd turned the poor, neglected thing upside down.

She'd dragged it into the light and warmed it up. Now I needed to figure out what I was going to do with all the heat and brightness she brought into my world.

After all, my faults and failures were much easier to see when they weren't hidden in the dark.

chapter THIRTEEN

Daire

Campbell's family was adorable. The boys, and the men raising them, were an entertaining mix of fun-loving and easygoing, with an inherent intensity that underscored everything they said and did. Vernon and Harlen were over-the-top hospitable, and the boys were little chatterboxes. They loved all things superhero, so I asked Vernon to find me some paper and something to draw with. I drew little characters of each brother displaying their dream superpower in no time. Lucas wanted to fly, and Eddie wanted to control the weather. The mini art session kept everyone occupied until Campbell and Delta joined the family.

The brother and sister strongly resembled one another. The ginger genetics were clearly dominant in both. I could tell Delta had been crying, but she had a strained smile on her face when she introduced herself. Her grip was firm and her gaze was direct as she sized me up. I returned the scrutiny with a grin, and instead of a mere handshake, I pulled her in for a tight hug.

I felt her jolt of surprise and how she quivered when I held onto her.

"We have more in common than you know. From one little runaway sister to another, I feel like I already know you. It's nice to finally meet you." I pulled back and gave her a warm look. "Your brother was really worried about you. I'm so glad you were safe and sound all along. I have a big brother I've been putting through the wringer lately. Watching things play out between you and Campbell was very eye-opening. I learned a lot."

Delta wrinkled her nose and made a very cute face. "I'm an example of what not to do. Don't learn from me."

I chuckled. "I'm always the poster child for what not to do. You're not alone. But nothing says we can't learn from our mistakes and do better in the future." I cocked my head to the side and felt my face settle into a serious expression. "I don't ever want to be the reason my brother looks like his world is ending the way Campbell has the last few days."

It was probably rude to lay it out for her bluntly after meeting her for only a few minutes, but I wanted her to know how deeply her actions wounded a man most would consider bulletproof.

Delta blinked in surprise at the harsh words. She tilted her head in the opposite direction of mine and cast a sideways glance at her older brother. "I see the resemblance to Karsen even more now." She sighed and looked around the room at her family. "It won't happen again. I'll be honest about everything, even if it's hard."

A murmur of agreement worked through the room as the younger kids ran up to Campbell and showed him their superhero drawings.

"Look what Daire made for us! Don't we look cool?" The excited voices broke any tension that was lingering in the room.

Vernon turned the conversation away from the heavy matter and asked, "Are you interested in a career in art? You're very talented."

I took the bottle of water Campbell handed me and absently scooted over to make room for him on the couch next to me. I didn't even realize how natural the move was. I just automatically wanted him next to me, so I made room. Everyone else in the room was keenly aware of the action as well.

People usually tried to keep their distance from Campbell. Not me.

"My dad is an artist. He owns the Marked Men Tattoo franchise. When he was my age, he was a big name in the tattoo industry, but now he's branched out into other forms of art. I've always been interested in drawing, and I inherited his talent. I thought I would take over the tattoo shop in Denver when I was done with college and went through an apprenticeship, but those plans went haywire after my brother's accident."

Harlen sat forward, and his eyes lit up with interest. "Your dad is Rule Archer?" After I nodded affirmatively, he exclaimed, "Then your brother is Ry Archer, and your uncle is Remy Archer?"

Again, I nodded.

Harlen clapped his hands together like he had a revelation. "A bunch of guys I used to play with had standing appointments at the Marked Men or Saints of Denver when we had games in Colorado. I've heard your dad's name tossed around for years. I followed your uncle's career when I was younger, and I kept an eye on your brother because they were related. He was always touted as a potential Heisman candidate."

I was struck speechless once again by the short the distance between my world and Campbell's. Every point we touched on this trip brought us closer to a middle ground rather than driving us further apart, as I initially assumed it would.

Vernon leaned back on the sofa and ruffled the dark hair of the youngest. "College is always there when you're ready to go. But it's not the universal answer for everyone. Hands-on experience is unbeatable when it comes to some career choices."

I nodded in agreement. "That's true. My dad never went to a formal school for art. He started tattooing and learned along the way. I think he wants a different start for me, and for me to get some life experience before I jump into the family business." I sighed and pushed my hair off my face. "Now that my brother is in med school, taking after my mother, I think my dad wants to make sure I'm doing what I want and not what's expected." Tired of being the center of attention, I asked Delta, "Do you know what you want to focus on in the future?" I was curious since we were close in age.

"I want to be a lawyer, like Karsen. I'd like to specialize in women's rights." Her voice was soft, as if she'd never spoken the wish aloud. "I know it's going to be a lot of work, but the more I learn, the more passionate I am about pursuing that specialty."

"Karsen seems like she's a force to be reckoned with. She struck me as someone who is very powerful and incredibly devoted to her family. I can see why you want to follow in her footsteps. I'm sure she'll be honored when she hears how she inspired you." As far as role models went, Karsen Booker might be the scariest one Delta could pick.

Delta huffed out a breath and gave her head a little shake. "It sounds like you didn't encounter Karsen's scary side while you were there."

I laughed. "You mean she has a side that isn't scary?"

Harlen broke into the playful banter by telling everyone to get ready for dinner. He promised a holiday-worthy spread since everyone was interrupted and upset over Christmas. Initially, Campbell said we wouldn't stay at the house, but Vernon insisted we use the guestroom. The only catch was that we would have to share a bed for the night. I was okay with that arrangement. I knew he wouldn't do anything while under the same roof as his siblings, but Campbell seemed slightly uncomfortable. I was going to offer to sleep on the couch; this house was immaculate and amazing. The big, plush couch in the family room was nicer than the motel bed I'd slept on the first day of this trip. Campbell cut me off before I could get the words out and assured Vernon we would be fine sharing the guest room.

Dinner was delicious and was indeed worthy of being called a spread. The atmosphere was warm and lively. It was the first time I saw Campbell smile repeatedly. He even tossed back his head and laughed at a story one of his brothers told him. Vernon was ridiculously charming, and Harlen felt like an old family friend when the subject turned to football. He knew more about my Uncle Remy and his short-lived football career than I did.

Overall, it was a pleasant experience, and I was very grateful Campbell trusted me enough to introduce me to his family. When it was time to clean up, I admitted the meal made me a little homesick.

I helped Campbell do the dishes, then tactfully made myself scarce so he could spend time with his siblings.

I walked out the back of the house, wrapped in the oversized hoodie from the lost and found, and wandered down to the semi-frozen waterfront. It was dark and cold, but it felt like the perfect environment from which to call home for the first time since I'd left on Christmas. I tucked my hair into the giant hood, pulled the sleeves down over my hands, and called my mom.

She picked up on the first ring. "Daire. Are you okay?"

"I'm fine. I'll be home in a couple of days. I know everyone is worried about me, but I'm all right. You deserve an explanation, and I owe everyone an apology. I wasn't thinking about anyone but myself when I left. I know I'm a terrible daughter."

My mom sighed, and I could picture her rubbing her forehead the way she did when she was really stressed and had a headache.

"I don't know what to say to you right now, Daire. Do you know I've aged ten years in the last week? I have never been as disappointed in you as I am right now."

The words stung, but they weren't a surprise. Getting what I wanted from her didn't feel nearly as good as I thought it would. Wanting my family to view me as a screw-up felt very different when they actually did it.

"You should be disappointed in me. I was thoughtless, and I messed up. Exactly like the night Ry got hurt." I blew out a frustrated breath and gazed out over the dark water. "I needed a way to show you how deeply I've been hurting. It felt like no one would listen to me. None of you would blame me for putting Ry in danger. I didn't know what else to do, Mom. I was desperate."

I started crying at some point. The tears were icy against my cheeks, and my heart felt frozen.

My mom sighed again, and her voice softened. "You have a certain knack for getting your point across. You must've inherited that from your father. Speaking of your dad, he wants to talk to you."

I heard my parents talking to each other in low tones and some shuffling as my dad took the phone and moved away. A moment later, his deep, reassuring voice came across the line.

"Daire."

I burst into loud, uncontrollable sobs at the sound of my name in that familiar voice. I hated myself for hurting them. Hurting them hurt me the most, so the punishment I was seeking finally came to fruition.

"I need you to listen to what I'm about to say to you. Not just hear it, but really listen to what I'm saying. Can you do that?"

I nodded even though he couldn't see me.

"When I was your age, your grandma and grandpa told me that I was a bad son and a bad brother all the time. For a stretch of time, that was the *only* thing they said to me. They were in a lot of pain because of your Uncle Remy's accident. The only reason he was out on the road that night was because I called him to come to pick me up. I knew the roads were bad, but I asked him to come get me anyway. It was selfish and stupid." My dad cleared his throat, and I could hear how emotional he was on the other end of the phone when recalling the night he lost his twin brother, and his life changed forever. I wanted to give him a hug. "They told me the accident was my fault. They told me Uncle Remy would still be around if it wasn't for me. They told me the wrong twin was taken from them. It felt like they wanted me to be the one who died in the crash. Part of me knew they didn't mean what they were saying, but the words still hurt. And I believed them. If you think for one second I would ever put you through that, you've lost your mind. I wouldn't wish that experience on my worst enemy, let alone my daughter. I've been in your shoes, Daire. I was told I was a 'bad' Archer for a long time. When your mom and I had you and your brother, we promised each other we would never make our kids carry a burden that does not belong to them. Do you understand why your mom and I wanted to help and not hurt you? Because the sins of the father will not be visited upon the son or daughter on my watch. I won't allow it."

The sobs shook my shoulders, and I almost fell to my knees.

"Grandma and Grandad don't treat you that way now." They were actually really good to my dad and my Uncle Rome. And they had been an active part of my life for as long as I could remember. There wasn't a hint of friction in the relationship, that I could recall. It hurt to hear they had treated my father so poorly when he was at his lowest. Thank goodness my mother was there to fight for him.

"No, they don't. Because I forgave them, and I forgave myself. It didn't happen overnight. We were angry at each other for quite a bit, but your mom and you kids helped everyone realize it was more important to be a family than to be angry at each other. You think you want us to blame you for an accident, but you don't know what that looks like, Daire. And you have no idea how hard it is to come back from if the family fractures like that."

"But it's all my fault." I wailed the words into the night and finally stopped trying to stay upright. I collapsed to the cold ground and lowered my head, sobbing uncontrollably.

"It was an accident. What if you were trying to change your tire on your own? What if you called Zowen instead of Ry? Or what if Ry had shown up five minutes earlier or later? There are too many factors for you to take the blame for what happened. The only thing you're responsible for is what led you to make the choice to drink and drive that night. We aren't going to gang up on you for asking for help when you needed it. Even after the accident, your brother is still showing up whenever you call him. So am I. So is your mom. So are your aunt and uncle and all your cousins. No one in this family is abandoning you. Even after this dumb stunt you pulled." He scolded me. "I got your car off the mountain, by the way."

Something about that final sentence snapped me out of my self-flagellation. I choked on a laugh and rubbed the sleeve of the hoodie over my wet face.

"Thank you. I didn't plan to leave it behind. I didn't even plan to leave. The first thing Campbell said when he found me was that I suck at running away from home."

"Campbell, huh?" My dad's tone of voice changed, and the hair on the back of my neck lifted in alarm. "You'll have to bring him by the house when you get back to town so your mother and I can thank him."

I sniffed and pulled myself together before climbing to my feet. "Why does it sound like the last thing you want to do is thank him?"

My dad grunted and sounded thoroughly annoyed when he replied, "My daughter disappeared with some guy none of us know anything about, and he helped her go totally off the grid. My first question is, why does he know how to do that? Of course, we have questions about his motives and intentions. I don't care that Benny vouches for him, or that Remy says he's a good guy who was only trying to help. I want to make that judgment myself."

"I've learned a lot traveling with him this week. I'm glad he's the one who found me first." I could hear the stark truth in the words, so there was no way my father couldn't.

My dad grunted again, and I could clearly picture the scowl on his face. "Don't expect your brother to be as understanding as your mom and me. You really hurt him, Daire. And you hurt Bowe's feelings, which made him doubly upset. He won't take his anger out on you, but that boy you're traveling with might become a substitute target."

"Campbell can hold his own. But you might want to tell Ry to pick an easier outlet for his anger. He should bring it to me. I'm the one who fucked up." It might be cathartic if we finally faced each other with our raw emotions and acknowledged the fallout from the accident. Ry was too used to coddling me. He always let me have my way. We'd never gone toe-to-toe over anything. We'd never even had a typical brother/sister conflict.

It was past time Ry was real with me.

It wasn't fair that I dragged Campbell into the middle of a family firefight.

"If your brother wants to pick a fight he can't win, let him. It's good for him to know he can't always come out on top. It'll humble him. And if that boy is willing to fight for you, it's a little easier for your old man to swallow that you seem overly interested in him. I love you, Daire. No matter what. No amount of rebellion is going to change that."

"I love you, too, Dad. No matter what." I didn't want to tell him I wasn't rebelling; I was just finding out who I was. And it was starting to look like that girl thrived on chaos. I probably inherited that from him right alongside my ability to draw.

"Tell your mother you love her, and promise her you will never put her through this again. Then get your ass home so we can hug you."

"Okay." I waited until my mom was on the phone and then parroted what my dad told me to tell her. Her reception was colder than my father's, but I knew it was because she was worried sick about me.

I took a couple minutes to get my head on straight before I walked back toward the house. I was cold and tired, and I wanted to take a scalding hot shower and go to bed. I was looking forward to spending the night next to Campbell.

I don't know when it happened, but I felt safe and comforted when I was near him.

A man who oozed danger and alluded to a violent, destructive past shouldn't be my safe space, but he was. I wondered how he would feel if I disclosed that particular revelation.

Would he welcome it or feel like I was another burden?

Lost in thought, I didn't notice the person standing on the back patio watching me in the dark.

It wasn't until I almost bumped into him that I saw Campbell. He caught my shoulders and let his gaze rove over my swollen eyes and the dirty knees of my pants.

He didn't ask why I was so unkempt. Instead, he pulled me into a tight hug and rested his chin on the crown of my head.

"Family is tough." His rough voice was as quiet as the night that surrounded us.

I wrapped my arms around his waist, closed my eyes, and leaned into him.

"Yeah. Really tough."

"You're tough, too, Princess. Don't forget that."

I held him even tighter and whispered, "I won't."

I sure didn't feel like a burden when he held me like this.

chapter FOURTEEN

Campbell

"Slow down!" Daire's scream startled me and I slammed on the brakes. The SUV careened to the shoulder of the road as Daire's fingers clamped onto my arm in a death grip.

I was going to scold her for the dangerous move, but when I caught sight of her, the words died on my lips. She was pale to the point of looking unwell. She was sweating and shaky. Her eyes were twice their normal size, and her breathing was slow and shallow. She looked like she was in the middle of a panic attack.

"It's okay. We're fine, Daire."

The roads were way better on the return trip back to Denver. We were near the spot we had originally stopped in Kansas when an accident occurred on the opposite side of the interstate. It looked like a minivan tried to pass a semi-truck but miscalculated how much clearance they needed. Both vehicles ran off the road and caused a few of the cars behind them to smash into one another. The minivan didn't look so good, but the rest of the damage seemed minor. Several people were walking along the median between the two directions of traffic, and as soon as Daire saw them and heard the sirens from the first responders, she started to freak out.

She put her hands over her face and continued to shake violently. She looked like a shell of the vibrant, lively girl who rang in the New Year with my family. She looked frail and fragile, and nothing like the girl who'd slept next to me and tempted me to no end the last couple of nights. She had naughty hands and a wicked mouth when she wanted to.

"Someone is hurt. Do you think they're going to be all right?" Her voice quivered, and it sounded like she was choking back tears.

It dawned on me that seeing the accident was a huge trigger for her. Even involving strangers she would never see again; it obviously still took her back to the night she nearly lost her brother. She hid her trauma well under her flirty and flippant attitude. I didn't know how deep her issues ran and how tormented she was until I witnessed her total breakdown.

She was far from a pretty, perfect princess at the moment. She was almost unrecognizable.

"The motel we stayed at on our way to Nowhere is off the next exit. Can you hold it together for a little while longer?" I was worried she might pass out because her breathing was so shallow.

"So much blood. There was so much blood." Her voice cracked, and she started to silently sob.

I reached out and caught her hand. It was ice cold. I squeezed her fingers and pulled the SUV back onto the road. It took longer to get to the exit than anticipated because traffic was backed up. When I parked, booked us a room, and carried her inside, she was practically catatonic. She was muttering nonsense, shaking uncontrollably, and her eyes were unfocused and wild. I called her name repeatedly and got no response. I gently shook her shoulders, which only made her cry harder.

I could handle a flood of regular tears and normal waves of deep emotion, but this was complete devastation. I was at a loss as to what to do.

I wrapped her in the comforter and called Remy.

She answered on the first ring. "Hello, Mr. No First or Last Name. I hope you're taking very good care of my cousin. My brother and her brother are eager to speak with you when you get back to Denver." The taunt was classic, sassy Remy.

"Remy, something is wrong with Daire." Typically, I liked Remy's playful attitude, but there was no time for it right now. "We passed an accident on the interstate, and she started to freak out. She's shaking and crying. She's struggling to breathe. I don't know what to do."

In a split second, Remy's entire persona changed. Her tone was serious; I could feel her concern from a thousand miles away.

"She left Denver so quickly that she probably didn't take any of the anxiety meds her mom prescribed. Just in case, check her purse. If you can't find anything, put her in a cold shower. Once her breathing rate picks up, focus on making her breathe with you. Calm, even breaths. You need to shock her system and restart it. Once you get her breathing evened out, she should calm down and come out of the attack. She should be okay once she relaxes and gets some rest." I scrambled to look through the tiny purse that still carried the GPS tracker and came up empty-handed. Remy swore softly. "This is another teachable moment for her. She should have made sure she had her medication with her. Not having it isn't an option when your mind is your own worst enemy. If you can't get her heart rate and breathing under control, you might have to take her to the ER. Her symptoms can become dangerous if they last too long."

She sounded like she was speaking from experience.

"Okay. I'll toss her in the shower and see where we end up. Tell the Archer boys they can have as many words as they want with me when I get back. It's better if we all agree to keep it civil." I looked down at Daire and frowned. "You may want to let them know, though, that I don't think Daire will handle it well if her brother ends up back in the hospital."

Remy clicked her tongue. "Confident. I love that for you. Ry generally plays by the rules, so he might agree to be civil. Except he is a lunatic where Daire is concerned. My little brother is kind of a wild card. Usually, he's the most rational of all of us kids, but occasionally, he goes feral. He gets that from my mom. Keep me updated. Call me back if she doesn't get any better. I can get her mom involved if need be."

I hung up the call and hauled Daire, blanket and all, into the bathroom. I awkwardly held her with one hand while cranking on the water. The icy stream drenched my arm and part of my shoulder, so I just climbed under the spray with her in my arms. In a matter of seconds, we were soaking wet, and our teeth were chattering. I tossed the soggy comforter on the floor and wrapped an arm around Daire's waist to keep her upright. I used my thumb to tilt her head back and watched as she gasped and blinked spiky lashes as the water hit her directly in the face.

Thankfully, it seemed to do the trick. Her chest moved more rapidly as her lungs were shocked to react. Some of the haze cleared from her vision, and her shaking hands clutched at the drenched cotton of my long-sleeved shirt. Her tears mixed with the water, and her lips parted with a soft moan.

"Daire. I need you to breathe with me, okay?"

She stared at me silently and acted like she couldn't hear me.

I sighed and lowered my head so my lips almost touched hers.

"In and out. Follow me." I exhaled against her mouth and felt her inhale with a soft sigh. I was cold as fuck, with the water hitting me directly in the back, so I was breathing faster than normal. But I made a conscious effort to slow it down.

It took a minute, but eventually, Daire matched me breath for breath. She was still shaking, but I could tell it was from the cold and not because her body and mind were in crisis. Her hold on my shirt tightened, and she pulled me closer.

Our lips were no longer *almost* touching.

The kiss was icy, but the inside of her mouth was warm. She shuddered when our tongues slicked against one another, and she willingly moved closer when I put my hand on her ass and pulled her into my arms. I could feel the pointed tips of her nipples through her clothes. The frigid shower must have woken them up and made them tighten. I used my other hand to push her wet, clingy hair away from her face and pulled back to look into her eyes. They were finally clear and looked less frantic.

"Feeling better?"

She nodded slowly and turned her face to rub against the palm of my hand like a big cat searching for affection.

"I don't know what happened. I haven't reacted that badly since the night of the accident. It came out of nowhere." She exhaled, wrapped her arms around my waist, and held tight. "I guess I need more help than I thought."

I skimmed my hand down her soggy hair and kissed the crown of her head. "Remy said you have medicine that helps. You need to keep it with you from now on. You never know when you might be triggered, and if you're on your own, you need to be able to manage by yourself." I didn't mean to lecture her, but the words came out more forcefully than intended.

I was worried about her, not just at the moment, but about how she would operate in the future. I didn't want anything bad to happen to her when she was in a vulnerable state.

She nodded, bumping her forehead against my chest. "I'll be more careful. Thank you for helping me through this one."

"It was Remy. I called her because I didn't know what to do. You gave me a good scare, Daire."

She leaned back and looked up at me. I needed to turn off the cold water and get us into dry clothes.

"I didn't mean to scare you. I was also scared when you came back from dealing with your dad and were bleeding. Does that mean we like each other?"

"It means something." I'd never been frightened for anyone other than myself and my siblings before her. I was used to having people be scared of me, not for me. It was an entirely new experience.

Daire reached past me to turn off the water. When she did, our bodies were plastered together.

"Did Remy tell you that distracting me and forcing me to focus on something else is also a good way to stave off a panic attack?"

"She did not." The words tripped out of frozen lips, and my entire body quaked when she pushed her hands under the sodden fabric of my shirt and tugged it over my head.

"I'm not surprised. She probably knows exactly what kind of distraction I would respond to best." Her stiff fingers dipped decisively to the fastenings on the front of my jeans.

I caught her hand and stilled her movements. "I'm not sure that's a good idea. You were pretty out of it a minute ago."

She shook loose from my hold and worked my zipper down. I might still be thinking straight, but my dick didn't have that luxury. It got hard and reacted to her intent before I could talk some sense into Daire.

"It's a great idea. I think it's a surefire way to make me feel better. I'm fully aware of what I'm asking for. So, go on and distract me, Campbell. Keep my mind on you for the rest of the afternoon and through the night if you think you're up for it."

There was no missing the challenge in her voice.

I exited the tub and pulled off my wet boots and jeans. I helped her carefully step out, and watched with heavy-lidded eyes as she stripped down to her bra and underwear. We left everything in a soaked heap with the comforter on the bathroom floor.

I picked her up when she moved to wrap her arms around my neck. With a little hop, she wound her long legs around my waist and settled her lips over mine. She kissed the breath out of me as I carefully maneuvered us toward the bed.

After sleeping next to her for several days and not touching a hair on her head, I was hungry for contact. I was starving for a taste of her.

Honestly, all roads, both in and out of Denver, led to this. It felt like one of those situations that was unavoidable from the start.

We kissed deeply, thoroughly, and roughly until we reached the bed. I let her drop, and she landed with a slight bounce. The mattress squeaked, and her pale eyebrows lifted in amusement.

"I guess it won't be a dirty secret when we fuck. It sounds like the whole motel is gonna know."

"Doesn't feel like it was ever gonna be a secret. That's why your brother is so anxious to talk to me when we get back."

She sat up and reached for the waistband of my underwear, her eyes bright as they hovered over my body.

"I really want to draw on you. Do you know that? You have such nice skin. I want to put color all over it to break up some of the black and gray. You don't have to live your life in the dark anymore."

I leaned over her once she had me naked. I was going to kiss her, but she moved her head, and I felt the tip of her tongue flick over the moth tattooed across my throat. The touch was as light as the brush of a feather.

While she was busy tracing the outline of my tattoo, I unhooked her bra and let my fingers skate over her soft skin.

She was tall and lean, the same way I was, but she had more than a handful of curves in all the right places. Had I known what was under the towel the first time she decided to tempt me, I don't know that I would have had the willpower to walk away.

"If I let you draw on me, what do I get to do to you in return?" My voice was ragged, and I could feel my heart trying to launch out of my chest.

Daire grabbed one of my hands and kissed her way over the ink that decorated the back, taking her time to lick each and every raised mark and scar the tattoos covered.

"Anything you want. You can do anything you want to me." She said it confidently, but I don't think she understood how much trouble an open invitation like that could get her into.

I plunged my hands into her hair and tilted her head back. I kissed her until neither of us could breathe and flinched when her fingertips moved to trace my abs. The tip of my cock gave an excited kick when it grazed her palm. She tickled her way down my happy trail and brushed her fingers along the underneath side of my erection.

I stepped back to slide her wet underwear off. Our eyes met, and hers were electric, glowing like a neon sign.

"Lift your ass." The command was gruff, but she obeyed without argument, leaving us both naked and covered in goosebumps from the icy shower.

I needed to warm her up.

I kissed her forehead. The tip of her nose. The point of her chin. I licked my way down the side of her neck and nibbled on her collarbone. I skimmed my hands over her breasts, palming one and lifting her waiting nipple up to my mouth.

Because her skin still carried a chill, she tasted like winter.

I rubbed my other hand along her ribcage until I reached her hip. I hooked my palm under her thigh and lifted one of her legs to curl around my waist.

"I don't have protection." Having sex was the last thing on my mind when I'd gone after her.

Daire wiggled closer and threw out a hand to grope for the purse I'd left on the bed. After a minute of searching, she pulled out a small foil packet.

"I do."

Now wasn't the time to lecture her on being prepared for sex and not a panic attack, but I would remember to mention her priorities later. At the moment, I was very thankful they were askew.

I worked my teeth to tease her nipple and ran my hand down the center of her body. I used my thumb to trace the soft, outer edge of her belly button and sucked even harder on the puckered tip of her nipple between my teeth.

Daire whimpered and wrapped her other leg around my waist. I could feel the heat from her body bleeding into mine. I could feel that she was getting wet and impatient the longer I used my mouth and hands to tease her.

I dragged my fingers down her lower stomach and watched the way the caress made her muscles clench. I brushed my fingers over the delicate folds that covered her inner heat and cupped my palm over her entire center. Her body quaked in response, and I felt my hand get damp. I pulled away and used her desire to slick my fingers before I slid two inside her.

She jerked underneath me and dug her hands into my hair. She lifted her hips eagerly and moaned my name in a low voice.

I bit down with more force on the tender peak than she was prepared for as I dipped my fingers inside her excited pussy. I smiled against her skin when I felt her body quiver against my tongue and pulse in anticipation.

She felt so good. Like life and promise. Like color and joy. Like happiness and anticipation.

She felt like all the things I'd never been able to hold in my hands before.

"You feel better than I imagined." I kissed my way back up to her neck and kissed the hollow of her throat. I felt her pulse flutter in response.

"You imagined how I felt? That's some poker face you've got, Campbell." I bit her earlobe and cut off her playful giggle.

"How could I not? What were you trying to do while we shared a bed the last few days? Drive me out of my mind?"

"I was trying to get us here. I'm exactly where I want to be. Don't have any doubt about it." She lifted herself up, and the tip of my overly excited cock bumped against the hand that I had buried inside of her. Her eyes were luring me to do every possible thing I could think of to her. Her gaze was more than willing. "Hurry up. I feel like I've been waiting for you forever."

She told me earlier on our journey that she usually treated sex like a game. It was a power struggle between her and whomever she was with.

Not now. The two of us on this bed were completely equal. We wanted each other the same way. Our hunger was the same. Even our desperation and darkness were the same.

I shifted away from her so I could put on the condom. Every breath, every glance, every shivery touch told me she was ready. Not to mention that my fingers were drenched in a clear sign of her want and need.

When I slid into her, Daire threw her head back and clutched my shoulders. Her nails dug deep into my skin, and her eyes drifted closed. Her legs tightened their hold on my waist as I braced myself over her, with an elbow above her head and a hand on her butt. It was sort of like our first kiss, wet, wild, and uncoordinated. We clashed against one another rather than moved seamlessly as one. We were both trying to take as much from the other as possible.

We were greedy, and it made the way we moved and touched frantic.

I kissed her cheekbones and moved my mouth to play with her ear. She writhed underneath me and whispered my name every time she caught a breath.

She was warm and soft, contrasting with all the sharp edges she normally liked to rub against me. I liked that she had both.

Typically, when I had sex, it was all about instant gratification. It was a rush to feel as good as possible, as quickly as possible.

Not with Daire.

I wanted to savor every sensation. I wanted to remember the look on her face when I touched her where she liked. I wanted to hear how she said my name when I made her come. I didn't want to miss a single moan or flicker of her eyelashes.

We finally found a rhythm that had us working together instead of fighting against each other. I felt her body pulse around mine with each thrust.

Faster. Deeper. Harder. More.

Like I said, we were both greedy.

It didn't take long before we both reached a shattering climax. Daire broke first. She wrapped all her limbs around me and locked her lips on mine. I felt her shake and shudder around me, which pushed my pleasure over the top. I thrust into her and collapsed on top of her with a low groan. I kissed the side of her head and felt pure satisfaction spiral from the base of my skull all the way to my toes.

"Are you feeling properly distracted?" I chuckled after the words worked their way out.

Daire turned her head and kissed me in the same spot I just kissed her. "It's a good start, but let's see what else you've got." She paused on a laugh and looked at me with wide eyes. "That was the only condom. You'll have to get creative with the rest of your distraction techniques."

I sighed and gathered her close so I could roll over and have her rest on my chest.

I never got creative during sex. It wasn't that important to me. As long as I left feeling good, I didn't care about what came before and after.

However, I could put some thought into it for Daire, because I wanted her to feel as good as she made me feel.

She was important to me... despite all my intentions to make sure she wasn't.

FIFTEEN

Daire

"Stop! What are you doing?!" I threw open the passenger door and jumped out of the SUV that had just pulled into my parents' driveway. I was fast, but my brother was faster.

Campbell didn't seem too worried about the conflict he knew was brewing upon our return to Denver, but being yanked out of the car by a former professional athlete was different than just speculating what Ry might do.

I darted around the back of the SUV and tried to get between the two young men.

Ry was bigger than Campbell, but he was still recovering from having a shattered leg and multiple other injuries from the accident. And Campbell was unpredictable. After we visited the farm, I didn't really want to speculate what he was capable of, but I knew it was much worse than what my brother was prepared for.

I was close enough to grab Campbell's jacket when I was jerked backward. I struggled against Bowe's hold, but she wasn't letting up, no matter how hard I pushed at her hands.

"Let me go. Ry has no reason to be mad at Campbell. He didn't do anything wrong. I was the one who screwed up." My voice raised as the sound of fists against flesh got louder. I heard my brother grunt and I tried to catch Campbell's eye. "Don't hurt him." I couldn't tell whether he registered my plea or not. At this point, I wasn't sure which boy I was begging not to hurt the other.

Bowe wrapped me up in a back hug. She was strong from hauling musical equipment in and out of venues and jumping around on stage. She wasn't letting me loose no matter what I did.

"Let them work it out between themselves. If you don't let Ry see that Campbell's willing to fight for you, whatever the two of you have going on isn't going to go anywhere. Your brother is stubborn. He won't hand you over to some guy who isn't willing to put himself in the line of fire for you. He's always let you have your way, but he won't when it comes to something like this."

I huffed out an annoyed breath and cringed when I saw Campbell's head snap back after a vicious uppercut. He spit out a mouthful of blood, but otherwise looked unfazed as my brother launched himself at him again. I was worried about the wound on Campbell's arm opening back up, but there was no way to intervene as long as Bowe held me in place.

I contemplated grabbing a handful of her rainbow-colored hair and pulling with all my might, but she was still on my list of people I needed to make amends to, so starting a fistfight with her would be counterproductive. Plus, she could probably kick my ass. The girl had been playing in some rough dive bars and honkytonks in Texas before she moved to bigger venues.

"Hey. You know me leaving on Christmas Eve had nothing to do with you and Ry dating, right?" I peeked over my shoulder and watched her eyes widen in alarm as one of the boys hit the ground with a low groan. "There's been a lot of change in my life lately. You just got caught up in the whirlwind. I love you and couldn't ask for anyone more perfect for Ry. I don't think he would've been half as motivated to get back on his feet if it wasn't for you. I've never seen him so happy."

Bowe swore and dodged the elbow I'd tossed back toward her tummy while she was distracted. Ry was the one on the ground. Campbell stood over him, watching to see if he would get up or stay down. His shirt was torn, and his hair was messy, but other than that, there were very few signs my brother had done his best to remove his head from his body moments ago.

They were both bleeding, and my brother looked alarmingly pale. Something shifted in the air, and Ry seemed to realize that although he fought back, Campbell did not want to hurt him.

"He is happy, but that doesn't mean anything if you're miserable. One without the other doesn't work, Daire."

"I'm not unhappy because of anyone other than myself. And it's not something I can control. It's similar to what Remy deals with. The chemicals in my brain aren't working right at the moment. It's my problem to fix, not Ry's."

Bowe sighed, and her hug turned from one of capture to one of comfort. "I thought we were friends, Daire. It hurts my feelings when you struggle with all this on your own. You've always been there for me, even when it involved your brother. I'm angry you didn't allow anyone to be there for you. You need to be nicer to yourself."

I wrapped my hands around her arms where she was holding me and watched Campbell extend a hand to help Ry back to his feet.

My parents exited the house and took in the scene with serious expressions. My father locked his gaze on Campbell while my mother looked at me and frowned.

I turned in Bowe's arms and gave her a fierce hug. "I thought struggling with it on my own was what I deserved. I'm in a better place right now, but I had to travel to get here. I know I was wrong."

"Everyone, get in the house. Now." My mom's voice was sharp, and the frown on her face grew fiercer when she saw Ry bleeding. Her gaze scanned over Campbell, and I could feel the frost from where I stood. "Go home, Campbell. I want to thank you for bringing Daire home and making sure she was safe. But I'm too angry to do it properly at the moment."

Campbell wiped the back of his hand over his bloody lip and looked at me. I gave him a tiny nod and watched silently as he collected my meager belongings from the back of the SUV and set them down near the steps to the front door.

I wanted to tell him I would talk to him soon. I wanted to tell him I appreciated everything he did for me, including all the creative ways he kept me distracted after my panic attack. The boy was very good with his hands, and even better with his mouth. I finally learned what it meant to really play games with a sexual partner, and I'd never had more fun in bed. On top of everything, feeling good and experiencing more orgasms in a row than I knew was possible, it felt serious. It felt like Campbell was invested in me, mind, body, and soul. I didn't want him to drive away without a word like he was the hired help, but my brother didn't give me a choice.

Ry caught my bicep and frog-marched me into the house like I was a little kid who misbehaved.

"Stay away from him, Daire. He's dangerous."

I shook free from Ry's hold and pushed my messy hair away from my face. I stared at my brother and crossed my arms over my chest.

"You pulled him out of the car as soon as we stopped. You threw the first punch."

My brother swore and stared down at me. "I had Zowen dig into him. And Campbell doesn't exist. There are zero internet records of him. Not even a birth certificate or Social Security card. He's not real, Daire. You don't need someone like that in your life."

I sighed. "I know all of that. And I know why he doesn't have a digital footprint. There is always more than what's on the surface, Ry. Why are you being so judgmental?"

"He's sketchy. The first guy you decide to get serious with shouldn't be a guy like him. It should be someone reliable. Someone trustworthy. I want you to date someone who can take care of you, since you've been doing such a shit job of taking care of yourself lately."

I gasped and gave him a dirty look. "I could take care of myself if everyone in this family didn't treat me like I was a porcelain doll. And for the record, I trust Campbell. He did a good job taking care of me after he got me off the mountain."

Ry looked like he wanted to hit the wall. His frustration was coming off his tense body in waves. "You don't know anything about him."

I shrugged indifferently, even though I knew it would rile him up even more. "I learned a lot about him and myself this past week. I like him. I liked things about him even before he found me in the blizzard. I like the way he sees me. Campbell doesn't even know what rose-colored glasses are." He always saw my true, authentic, and deeply flawed self. In fact, every time I let him witness one of my weaknesses, it brought us closer together. The further away from perfection I was, the more he seemed to appreciate me. "He likes me too," I said the last part with confidence, which obviously ruffled my brother's feathers.

"How do you know?"

I snorted a sharp laugh. "Because you're still in one piece. I know you landed a few lucky punches. He let you hit him, Ry. You don't know anything about him. He let you hit him so you could hold onto your pride. It's because he likes me and didn't want to hurt my brother. That might be awkward if you're around each other in the future." I smiled cheekily, which made Ry grind his teeth together. I watched a muscle twitch in his jaw.

"I don't want you to see him again." Ry's tone was flat, and his eyes were like ice shards.

"You're being ridiculous. What if I'd told you to turn around and come back to Denver when you went after Bowe?"

My brother opened his mouth to argue. I'm sure he was going to tell me that Bowe was a family friend and we'd known her since we were young, but he was interrupted when my parents walked into the house.

"Ry. Daire is an adult. You don't get to dictate who she spends her time with." My father's voice was low, and his eyes were deadly serious as they clashed with my brother's. They both had pale, icy blue eyes. It was like being caught in the middle of another blizzard when they argued and glared at each other.

"She's not acting like an adult. She's acting like a spoiled, irresponsible child."

I rolled my eyes and silently thanked Bowe, who lifted a finger and placed it over his lips to quiet him down.

"Stop talking." Bowe was the only one he would listen to when he was this worked up. "You're going to say something you don't mean and won't be able to take back. I know you and Daire don't normally fight, so I'm going to stop you before you go too far. Let's go clean up your face. You look scary standing there yelling with blood all over the place."

Ry scoffed but obediently let her lead him away. "I looked like this after most of my games."

She made a disgusted face and pulled him toward the bathroom. "How did you ever have a girlfriend then?"

Ry's response was muffled when the door closed behind them.

My dad sighed and pulled me into a hug. He ran his hand over my hair and squeezed me so tightly that it made me squeak. "I'm glad you're home."

I closed my eyes and hugged him back. "Me too. I'm sorry I made you worry."

I stepped back and looked at my mom. She still hadn't said anything directly to me. She was looking at me like I'd sprouted alien antennae or something. She looked at me like I was a stranger.

"I agree with your brother. I don't think it's a good idea for you to spend any more time with Campbell." My mother's elegant features were set in steely lines, leaving no room for argument. "You're in a vulnerable state. I'm thankful he went and found you right away, but he should've turned around and brought you home. That would've been the right thing to do. The responsible thing. I don't know what happened this week, but I don't like the thought of that boy taking advantage of you when you aren't acting like yourself. You didn't even have your phone. You were totally isolated. I don't trust his motivations. Ry is right; we don't know anything about him."

I balked in surprise and felt my father stiffen in shock next to me. My mom never talked to me like this, and very rarely put her foot down in such a decisive way.

"Mom…" She cut me off before I could launch into a heated defense of Campbell.

"No. I don't want to hear it. I'm happy you're home safe and sound, but this isn't the end of whatever is going on with you, Daire. You don't get to turn this family inside out, then waltz back in here as if nothing happened. You need to focus on yourself and on healing, not some boy who doesn't even have a full name."

"I…" I didn't have words. I wanted this kind of reaction, this kind of scorn, but now that I was facing it, I had no idea what to do with any of it. Her disappointment drop like a led weight deep into my gut. "I'm an adult, Mom. You don't get to tell me who I can and can't spend time with. You don't get to dictate what I choose to focus on."

My mother gave me a look that froze me on the spot. "While you live in my house, you will obey my rules. If you don't make decisions that benefit you, I will. You were the one who decided to skip college. You're the one who has stayed holed up in your room like a ghost since the accident. You are making choices that make me think you can't be trusted."

"Okay. That's enough. Everyone needs to calm the fuck down." My dad interjected right when I was getting ready to lose all control. I couldn't believe my mom threw the my-house-my-rules rhetoric at me. Not after the way she grew up. I knew how controlling my maternal grandparents were. They *still* disliked my father and treated him like he was a loser and unworthy of being married to my mom. It was unbelievable that she was acting in the exact same way towards Campbell. This was more than of an alternate reality than being on the compound was. "Daire, go upstairs. We aren't doing this." He gave my mom a look and pointed at the stairway. "Separate corners. Now!"

I stomped up the stairs and went into my room. I slammed the door behind me more forcefully than necessary and picked up my long-forgotten phone.

There were endless messages and missed call notifications. My family must've been going out of their minds with worry when I disappeared. I needed to be more understanding with my mom. I put her through a lot, and she almost lost Ry not too long ago. Fighting with her didn't feel good. And it wasn't fair that Campbell was cast as the villain when he was the hero.

I sighed and texted Remy to let her know I was home.

> *~ Ry and Campbell got into a fistfight as soon as we hit the driveway. I think my mom just tried to ground me. I was expecting a different reception.*

I sounded whiny, and I knew it.

> *~ Not the reception you expected, but maybe the one you deserved. Your mom has been a nervous wreck, and your brother feels like it's his fault you left. Take it from someone who knows well; things will get worse before they get better. Don't you remember how far my mom went when she was trying to protect me?*

I flinched and bit the inside of my bottom lip.

> *~ I remember.*

My Aunt Cora begged and pleaded with Hyde to get out of Remy's life after a failed suicide attempt. Remy's actions weren't related to Hyde at all, but my aunt didn't care. She saw him as a threat to Remy's mental stability and practically ran him out of town. My cousin stopped talking to her mom and refused to come home for years after finding out what my aunt did. It was a mess, and the first real fracture in the Archer family since my Uncle Remy passed away.

> *~ Did you know Ry asked Zowen to run a background check on Campbell?*

> *~ Of course, I did.*

Remy sent a laughing emoji like it was a stupid question to ask.

~ Zowen was pretty upset when he couldn't find anything on Campbell. It hurt his little hacker heart. I trust Campbell because I've watched him with Hollyn, and because Hyde trusts him. But it is weird his background is completely blank.

I sighed again and tapped the corner of my phone against my forehead before texting her back.

~ He took me to his hometown, and I met his family. I completely understand why there's no information out there on him. His background might be more complicated than Uncle Benny's.

Remy sent a wide-eyed emoji.

~ You met the family already?! You move even faster than me when you finally find someone who interests you.

I laughed and let out a deep breath. I knew talking to Remy would make me feel better.

~ What should I do if my mom and Ry are serious about not letting me see him again?

~ You fight. For yourself. For him. For whatever relationship you want to have. If it's not worth fighting for, then stop worrying about it.

I dropped the phone without responding.

Bowe said I had to let Campbell fight for me, or my brother would never accept him.

Maybe Remy was right.

I had to fight for him as well. And I'd already boasted to Charley Booker that I would defend him if I had to.

I was a girl who always got what she wanted, but I'd never had to fight for any of it. When I set out to figure out who I was at my core, I never thought I was looking for a fighter, but that's who I needed to be if I wanted to keep Campbell. It seemed Waldo needed to come with boxing gloves and a steel spine now.

SIXTEEN

Campbell

"**I** told you to watch out for those Archers. They aren't as simple as they seem."

I twitched uncomfortably as Benny rebandaged the wound on my arm with a far rougher touch than Karsen used. When he reached for my face, which was now sporting a collection of bruises and a split lip, I flinched away and told him I would take care of it myself.

I poked at my eye in the bathroom mirror while he watched me from the doorway.

I didn't want to return to Hyde's house looking like I lost a fight. I was worried about scaring the baby and getting the third degree from Remy. As weird as it might seem to anyone familiar with the old Benny, he was the closest thing I'd ever had to a parental figure and confidant. My instinct was to turn to him when life felt like it was getting out of control.

Echo had answered the door and ushered me inside without question. She gave me a sympathetic look before handing me over to her husband. The stoic reaction reminded me of the way Daire handled her time on the farm. Echo always seemed to know when and what kind of questions to ask and what not to say. She also had a keen sense to keep her nose out of Benny's business if the information could prove dangerous to her and their marriage. It was one of the key foundations that kept their relationship rock solid all these years.

Benny ensured she knew what she needed to know, nothing more and nothing less. And he made sure she was safe. The woman was practically untouchable.

"If Daire's brother wasn't still dealing with mobility issues from the accident, it would've been a pretty evenly matched fight. A brother who doesn't want you touching his baby sister has a different kind of strength."

Benny chuckled. "But you let him get in a few lucky shots, even though you could've stopped the altercation before it started. Daire's gotten under your skin."

I glared at his reflection in the mirror. I turned on the faucet to wash the blood off my face and prod the cut on my temple that was slowly oozing fresh blood.

"Of course, she got under my skin. Wasn't that your entire plan when you sent me after her?" I braced my hands on the sink and watched him in the mirror. "As soon as the bits and pieces of Daire that were similar to Karsen became clear, I understood why you were adamant that I help her run away. You wanted me to see that she's not a princess; she's a warrior. Or at least she will be when she comes into her own. She's going to be a problem down the road when she gets her life figured out."

"She doesn't have to be a warrior to protect what's hers. A princess is more than capable of the task. Especially when she has a predator guarding the gates of her kingdom. The Archers are a unique breed. I like how they are willing to do whatever it takes to keep each other safe. It reminds me of some of the people back home. But Daire..." he trailed off, and the corner of his mouth kicked up in a grin that made him look slightly sinister. "She's got something that sets her apart from the rest. I know she hasn't suffered through struggle and strife, but I'm willing to bet she would come out on top when she does.. You need someone in your life willing to stand side-by-side with you, Campbell. Not someone who wants to hide behind you when things get tough."

I rolled my eyes and regretted the action when it made my head throb painfully. "Daire is more the type to jump right out in front of someone when things go south. She acts before thinking of the consequences."

Benny reached out a hand and slapped me on the shoulder. "Good. You've been jumping in front of bullets for others your entire life. Don't you think you deserve someone willing to stop a bullet for you?" He gave me a pointed look in the mirror. "You are not your father, Campbell. You don't have to atone for what that man did for the rest of your life. It's time to live for yourself and choose *you* for once."

I turned around and braced myself with my palms on the sink. Facing Benny when his full attention was locked on you was difficult. I looked at the scar that encircled his throat and asked, "Is that how you justify all the bad shit you did before you left The Point? When you had the choice, you became someone else. Why does the new you deserve a happy life and a normal marriage? Why isn't there a need to atone?"

Benny squeezed my shoulder to the point it hurt and stepped back to stare at me. "I don't justify what I did, and I don't apologize for who I was. I did what I had to in order to survive. So, I will not atone. I don't regret staying alive. And, believe it or not, I'm still the guy from The Point on occasion. He never completely disappeared. The same will happen to you, kiddo. You never know when you'll need to bring the old Campbell out of retirement, because the world is trash, and humans are fucking dangerous. Echo knows exactly who she married. She picked me regardless of my past. She knows that what matters is the future we share together. Daire will do the same for you if you let her. I don't think she'll make you search for atonement either. But if that's something you feel you need, then you have to find a way to do it on your own."

"You have a name." Albeit a fake one. The government had given him a new name when they put him in witness protection and entrapped him to be a high-level informant. He hardly ever used it anymore. Nicolas Bennington didn't suit a criminal mastermind the way 'Benny' did. "You have a birthday and a Social Security number. You exist, Benny. I'm a ghost. We aren't the same."

I couldn't even tell Daire how old I was if she asked. My father wasn't exactly keen on birthdays. If I had to guess, I was somewhere around twenty-three or twenty-four, but who knew?

Benny gave me a shake, snapping my head on my neck. "Pick a name, any name you want, and I'll get you all the paperwork you need to make it legal. If you want an actual birthdate, pick a number, any number. A Social

Security number is trickier, but I can still find you one of those. The feds owe me endless favors. I can make you as boring as any other guy you pass on the street. Take it from me, Campbell; none of those things are what building a normal life is about. They don't make you who you are. They won't make you happy or bring a sense of closure. Finding someone you can rely on, someone who loves you—all the parts of you—that's what living a normal life is like. If you let go of this girl because your father still has his hooks in you, then you've learned nothing from me over the years."

I swatted away his hand on my shoulder when his hold on me started to hurt. I rolled my shoulders and lifted a hand to rub my fingers over my scar. "I already told you, my dad is gone. When we went to the house to look for Delta, we found a girl held captive in the root cellar."

Benny let out a low sound of acknowledgment, and his smirk turned even more evil. "Karsen wouldn't let that slide. I've always admired how ruthless that girl turned out. Booker chose well when he picked her."

I rolled my eyes again and pushed away from the sink. "She picked him. But you're right. She wouldn't let him get away with this."

Benny chuckled and followed me down the hallway toward the kitchen. "She would be pissed about that, but she showed him no mercy because he shot you." He pointed at the red mark on my face. "That's enough for her to want him gone. I know you always saw them as people you were indebted to, but Karsen and Booker always viewed you as one of their own. Why do you think

Booker dislikes me so much? He's jealous you gravitated toward me and not him when it came to getting your hands dirty and learning the ropes of the underworld."

"No one likes you." I wasn't joking. Benny snorted a laugh at my dry comeback. "You're a liar, and you're shifty as hell. No one ever knows your real motivations, and you only care about yourself."

"And yet, you still decided to follow me and mimic my every move. You dropped everything and finally left Nowhere when I asked if you wanted to come to Denver. You should know I never set out to be liked by anyone, and neither have you. All that matters to men like us is survival and being able to take care of the people we love. We're cut from the same cloth, Campbell. I've always known that."

The bitch of it was, I'd always known that, as well. If I'd stayed in Nowhere, there was no doubt I would've become as cruel and apathetic as Benny. I would be fighting for my life on the streets or in prison. I'd have become a man people feared with nothing more than a name.

We were alarmingly similar, and I was terribly envious of the life he had now with his wife. I *did* want to follow in his footsteps, and by doing so, I had to acknowledge the past and come to terms with it. I had to accept that the guy who would do whatever he had to survive was never going away. He would always be there, waiting and ready. I would never fully be able to walk away from who I was and the things I'd done.

Benny's phone rang, and his expression turned dark and foreboding. I never met the Benny who came from The Point, but I'd seen glimpses of him over the years.

The expression on his face now let me know how close to the surface that killer lurked.

He excused himself and left me in the kitchen with Echo, who was making me something to eat. She wasn't a great cook, but throwing together a sandwich and some canned soup was doable.

When I asked if she needed help, she shooed me away and told me to sit down until it was ready.

She was such a contrast to Benny. He wore watches and rings that cost the amount of a mansion in Malibu; she wore a string friendship bracelet Hyde, her nephew, had made her when he was in elementary school. Benny kept his black hair slicked back and styled like a true gangster. Echo wore her dark curls wild and loose. She didn't even bother to dye the gray that was starting to speckle the kinky strands. The thing they had in common was their scars. Benny's were ugly and visible. There was no hiding the rough, white, raised skin that encircled his neck. Echo's were smaller and hidden under the flowy sleeves of her boho-style dress. She was a recovering drug addict who nearly lost her life to her habit more than once.

After she put a plate in front of me, she sat across from me and gave me a curious look.

"You let Daire's brother beat you up?" She reached out and gently touched my swollen eye. "I assume you had a good reason for doing that."

I shrugged and took a bite of the ham and cheese sandwich. "I think I like her. I figured I needed to make it look good if I ever wanted to see her again. If I beat her brother to a bloody pulp, what would that get me?"

"Does she like you?" Echo asked the question quietly, almost like she feared the answer. It was sweet. She was worried I let myself get punched in the face for no reason.

"She likes me." I wiggled my eyebrows. "Or, she at least likes the way I look." And the way I fucked her. She would eventually like the rest of me just as much.

Echo smiled and leaned back in her seat to watch me eat. "Benny is usually right about people. If he thinks she's a good match for you, it's not without reason." She sighed. "He never shows it, but he cares about you. He wouldn't send you after some girl if he didn't think she was worth it. He's always looking out for you in his own way."

"I know. He's infuriating but hardly ever wrong." It was damn annoying.

She made a light sound of agreement before leaning forward and placing her hand over mine.

"He is right about many things, but there are some that he'll never understand, like grief and regret. Benny won't tell you that it's okay for you to mourn the loss of your father, or rather, the loss of what that man took from you. You're allowed to grieve your stolen childhood, Campbell. You can be sad over all the normal experiences you missed because of him. Benny will tell you those emotions are worthless because you can't go back. But I think you need to acknowledge them before you can move forward. Don't let someone else feel those things for you. That's not the answer."

Echo's eyes told me she was grieving for all the things Benny may have lost in the past. It was a burden she didn't want to pass on to the next generation.

"I'll do my best to let myself feel everything." I'd kept my emotions tightly controlled for so long, there would be a learning curve. I wanted to let them trickle out, not rush over me in a flood. If that happened, I was going to drown.

Echo winked at me and got up to drop a soft kiss on the top of my head. "Good boy. There's nothing wrong with emulating the great things about Benny. However, we both know his bad side is not for the faint of heart. Be your own man, Campbell. Don't worry about who your father was. Don't try and be who Benny expects you to be. Just be yourself. That's all you need to do."

She left me alone to finish my sandwich in silence. When I got a text message, I was turning her advice over in my mind, wondering if I had enough pieces to build my own person.

I was surprised to see Remy's name on the display.

~ Don't be scared to come back to Hyde's. Hollyn misses you. This baby is about to start crawling. I need you around to teach me what to do when she's mobile. I promise not to harass you about whatever is going on with Daire.

I chuckled at the message and responded:

~ I'll be back tomorrow. I have a black eye and a fat lip courtesy of your cousin.

~ Ouch. Ry has a mean right hook.

~ That he does. He made it clear that he doesn't want me anywhere near his sister.

Remy sent the big eye emoji, and the phone rang the next minute. She started talking before I could say hello.

"Don't worry about Ry. He'll calm down and stop being psycho-overprotective now that Daire is home. It's her mom you're going to have to win over. She still hasn't dealt with the trauma of almost losing Ry, so she's going nuclear over this situation with Daire. I'd expect Daire to lose her phone and car keys in the next few days. Honestly, it's good for her. She's always been a troublemaker but never had to face the consequences. Everyone needs to set healthy boundaries. Don't worry; I'll break her out before things get too bad. But you have to promise me you aren't playing with her. If you're not serious, I'm not throwing myself on a live grenade for either of you."

I blinked as I tried to take in her rapid-fire words. I told her the same thing I'd just told Echo, but with more certainty. "I like her."

Remy laughed. "What a glowing endorsement. If it was anyone else, I'd tell you to take a hike. I know that for a guy like you, admitting you like her is practically one step away from putting a ring on her finger, and a bigger feeling than you're used to. I'll do my best to run interference. I'm a pro at navigating an overprotective parent."

"I don't want to be the reason there's more friction with her family." We weren't even in a serious relationship.

"Don't worry. It takes more than a boy with a troubled past to break the Archers apart. Everything will be fine. Expect a bit of a rocky road along the way."

I scoffed. "I've never even seen the path of least resistance. A rocky road is all I've ever walked." The only difference was, I used to do it barefoot and alone. This was a huge improvement; I had shoes and people to walk alongside me. The journey was much easier now.

"Daire is different from the rest of us Archer kids, Campbell. Ry has been in love with Bowe since the beginning of time. It was love at first sight for me and Hyde. My brother has been infatuated with Aston Wheeler since he started high school. Daire is the only one of us who waited and held onto her heart. She's the only one who fell for someone blindly. She is brave enough to love without knowing you. She didn't run just so she could find herself; she's been searching for you. You're the one, Campbell. Don't make her regret being patient."

I'd never felt like I was worth much of anything, let alone *the wait*.

"I want to be worth the wait." I didn't mean to say the words out loud, let alone to another person. If I spoke them into existence, I would have to put the words into action.

"That's a good start. Come home and kiss this baby and explain to Hyde everything that's been going on with you. He needs to know why you vanished without a trace. He may be your employer, but he let you into his home and trusted you with his child. You're smart enough to know that he thinks of you as more than just his nanny. He's very understanding, but his patience has limits."

"If he wasn't patient, how could he be with someone like you?" The sarcastic quip slipped out before I realized I shouldn't antagonize the only other Archer who was on my side.

Remy laughed and made a tsk-tsk sound. "Look at you. You sound like one of the family already."

She hung up the phone with a laugh, leaving me alone with my whirlwind thoughts.

Why did I feel like I was tossed onto a live grenade every time I talked to her?

chapter
SEVENTEEN

Daire

"I have a special delivery coming for you shortly." I stumbled as Remy pushed me into her loft and closed the door behind us. "You can thank me later."

I caught myself on the massive dining table and looked at her over my shoulder. "Why do I feel like a fugitive?" I glanced at the duffle bag of my stuff she dropped on the floor near her feet. I had no idea when she went to my house and raided my room, but it looked like she'd grabbed enough for me to be gone for at least a week.

Remy laughed at me and tossed her curly hair over her shoulder. "Because this was a jailbreak. I was supposed to pick you up from your therapy appointment and return you to your parents' house. I even promised Aunt Shaw I would stay with you until her shift at the hospital was over. She got called into emergency surgery, and your dad had a late appointment. It was the perfect time to get you out."

I lifted my eyebrows at her in admiration. "You're brave. My mom has been acting like a warden lately. She's going to be mad at you."

Remy shrugged and moved to the fridge to take out a can of soda.

"She can be mad at me. I don't mind. She's going to be madder at your dad. He was the one who told me she was working late, and he made his appointment take longer than normal on purpose. He doesn't agree with how your mom has kept you on lockdown the last few weeks, but anything he says isn't getting through to her."

I sighed. "I know. They've been fighting a lot. He even gave me my phone back after she took it away. He keeps telling her she'll push me away the longer she tries to control my every waking moment."

Remy hummed and motioned to the fridge to see if I wanted anything. I shook my head and looked around the loft.

It was a lot cleaner than normal. It had a beautiful view of the mountains out of the floor-to-ceiling windows. It was so nice to see something other than the inside of my house.

Other than the therapy appointments I'd been attending and venturing out to my dad's tattoo shop, I hadn't been anywhere in weeks. My mom forced my dad and his employees to babysit me during the day, and when she was home at night, she watched me like a hawk. I had a newfound sympathy for Campbell's ire when he found out I would be watching his every move with Hollyn. My mother took my keys, my phone, and all my means to get my hands on money. It was a tense and awkward situation that grew more uncomfortable by the day. I was trying to roll with the punches and be understanding, but every time she told me that what she was doing was for my own good, it ruffled my feathers.

I didn't like the none-to-subtle shade thrown at Campbell. She thought what was best for me was to stay away from him.

Luckily, I'd stashed my prepaid phone from Campbell. For the first week of my lockdown, that was the only way I could communicate with anyone outside the house. He was understanding and sympathetic to my situation. I think he even found it kind of funny. I was a legal adult, but here I was, being grounded like a child who'd misbehaved. The situation was ridiculous. Thankfully, my father was the voice of reason and gave me my phone back. He asked me to bear with my mom since she was obviously working through her own issues. I agreed because, at the end of the day, I owed them everything and loved them unconditionally. The same way they loved me.

I'd been to a handful of therapy sessions with the woman Remy recommended. After speaking with her in-depth, she suggested that I was dealing with Post Traumatic Stress Disorder on top of the anxiety and depression. The panic attack on the interstate was more than likely related to the PTSD. When I told her about the current situation at home, she suggested we consider family therapy, and alluded to the fact that my mother may be dealing with PTSD as well. She was surrounded by death on a daily basis. She had to have strong coping mechanisms to deal with the risks and rewards of her job, but may be more vulnerable when facing the same types of encounters in her personal life. Those shields weren't up, and the trauma caused by nearly losing Ry and my disappearance triggered her the same way the accident triggered me. My mom's desire to bubble wrap me and keep me from the dangers of the outside world was her own personal version of a panic attack.

I planned to play along, at least for another week. One good thing about being supervised twenty-four-seven was that all the time in my dad's shop rekindled my passion for art. It reminded me of the legacy waiting for me. It showed me how far I had to go, and I understood with a clarity I'd been lacking that I didn't want my dad to hand all his hard work over to me just because I was his daughter. I wanted to earn it.

I wanted to prove to him I deserved it.

While at the shop, I did more than answer phones and make appointments for his artists. I put together a portfolio and planned to reapply to art school. I also sent my portfolio out to some artists with exemplary reputations in the field. I didn't even use my real name. Taking a cue from Campbell, I sent everything under my first name alone. My first choice for an apprenticeship was at a well-known Bay Area tattoo shop run by a man named Cable McCaffery. His style was quite different from my dad's, but the work was award-winning. A big bonus, if he agreed to take me on, was that Aston was in California at Stanford. I missed her and loved the thought of getting to be so much closer to her.

I hadn't heard anything back yet, but I planned to go to San Francisco to plead my case in person. And if that still didn't work, I would head to Austin for a little while and work with my Uncle Rowdy. That was still too close for comfort, but it was better than nothing, and better than having my dad go easy on me during any apprenticeship I would have in Denver.

I'd already asked Campbell if he would get me a plane ticket to California with a promise to pay him back. I didn't want anyone in my family to know the full scope of what I was up to. Not even Remy. At least not yet. This was a venture I needed to accomplish—or not—on my own. I planned to crash with Aston in her dorm while I pleaded my case with Cable McCaffery, but Campbell surprised me by saying he wanted to go with me, so we needed a room for two. It was odd he wanted another vacation after our unplanned road trip, but I wasn't about to turn down any amount of time with him. This time I was planning on being honest and telling my parents I was going out of town so they wouldn't worry. However, I was not looking forward to the conversation, and was slightly worried my mom might go to extremes to keep me within arm's reach.

Not seeing Campbell for the last several weeks was torture. I missed him.

I missed his dry sense of humor.

I missed his dark eyes and hard-to-read expressions.

I missed his permanent frown and growly voice.

I missed the surprise in his eyes when I kissed him.

I missed all of his bits and pieces, and when I was alone at night and particularly frustrated, I missed how he filled me up and took me away from the rest of the world.

He was by far the best distraction I'd ever found.

"Moms are just like that. They go overboard in *our best interests.*" Remy sneered as if recalling her past conflicts with her mother. "It'll pass. Your mom is one of the best people I've ever met, and so are you. There is bound to be a big storm when two strong women collide. But all that bad weather eventually passes." She wiggled her eyebrows at me in a suggestive manner. "Hyde's parents have Hollyn for the weekend, which means adults only at his house for the next couple of days. Campell's services won't be needed. I'm sure you can figure out a way to keep him occupied. Stay here as long as you want. I'll stay with Hyde. Most of my stuff is at his place anyway. I'm sure your mom will figure out where you are, but you don't have to go home unless you want to."

She pushed the keys to the loft in my direction and playfully waved on her way out the door.

"Thanks, Remy."

She laughed but didn't turn around. "How many times did you cover for me in the past? How often were you the only one who didn't think I was a loser wasting my life? You've had my back since you could walk, Daire. Busting you out of house arrest is the least I can do. I love you."

"Love you too."

"You'll really love me once your special delivery gets here. Have the best weekend, darling."

She flounced out the door in a uniquely Remy way. Her hints were a bit too on the nose for me not to figure out; she had Hyde kick Campbell out of the house for the weekend so they could be alone. Sending him to me was a win-win situation for her, so I knew she hadn't done it entirely out of the kindness of her heart.

I dragged the heavy duffle bag toward the open part of the loft with the bed. There were hardly any signs that

Remy had been here. It looked like she spent most of her time with Hyde and Hollyn these days. I wondered if his house was now in a perpetual state of clutter and mayhem. Remy wasn't the tidiest person in the world. Her surroundings often reflected the chaos of her mind.

I was looking out the massive windows, thinking about the vast horizon and wondering why I never noticed how big the world was before when there was a knock at the door. Knowing who was on the other side, my steps were hurried, and my heartbeat sped up. I threw the door open and practically tackled Campbell to the ground.

It was good that he was stronger than he looked, or we both would've landed on the concrete floor.

Campbell wrapped his arms around my waist and lifted me off my feet. I grabbed onto his neck and wound my legs around his waist. Our lips touched without exchanging any other greeting. I could tell by the way he kissed me that he missed me as much as I missed him. There was a hunger there that differed from all the other times we touched and tasted each other.

He kicked the door shut with his heel and carried me toward the bed, his lips never leaving mine.

It was a kiss that spoke more than words ever could. There was so much emotion caught between our lips and tangled around our tongues, I didn't even notice how we both ended up naked. It was all a blur. My entire existence narrowed down to the points of my body that touched his.

He was fire and life.

He was damnation and temptation.

He was forbidden and promised.

He was so much more than a man who didn't have a name.

I tossed my head back and moaned when I felt his teeth tug at the skin on the side of my neck. He dropped down to the bed, so he was sitting on the edge with me on his lap. Campbell's cock was already hard and thick. I felt him nudge the opening between my legs and let out a needy, whimpering sound. I kissed him harder and carded my fingers through his copper hair. It was soft under my fingers and reflected the light through the windows, making it look like a flame.

I gasped when he flipped our position, so I was on my back on the bed. Campbell kneeled on the ground in front of me and hooked my legs over his shoulders. His teeth bit the inside of my thigh with enough force to leave a mark. I felt his breath flutter over my pussy every time he exhaled. The sensation sent shivers dancing all over my skin.

This wasn't the first time Campbell had gone down on me. When we were in the motel, he blew more than my mind. I knew he was good at oral sex, but it was a bit different to experience on my home turf with the sun shining down on us as it sank behind the mountains. It felt less like a secret. Less clandestine. Less like a dream.

As we watched each other before he lowered his mouth to cover my now-aching center, we silently acknowledged the choice we were making. Not because it was convenient. Not because it was easy or made much sense. But because we were exactly where we wanted to be.

Before the sun went down, we decided to choose each other.

Campbell used his hands to pull me closer to his face. I let out a strangled sound at the first swipe of his tongue through my wet folds. I didn't need to pull him closer or demand more. He came to me and gave without asking.

I felt him probe at my aching entrance with the tip of his tongue and the edge of his teeth against my excited clit.

The pleasure that followed was like a punch to the gut. I moaned and tossed my head from side to side. My thighs quivered on either side of his head, and my hands found the tips of my breasts to alleviate the tightness in my nipples. The puckered points pressed impatiently into my palms while Campbell's mouth worked to take me from wet to drenched.

His fingers dug into my ass and tilted my hips upward so he could go at me at a different angle. I closed my eyes and let the sensations he evoked wash over me. I squeezed my nipples between my fingers and whispered his name because I couldn't catch my breath to shout it.

He caught my clit softly between his teeth and flicked it with the tip of his tongue. The current that followed that small caress made my entire body feel electrified. I shifted my hands to the top of his head and pulled on his hair. I heard him breathe a soft chuckle and felt the vibrations of his amusement all throughout my core.

My body quaked with anticipation, and my legs tightened around his head involuntarily.

He was trapped. Not that he seemed to mind.

I made a noise that wasn't quite human when he slid a finger inside me and used both his hands and mouth to push me to the brink of an orgasm. My entire body shook, and I forcefully used a hand on his forehead to push him back before I came on his tongue.

He looked at me with a flash of confusion in his dark eyes.

I slid my legs off his shoulders and sat up to grab the back of his neck and pull him over me. He braced a knee on the edge of the bed and looked down at me with an intense gaze.

I reached up and pushed at the forever frown that marred his forehead.

"I missed you." I pulled him down so I could kiss him. "I need all of you. I'm greedy." I whispered the words against his lips and watched the frown finally fade. I tilted my head to drag the tip of my tongue across the scar on his chin. "I want more."

An unidentifiable expression touched his strong features before he dipped his head and kissed me breathless. He touched my face with soft, gentle kisses until he reached my ear. I felt his nose rub against my earlobe and felt his warm words more than I heard them.

"I'll give you everything for as long as possible, Daire. I promise."

Maybe it was a promise of sexual gratification in the heat of the moment. Maybe they were just pretty words he thought I wanted to hear.

Regardless, it was my favorite promise anyone had ever made, and it felt like he was handing himself over to me.

I doubted that I was worthy of such a great honor, but I vowed to prove to him that he made the right choice by picking me.

Campbell materialized a condom from somewhere like magic and adjusted himself between my legs. He pushed into my body with a rough thrust that moved us both up the bed. I grabbed onto his shoulders and dug my fingernails into his skin. I arched against him and struggled to catch my breath as he set a frantic pace, his body moving fast and hard within mine. It was like he couldn't get enough, or he was afraid I might disappear from underneath him at any moment.

I tried to match his movements, to let him know he wasn't alone in his desperation, but I was soon swept away by the pleasure pulsing through my blood. After all, he put in the work to prime my body with his talented tongue, so I was much closer to completion than he was.

My nipples rubbed against his chest, and my lips locked onto the moth inked on his throat. If I was going to do something silly like leave a hickey to mark my territory, I was going to do it in a spot that wasn't terribly obvious.

He grunted in satisfaction when he felt my teeth bite against his skin.

His hips moved faster, and he put a hand underneath my hip to hold me closer. Our bodies writhed together, becoming a sweaty, lust-fueled, sexy mess. The sounds that echoed off the loft walls should have been embarrassing, but they only served to make the atmosphere more heated and sensual.

When I wrapped my legs around Campbell's waist and moaned through a bone-rattling orgasm, he finally lost his rough rhythm. The pull of my body when I broke apart sent Campbell's search for his own release spiraling.

He moved over me, rough and with zero finesse. I'd never seen such a raw side of him before. He kept himself so tightly locked down that the wildness was a nice surprise. It felt like I was forever learning something new about him.

I knew I would never get bored when I was with Campbell.

When he finally came, his teeth bit down, and his hands held me hard enough to leave marks. He panted my name a couple of times, and I was enamored with how his big body shook.

He was so cold when we first met, so I definitely wanted to see more of this side of him.

I was sure I would follow him anywhere when he let some of his inner fire spark to life. He was warm; you just had to get close enough to feel his heat.

He collapsed on top of me, still buried deep inside. The soft pulse as his orgasm faded out made me shiver in delight. He turned his head so we could look into each other's eyes and gruffly uttered,, "Hello, Daire. It's nice to see you. I missed you too. Do I want to know what would've happened if someone else had been at the door?"

I laughed at his dry tone and curled an arm around his head. "Remy told me a special delivery was on the way. I knew it was you."

He smoothed a hand down my hair and hugged me tightly. "How will your family feel about you running away from home again, Princess?"

I sighed and cuddled closer. Who knew that scary and silent Campbell would be such a softy after he got off? It was adorable.

"They won't like it. But this time, they'll know where I am because I'm going to tell them I'm leaving. I won't avoid their calls or refuse to see them if they show up." Ry left with Bowe the first week I was on house arrest. I don't know whether it was planned or Bowe threw me a bone by dragging him to a show in Nashville. His reaction to my return was somewhere between my mom and dad's. He was the only Archer I didn't have to worry about showing up at the loft before I got on the plane to San Francisco. "No more running from my problems."

"Wow. The princess gets locked in the tower for a few weeks and grows the fuck up."

I snorted and rolled over to look at the ceiling. "I realized there is a lot of world out there for me to search for Waldo. I'm not running away; I'm running toward." I reached out to stroke the scar on his chin. "How about you? Are you ready to stop standing still and start moving somewhere, anywhere, as long as it's not Nowhere?"

Campbell kissed my shoulder and threw an arm across me in a protective manner. "I've been chasing you since Christmas. Hard to stand still when your girl is running full steam ahead."

"Hmmm...you can be very sweet when you want." I laced our fingers together and looked at him again. "Speaking of, how come you decided to tag along to San

Francisco with me? Don't get me wrong, I welcome the company, but I'm surprised you want to go."

His gaze drifted away, and he stiffened next to me. I paused and watched as a myriad of emotions crossed his handsome face.

Finally, he sighed and told me, "I promised your brother I would go with you."

"What?!"

When did he talk to Ry?

And how could he leak my plan when I told him how important it was to keep secret from everyone?

All the warm, squishy feelings I had a moment ago vanished into thin air. I definitely wouldn't have jumped all over him like a sex-starved fiend if I'd known he sold me out.

Traitor.

chapter
EIGHTEEN

Campbell

The moment was ruined.

Daire went from sweet and pliant to angrier than a swarm of hornets in a heartbeat. I had every intention of telling her that her older brother stopped by Hyde's place to see me before he left town, but she was all over me the minute the door opened. I wasn't trying to take advantage of her. I would've told her the truth before we landed in bed if she'd given me a chance, but I was a man, after all. Given the opportunity to listen to my cock instead of my brain, the organ with the most blood flow at the time would always win out.

Daire grabbed my t-shirt since it was the closest article of clothing and pulled it over her head. She threw my jeans at me with enough force to make me grunt while glaring at me like she was trying to peel off my skin with her eyes.

"I told you I wanted to try and get the apprenticeship independently. I can't believe you told Ry I'm going to California." She kicked the edge of the bed, then swore up a storm when her toes smashed into the metal frame. "I get that you have some big brother code you live by and that you relate to what I've put Ry through, but you're not *my* big brother, Campbell. If that's the role you want to play in my life, then what just happened in that bed can never happen again."

"You've got a good brother; you don't need another one. Of course, I don't want you to see me that way." She was so huffy and puffy; it was kind of cute. If she didn't look ready to take my head off, I would've grabbed her and tossed her back on the bed. She marched into the bathroom, and I yelled so she could hear me over the toilet flushing, "I didn't tell him why you want to go to California." I sighed and stood to clean myself up and pull on my pants. I ran a hand through my messy hair and looked around the loft. "Did Remy leave anything to eat? I'm starving." Now that Hollyn was mobile, watching her took more work.

And I forgot to eat lunch earlier because I was on the phone with Vernon. Lucas fought at school today because someone made fun of him for having two dads. Harlen being a local hero didn't make him exempt from small-minded people who passed their prejudice onto their children. I told Vernon to handle the situation the way he thought best. I knew he would find a proper punishment for Lucas and take care of the parents of the kid who started the fight. Vernon was going to destroy them in a very low-key way.

Daire grumbled under her breath but moved to search the kitchen. After a few minutes, she pulled her head out of the freezer and declared she could cobble together some French toast and bacon. I offered to help, but she continued to glare at me and told me to back off.

After running to the bathroom to roughly clean myself off, I grabbed an energy drink from the fridge and leaned against the big dining room table to watch her.

"Your brother came to see me before he left town. He apologized for starting the fight. I told him I understood where he was coming from because I have a little sister of my own. I know Ry isn't a bad guy. Maybe a bit overprotective, but there is nothing wrong with that."

I chugged back the fizzy drink and tracked Daire's every move.

"He told me you were going to break out of the house sooner or later. He knows there is no way you'll be happy under lock and key like that. He asked me to watch you when you made a break for it. I told him I already planned on doing that." I snorted. "He got a call from someone named Aston while he was there. She's the one who told him you were coming to California."

Daire slammed the pan down on the stove and turned to grab the edge of the counter that separated us.

"You're sure it was Aston who called him?"

Her glare was fierce enough to frighten the strongest man, and I was weak when it came to her, so I shivered.

"Yeah. They sounded close. From what I could understand, she only wanted to make sure Ry knew that you were going to be with her when you disappeared again. He promised not to tell anyone that he knew where you were headed. When he got off the phone, he asked me if I knew what you had planned. I told him I did. Ry asked me to keep you safe, and I promised him I would. He knew you were going to run again. It was just a matter of time. I was already planning on going with you because I don't love the idea of you taking off for a city you've never been to before to meet some man you know nothing about. But when Ry made me promise to go, I couldn't say no. Not when I put myself in his shoes. I would never try to stop you from doing what you think you have to. And you can't stop me from doing the same. I never said a word about you contacting other tattoo shops or reapplying to art school." I gave her an odd look as I watched her dip pieces of bread into melted vanilla ice cream. I'd never seen French toast made that way, but I guessed it could work. "Aside from Denver and San Francisco, where else did you apply to school?"

She shrugged and turned back to the hot pan. "Boston. New York. Chicago. Seattle. Paris. London. All over." She looked at me over her shoulder with a scowl. "Aston and Ry dated throughout high school. They were two peas in a pod. I'm not surprised she ratted me out to him. I'm starting to feel like I can't trust anyone to keep a damn secret from anyone named Archer."

I got up and walked behind her. I wrapped my arms around her waist and looked at the Willy Wonka creation she had on the stove in front of her. I rested my chin on her shoulder and told her, "No one gave away your secret. Ry knows where you're going, not why. That sounds like a fair trade-off. You'll have to compromise a bit going forward, Princess." I hated the idea of her family being at war over unnecessary battles. "If Delta told me she wanted to miss Christmas, that would've been enough for me. Knowing why helped me understand the situation better, but just knowing where she was and that she was safe would've been enough. Do you get what I'm trying to tell you? No one wants to prevent you from living your own life. They just want to be included."

She sniffed in irritation, pulled the sweet-smelling bread out of the pan, and plopped it on a brightly colored plate. I got an elbow in the gut as she pushed me back to carry the concoction to the table. She didn't say anything while she searched for butter and syrup.

When Daire finally sat across from me at the massive table, she looked less aggravated. She pushed a plate in my direction and pinned me with a serious look.

"What do you think about all the different places I applied for school? What if I get into one that's outside of Denver?"

I picked up a fork and poked at the strange breakfast for dinner. "I don't think anything. That's your future. You go wherever you want." The first bite of the toast surprised me. It tasted like French toast on steroids, and the ice cream made it extra custardy. It was breakfast and dessert all rolled into one. "This is fucking delicious."

She cocked her head to the side and pushed her food around with less enthusiasm. "So, what happens if I'm in California and you're in Colorado?"

"What do you mean?" I honestly needed clarification on her question.

She muttered something under her breath and pushed the plate away. "I know whatever we're doing with each other is new. I don't need a label or a time frame, but I do need to know that you aren't going to forget about me the minute I'm out of sight."

I blinked in surprise and pushed my plate away as well. "Daire. You're unforgettable. Nothing is going to change if we're in two different states, or even if we're in two different countries. I told you I've been chasing you since I decided to help you run away from home. I'll chase you all over the globe until I catch you." I wasn't the kind of guy who gave reassurances. And I didn't say things I didn't mean.

When I told her I would give her everything for as long as possible, I thought she understood that meant she was mine. And I was hers.

"My contract with Hyde is only for a year. By then, he and Remy should have a better handle on how to care for the baby. Truthfully, Hyde already does everything the baby needs; I'm just there when they have to work. When my contract is up, I can come to you, or maybe you can come to me. I still haven't decided where I want to end up long term." As long as it wasn't Nowhere, I could call any place home. "I'll come see you as often as I can."

Even if she didn't leave for school, she still planned to take an apprenticeship before she started classes in the fall. We were bound to be separated. However, since we'd barely declared a truce and decided to choose one another, it didn't occur to me that she would be insecure about the distance. If I was only after a quick fuck, I could understand her insecurity. I thought I made it clear that I was after far more than her body and pretty face. I was ready to tackle all her problems and help her track down Waldo until the very end.

Daire got up and walked around the table. She sat herself in my lap and rested her forehead on my shoulder. "I'm overthinking things. My new therapist told me I do that to distract myself from being in the current moment. I worry about what might be instead of focusing on what is."

I skimmed a hand along her spine and rubbed her cheek with mine, careful not to be too rough because of my stubble. "I'm not a good person, Daire. Right now, you like me, but when you know all there is to know about me..." I trailed off and held her closer. "You'll see I'm no hero, and I'm definitely not qualified to save a princess. You and I need to take things one day at a time. Each day you can decide if you still like me, and we'll go from there."

Was it possible for the princess to fall for a villain? I guess we were about to find out.

She hugged my neck and looked me in the eye. "I'm going to like you every day. I liked you even when I didn't like you, Campbell. I liked you when I didn't like myself. Liking you is easy for me."

I never thought anyone would say those words to me.

I wasn't likable. I went out of my way to make that the case. Only someone who knew the ins and outs of a hard life like Charley could like me and mean it. We were too similar. I wondered if the fact Daire found it easy to like me said more about her than it did me.

"I've never liked anyone before. I can't say liking you is easy, but it doesn't feel as hard as everything else in my life. I promise you I'll be wherever you need me in the future. How about that?" It felt like a reasonable compromise. If she wanted me by her side, I could figure it out. And if she realized I was not the kind of guy she should build her future around and needed space, I could give it to her. "You only have to worry about finding yourself, Daire. You won't have to look for me. You'll always know exactly where I am."

I pushed her hair off her face, and we stared at each other for a long, silent moment. I could tell she was still worried, but she forced a smile and touched the scar on my chin with a fingertip. I did the same thing when I was anxious. It gave me a little thrill that she picked up the habit from me. Her soft fingertips felt far more comforting than mine when I touched that spot.

"Okay." She kissed me softly, and her green eyes started to glow from within. "I'm going to focus on what's in front of me, just like the therapist said."

Since Daire commandeered my shirt, I was still naked from the waist up, which made it very easy for her to move her light kisses from my mouth to my throat, to my chest, and all the way down my stomach as she sank to her knees in front of me.

The floor in the loft was painted concrete. I didn't want her to sacrifice her comfort for my pleasure. I reached to pull her back up so I could take her over to the bed, but before I got the chance, she whipped my shirt over her head and used it as a thin cushion between her knees and the ground. Daire leaned forward and tickled the tip of her nose with the fine hairs that arrowed down into my pants. She blew into my belly button, which made my abs lock, and I stopped breathing for a second when she pulled down the zipper of my jeans.

I sent a silent thanks to the universe that I took the time to rinse off in the bathroom so my dick wouldn't taste like a balloon at a kid's birthday party when she put it in her mouth. And she was most definitely going to put my cock in her mouth.

She licked her lips and then the tip of my erection. I felt the faint flick deep in my gut. I reached out to thread my fingers through her hair and hold her too-pretty face between my hands.

She let her tongue play lightly along the length. Teasing and tasting softly and slowly. It was the complete opposite of the way we'd just fucked. All her attention was on the hardness filling her mouth and touching the back of her throat. I appreciated Daire's attention to detail, but even more than that, I appreciated the way her eyes heated and her pale skin turned pink with pleasure the deeper she took me in and the harder I held her face. She really did like me. She liked doing this to me.

That thought alone was almost enough to have me coming down the back of her throat.

I had no idea how she managed to tap into all the emotions I'd long kept buried. Now that they were free, all those feelings wanted nothing more than to rush at Daire, tangle around her, and tie her to me forever. I was starting to realize that emotions were dangerous when you couldn't control them.

Once Daire had my dick slippery with saliva, she focused on using her mouth on the tip while her fist slid up and down the throbbing shaft. Her thumb pressed against the pulsing vein, which ran the length of the underneath side of my erection; simultaneously, her tongue dipped into the leaking slit on the tip. The dual sensation made my head spin, and I couldn't stop myself from thrusting farther into her mouth.

She gave me a playful glare when the pointed tip hit the top of her mouth. She squeezed the base of my cock with more pressure than was pleasurable as a warning. She was in control of this experience, and I better let her have her way, or I would regret it like those stupid boys before me who tried to push her and paid the price.

She pulled back so she could circle the flared head with the tip of her tongue and used her hand to slide into the opening of my pants to lightly rub her fingers over my tingling balls. Her tongue caught another drop of liquid that leaked from the tip and swallowed me back down so fast I couldn't keep up. The pace was steady, and her mouth and hand met in the middle, so not an inch of my cock was left unattended.

Her cheeks hollowed out, and her nostrils flared as she practically choked on my length. She was still gentler and more patient than I'd been with her, but what she was doing was effective. I was going to remember this moment forever. It was going to linger.

As I said, she was unforgettable, and so was the way she made me feel.

The phrase *killing them with kindness* existed for a reason. I felt like I might die if she didn't finish me off in the next minute.

"Daire." Her name came out in a gasp. I threw my head back and pulled her closer. I couldn't help it. I wanted to bury myself inside of her. "I'm so glad you like me." It was like getting one big gift to make up for all the ones I'd never received when I was younger.

She squeezed the base of my cock and did a swirly thing with her tongue that made my eyes roll back in my head. I didn't have time to warn her before I came into her mouth.

I hadn't lost control of myself like that since I was a pre-teen. Daire made a strangled sound as I finished. I pulled her back onto my lap and rubbed a hand over her red knees.

She looked at me with knowing eyes and touched my cheek. "I'm glad I like you, too, Campbell. I have a feeling when I do find the version of myself I want to be, she'll be standing right next to you, regardless of where that might be."

I held her to my chest and waited while we both took a minute to catch our breath.

I didn't bother to tell her no distance would keep me from her as long as she wanted me around. Instead, she should worry about how close I wanted to be to her at all times, not how far away we might end up.

chapter
NINETEEN

Daire

"I'm getting on a plane to California on Saturday." I was fully embracing the ask for forgiveness instead of permission attitude when dealing with my mother these days. I looked at her over the cup of coffee I held between my hands and watched a hundred different emotions cross her face. She looked tired and older than she ever had before. Seeing her look so defeated was like a knife in my heart. I never meant to break her in the process of fixing myself.

My mom was hysterical when she realized Remy had abducted me. She was so upset that my dad had to intervene. He told me he would take care of her and not to worry about coming back to the house until I was ready. I waited until I thought she had enough time to calm down and called her to ask if she wanted to meet me for coffee in a neutral location. I told her I wasn't coming home as long as she felt she had to keep me under constant supervision, but I wanted to see her and try to set things right. She agreed but didn't sound happy about it.

My mom fiddled with her wedding ring, turning the band around her finger while watching me as if trying to peer inside my mind.

"You just got back to Denver. Why are you leaving again?" She cleared her throat, and I could tell she was struggling to keep her cool and stop herself from snapping at me or bursting into tears.

"I'm going to see Aston and look at some art schools. I reapplied to college. My first choice is in San Francisco." Mostly because it would allow me to go to school and complete an apprenticeship if I convinced Cable to take me under his wing.

"I decided to check out the area and see if I like it. You know I haven't traveled much. There are a lot of places I want to see, and I miss my best friend." I sighed and reached out to hold her fidgeting hands. "It doesn't have anything to do with you, Mom. I need to start making decisions for my future on my own. Your input is welcome because I know you only want the best for me, but the final choice has to be mine." Campbell's warning to keep my family included was ringing in the back of my mind.

She gulped nervously, and I could see the struggle to be understanding and supportive in her eyes. "San Francisco is really far away. It's also expensive. How much research have you done about these choices you want to make?" Her voice was shaky, and her eyes glazed over with unshed tears.

I patted her hands and gave her a reassuring smile. "San Francisco isn't any farther away than Ry in Texas. You didn't have such a big reaction when he changed majors and schools. You were proud of him for deciding to go into the medical field. I don't understand why his choice was admirable and mine is reckless." I tried to keep the hurt out of my voice.

My mom blinked wide eyes that were a mirror image of mine. I watched as realization suddenly dawned in the glittering green depths.

"Oh. I...you're right. Of course, your dad and I worried about Ry moving so far away. I worry about him daily and miss him like crazy, but I didn't question his choice to move out of state. Not once. That isn't fair to you at all."

I let go of her hands, lifted a shoulder, and let it fall in a careless shrug. "It's okay. I know you've been anxious over my choices since the accident. And I can understand that if I leave, it'll be you and Dad alone. That's a huge adjustment. But Mom, no matter where Ry and I go or how long we stay there, you and Dad are home. We'll always come back to you. You did your job. You raised us right and taught us to go after what we want. You can trust us because neither of us want to disappoint you. We want the opportunity to prove to you that we turned out all right." I sipped my coffee and gave her a grin to ease some of the tension between us. "And just because I want to get into the school in San Francisco doesn't mean I will. I applied to a bunch of different schools all over. I want to have options."

My grandparents on both sides of the family had set aside funds for Ry and me to go to college. Tuition wasn't going to be a problem if my parents ever decided to really cut me off. I doubted it would ever come to that, but lately, I'd started to question my relationship with them. I knew it was mostly growing pains. However, there was still a small part of me that wondered if I could push them to a breaking point.

"Mom, I know I handled what happened over the holidays incorrectly. I know I've been off since the accident. But I recognized the problem and am doing my best to address it. If you acknowledge that, it will go a long way to making things better between us."

My mother sat back in her seat, dragging a hand down her face. Her shoulders slumped, and she gave me a wry grin. "I wish you were old enough to drink. This conversation deserves whiskey, not coffee." I giggled and felt some of my tense muscles relax. "Your dad and I had a long talk the day Remy came and got you. I don't know when it started, but I can't stop seeing you and your brother in every patient that comes through the ER in critical condition. It doesn't matter if they're young or old; all I see is you kids fighting for your lives... and losing. It makes my hands shake, and I feel like I can't breathe. It's been hard to do my job properly. I didn't realize I was bringing that home with me until I tried to lock you away from the world so nothing would ever hurt you again." She sniffed a bit, and a single tear rolled down her cheek. My heart clenched. It felt terrible to be the reason my mom was crying. After all she had given me, I never wanted to be the cause of her distress. "The problem is with me, Daire. Not you. You became a casualty because I didn't want to admit I was struggling. I've promised your father I'm going to take some time off and reevaluate where I am in my career and if what I'm doing is making me happy. I know I make a difference, but that might not be enough for me anymore." She gave a pointed look and sighed heavily. "I told myself I would never treat you kids the way my parents treated me, and that's exactly what I've been doing. My mom ruined our relationship by trying to control me and by using money as a weapon. I never want that to happen to us."

I shook my head. "I'm at fault too. I was selfish and didn't think about anyone else when I left. I'm sure that didn't make what you're going through any easier."

My mom reached out, smoothed some of my hair, and pinched my cheek like I was a toddler. "We had it pretty easy with you kids growing up. I was overconfident that it would always be a breeze. You and your brother were bound to grow up and become your own people. I should be teaching you to fly, not trying to clip your wings. I don't want history to repeat itself. I don't want you to beat yourself bloody against a cage trying to escape the way I did when I was your age."

I pushed her hand away and gave her a fake scowl. "We're all bound to make mistakes. That's what makes us human."

She changed the subject while she collected herself. "Are you staying with Aston when you get to California? I was surprised she didn't come home for Christmas."

"I'm not. Her mom didn't love that she left for college either. There's some tension there. Plus, she might've been the one who broke up with Ry, but that doesn't mean it doesn't hurt her to see him with someone else, especially over the holidays. I don't blame her for staying in California and not wanting to face everything she was trying to avoid back here." I shifted my gaze away and tapped my fingers on the table between us. "I'm not going alone. Campbell is tagging along, so I can't stay with Aston."

My mom froze, and I watched her stiffen. "Don't you think you're moving too fast with this guy, Daire? You've never even dated someone seriously before. You're still so young. I hate to see you getting in over your head with someone too quickly. Do you even know how old he is? What's his family like?"

I couldn't fault her for feeling that way. Campbell and I hadn't even gone on a real date, but we'd already been on a road trip together and met each other's families. Our short time together had been intense, which made it feel longer than it was.

"He's in his early twenties but has an old soul. He's very mature because his childhood wasn't easy. I didn't ask him to go to California with me; Ry did. He'll ensure nothing happens to me in a strange city where I don't know anyone. I would think you should appreciate that instead of condemning him."

I would bite my tongue off before admitting I didn't know his exact age because he didn't know his real birthday. I didn't want to give my mom more ammunition to use against him.

"Your brother got over his resistance to you seeing Campbell pretty quickly, didn't he?" She didn't sound thrilled about the fact.

"They came to an understanding because they both have stubborn little sisters. I like Campbell, Mom. That feels like the one thing I've gotten right since the accident. He's far from perfect, but he feels like the perfect guy for me."

My mom gave me a startled look and let out a shocked laugh. "I'm almost positive I said the same thing about your father when both your grandmas tried to warn me about getting involved with him. I can't believe we've come full circle." She shook her head and tossed her hands up in surrender. "I give up. If you want to be with him, do it. But if he ever mistreats you or drags you into a dangerous situation, you must promise me that you'll protect yourself. You come first—always."

I could tell she was serious and wouldn't let the subject drop unless I agreed. I got up and walked to her side to wrap my arms around her shoulders and hug her tightly. "I'll keep myself safe, Mom. Campbell isn't the one you need to worry about; his motives are always crystal clear."

She hugged me back, and the rope around my heart loosened. It felt good to have her finally understand me.

I would never wish for my family to hate me and blame me for my mistakes again. I would never undervalue the importance and power of their forgiveness and love. My family taught me that understanding was the greatest gift you could give to someone who felt unworthy.

She gave me my debit card back and told me she would transfer some money so I could afford at least a week in California. I didn't tell her I'd already borrowed money from Remy for the trip. I'd pay them all back eventually, anyway. After promising to call her once I was in California, and swearing up one side and down the other that I would check in regularly, I left and made my way back to the loft. I needed to go through the stuff Remy snagged from my room and pack for the short trip. When I dumped my purse on the bed to clean it out, I rolled my eyes at the GPS tag still mixed in with the other junk. I owed a lot to that little device, so I kept it as a memento and shoved it back in a pocket when I repacked everything.

Looking at my wallet, I paused when I thought about going through security at the airport. Campbell didn't know if Campbell was his first or last name and he didn't know his birthdate. When Zowen tried to look into him, it was like he didn't exist. Belatedly, I wondered how he planned to travel with me if he was a ghost. I frowned as it became clear how difficult it must be for Campbell to operate with his odd background. I wondered if this was an area I should ask questions about, or look the other way. I had a feeling I was going to run into a lot of these uncertainties in the future. I shook my head and reminded myself that I was trying to take things with Campbell one day at a time. There was no use getting worked up or worried over what might happen, and since he was the one who booked the tickets, it made sense that he had some sort of identification he could use to fly.

I made a mental note to ask him if I needed to call him by a different name so as not to raise suspicion. I laughed to myself as I cleaned up the loft and messaged Aston to make sure she had the correct dates that I'd be in California. It was interesting being with someone like Campbell. I had to stay on my toes to keep up with all the idiosyncrasies that came with a guy who literally came from Nowhere and had nothing. It was almost as if he had the opportunity to constantly reinvent himself. I envied that about him.

But I also hoped all the versions he would eventually become still liked me.

I spent the next day stalking my email, hoping to hear back from Cable, and researching him and his shop as much as possible. I made a list of places I needed to visit while I was in San Francisco. Hyde had to go out of town for work, and Remy was on a deadline, so I didn't see Campbell until he picked me up for our early morning flight.

He kissed me hello, but I noticed he was distracted all the way to the airport. I filled the silence by telling him about making up with my mom and peppering him with easy questions about Hollyn and how he had spent the last few days. He gave terse one-word answers and never stopped clenching his teeth. A muscle in his cheek fluttered from how hard his jaw was grinding. He looked seriously stressed out but didn't tell me why. I thought for sure he was going to get picked by TSA for extra security screening because he was a sweaty, nervous wreck all the way to our gate.

I didn't realize he was nervous about flying until we boarded, and he looked like he might throw up.

The boy was turning green right before my eyes.

His rough condition didn't slip past the older gentleman seated on the aisle next to me.

I put my hand on the back of Campbell's neck and gave him a gentle stroke to try and calm him down.

"Why didn't you tell me you don't like to fly?" I couldn't hold back the hint of humor in my voice. He was such a tough guy. I couldn't believe he had a common, everyday phobia like any other human.

"I didn't know I was afraid to fly until I woke up and realized I had to get on a plane this morning. I've never flown before." He gave me a look that solidified my suspicions that it was challenging for him to get the kind of documents he needed to get through the airport. He put in the work for me, and because he promised my brother he would.

I leaned my head on his shoulder and reached for his hand. I laced our fingers together and reassured him, "It'll be fine. I won't let anything happen to you. Just squeeze my hand when you're afraid."

The older gentleman smiled in our direction and looked relieved when Campbell started to relax.

"Are you going to keep the plane in the air by sheer force of will, Princess?" Campbell cleared his throat and rolled his head around on his neck to release some of his tension. He was still grinding his back teeth together, but his pallor began to look less sickly.

I arched an eyebrow in his direction and taunted, "You don't think I can?"

He snorted and sank down in the seat. He was tall enough that his knees were right up against the seat in front of him. A woman with a speak-to-the-manager haircut turned to glare at him, which made Campbell snicker.

"I think you can do whatever you put your mind to, but telekinesis might be a stretch." His tone was so dry it could start a forest fire.

"If she can't keep the plane in the air, I can. I'm a retired pilot." The older man interjected quietly. "I don't mean to interrupt, but I wanted to offer reassurance because you looked a touch queasy a minute ago, and we haven't even taken off."

I laughed and rubbed my thumb over his. "See. You're covered on all sides. Your first flight will be a piece of cake."

Campbell grunted but dipped his chin in a nod and offered a quiet 'thanks' to the older gentleman. His fingers tightened around mine, and he closed his eyes and leaned his head back against the seat.

"Did you hear back from the tattoo guy about your portfolio?"

"Not yet. That's why I'm going to the shop to see him in person."

"You aren't worried that might come across as pushy?" He asked me the same question before he bought us the plane tickets. He wanted to make sure I really thought it through.

I shook my head. "No. I think it'll come across as persistent and passionate. No one can plead my case better than me. I'm very convincing when I want to be."

He lifted a hand to cup my chin and brushed his thumb across my bottom lip. "I don't want you to be disappointed if things don't play out how you want. It would've been a lot easier to send your portfolio with your full name attached to it. No shame in using any advantage you have."

"I don't want to use my name any more than I want to use my face to get ahead. I want to prove my talent and deserve to step into my father's shoes when he's ready to step down."

"You're going to ignore my advice about living an easy life, right?" He sounded resigned to the fact.

I lifted his arm and wrapped it around my shoulders so I could lean more fully into his side. I stroked a hand up and down his thigh when the plane pushed back, and he went stone still next to me.

"I'm going to live *my* life. It's going to be easy and hard. I'm okay with that." I guided the tip of my nose along the curve of his jaw and whispered, "I'll try to make liking me easy for you since everything else has been so hard." The guy deserved a break in one aspect of his complicated existence. I didn't mind being the eye in the middle of his raging storm.

The plane rattled and shook as it raced down the runway, and Campbell rested his head against the side of mine. "Doesn't matter if it's easy or hard; I like you, Daire."

The fact that he was on this flight, which clearly freaked him out and made him seem so much more relatable than he ever had, proved he wasn't talking out of his ass and saying what he thought I wanted to hear.

So far, it'd been easy to like him, but just like he said, I knew I would like him even when it was hard.

Now, I just needed to figure out how to treat myself with the same kind of certainty and compassion. Then all would be right in *my* world.

TWENTY

Campbell

I quickly learned that whatever was next for me in life, being a tourist was not it.

I hated the congestion of people.

I hated the noise.

I hated how everything was overpriced and gimmicky.

I hated that strangers felt like they could get in my personal space and randomly hand me their phones while asking for a family photo.

I was in San Francisco for less than a day and was already over it. And it was clear Daire was having more fun watching me squirm and sweat my way through a walk along Fisherman's Wharf than visiting any of the attractions she wanted to see. I was glad she found my discomfort amusing because I was never going to a tourist hot spot again. And it would take an act of God to get me willingly on an airplane in the future. I'd much rather drive up the side of a mountain in a blizzard.

On the second day, I escaped a visit to Chinatown and a ride on the trolley because Daire's best friend, Aston Wheeler, showed up to keep her company. I promised Daire I would be fine on my own and sent the girls off with a reminder to be careful and to stay watchful. I wasn't too worried about Daire, but her friend looked like a stiff wind could blow her over.

I knew Daire was staying busy because she was worried about showing up at the tattoo shop unannounced, but I couldn't keep up with her frantic pace. There was such a thing as too much of a good thing.

Plus, since San Francisco was so close to The Point, I'd gotten a message from Karsen's brother-in-law, Race Hartman, to meet him almost as soon as the plane touched down. I had no idea how he knew I was in town, but he wasn't the type of guy one got to ignore.

I would never take Daire to The Point. It was bad enough she had to visit Nowhere with me. I took the opportunity to set something up with Race while she was occupied with her friend. The timing was a blessing.

A place like The Point wasn't somewhere you could take an Uber to. It was the type of place people didn't want to acknowledge, and if they did, it was with a look of disgust or fear on their faces. I wasn't sure how Race expected me to find him, but I realized it was dumb to worry about something so mundane. A man like Race didn't leave anything to chance. As soon as I stepped out of the hotel, a sleek, low-slung sports car was waiting at the entrance. There was an army of black SUVs surrounding the expensive car. It wasn't a subtle welcome.

I nodded at the doorman, who was looking at the expensive car with obvious admiration and slid into the passenger side. It was a safer bet to jump in one of the

SUVs. However, since Race made an effort to pick me up in person, I had no choice but to get into his car.

Race didn't look like a man who ran an underground empire the way both Benny and Booker did. He was polished and carried himself with every inch of privilege and power he possessed. In another world, he would've made a good politician. He had prestige and was really fucking good at breaking the law and not getting caught. I'd only met the man a couple of times while I was growing up on the compound, but he left a lasting impression. No one got under Karsen's skin the way he did. And no one put Booker on high alert the way he did. I understood in a hot second that while Race might be family, he could still be considered an enemy.

I couldn't think of a single reason why he wanted to see me while I was in California, and I wasn't going to ask until he gave me a hint.

"You're in town with your girlfriend?" Race's voice was smooth and held a hint of his rich-kid upbringing. He sounded like a blue blood-country-club-designer-suit kind of guy.

I looked at him out of the corner of my eye. His hair was mostly white and slicked up off his forehead. His watch was as expensive as Benny's, but his eyes were twice as cold when they met mine. "I came with the girl I like." That seemed more significant than labeling Daire as something so common as a girlfriend. The idea of having a girlfriend wasn't so far-fetched. However, I never imagined I would have a girl I liked, who reciprocated my feelings, in my lifetime. It was hard to picture when there wasn't anything particularly likable about yourself.

Race made a sound of acknowledgment as he guided the car to the city's outskirts and closer to the water. "Let me know if there's anything in particular you want to do while you're here. I'm happy to set the two of you up. This is probably your first vacation since Karsen got her hands on you, right?"

"Yep." I wished I smoked so I would have something to do with my hands. "Daire's got everything planned while we're here. I'm just tagging along to make sure she doesn't get herself into any trouble. She has a knack for that."

"Trouble is fun." Race chuckled as he pulled the sports car into the parking lot of a diner. It wasn't all the way in The Point, but close enough that the people walking in and out were not the type you'd want to run into in a dark alley—or a well-lit one, for that matter.

I sighed. "Trouble is fun, until it isn't." I followed him into the retro-themed diner and tried not to stare at the burly bodyguards who flooded in after us. "This place seems a little low-key for you, Hartman."

Race lifted an eyebrow and motioned for me to sit across from him.

"This place is an institution. It has survived no matter who is running things in the city. It's always been a safe place. My wife even worked here when she was younger. It's close enough to The Point I can enjoy lunch without worrying about getting a bullet in the back of the head, but far enough outside city limits that Karsen won't murder me when she finds out I met with you."

"Why did you want to meet with me?" I watched him with careful eyes, not that I stood a chance if he decided to take me out. I could hold my own one-on-one, but he had a legion of armed badasses at his beck and call. It wouldn't be a fair fight.

"Any threat that comes close to The Point is my responsibility to take seriously."

I blinked and slumped back in the booth. "Me? A threat? To you? I think you're giving me too much credit."

Race tapped his fingers on the old laminate tabletop and gave me a sharp grin. "Karsen and Booker took you in; Benny taught you everything he knows. Your roots are razor sharp and bone deep, Campbell. Only a fool would underestimate you."

I swore and shook my head. "I don't want anything to do with The Point. I'm only here because the girl I like has business here."

Race gave a slight nod. "I know that. But I also know your girl applied to a college near here. If she moved to the Bay Area permanently, are you planning to follow her?"

"How do you know everything?" I was alarmed and frustrated by how well-informed Race appeared to be.

"It's my job to know everything. That's how I keep the people I love safe."

"I don't know what I'm going to do if Daire leaves Denver. I'm still under contract for the family I'm working with. I'll make decisions when the time on that is up. Who knows if she'll want to be with me by the time that rolls around. She's young and impulsive. She likes me today. She could hate me tomorrow."

"True. But what really matters is if you like her or not. She could hate you with every fiber of her being, and if you still like her, you'll do anything to make sure she's okay. You'll end up awfully close to my doorstep sooner or later. Before that time comes, I want to make sure you know it's better to come as a friend than a foe."

"You're threatening me?" I shouldn't be surprised. There was no question that Race was a threat. There was a reason he and Karsen constantly butted heads and clashed like two titans.

"I'm not. I'm warning you. I'm not as young as I used to be. The Point, like everywhere else in the world, has evolved. No one can keep control of it forever."

"You're delusional if you think I want to challenge your authority. I'm doing my damnedest to leave the type of life you and Karsen live behind me. I don't want to be a threat to anyone anymore."

A server came by, and Race ordered us two house specials. He also got himself a chocolate milkshake, which would've made me laugh if he was someone else. I felt like letting a chuckle slip at the wrong time during this conversation was a surefire way to end up with my throat slit.

"You will always be a threat, Campbell. Surviving what you have proves how strong you are. You've learned from the best. That knowledge will never leave you. You'll react before you even realize what you're doing. I've seen it a thousand times when someone thinks they've left The Point behind. It's not possible to forget your origins. And I'm not asking you to. I'd like to gauge how we will get along if you end up living in my backyard. You know they say, 'two tigers can't live on the same mountain' for a reason."

I grunted and reached for the glass of water the server dropped in front of me. "If, and that's a big if, I end up on the West Coast, I will do everything I can to stay out of your way. I don't want Daire to get curious about The Point. I don't want any part of it to touch her. I don't want to be your enemy or your ally. I want to be my own man." I was tired of answering to anyone more dangerous than I was. So be it if that meant I had to become the *most* dangerous of them all to secure my freedom.

A giant sandwich on fresh sourdough was put down in front of me. It looked good, but I didn't have much appetite. I shoved a fry in my mouth and waited for Race to pass judgment on what I just said.

"Okay. I can respect that you want to remain a neutral party for now. I assume that will change if Karsen decides she wants to expand her operations into my territory."

I sighed heavily and reached up to rub the scar on my chin. "I owe Karsen more than I can ever repay. If she asks me to get involved in something, I can't tell her no." Holy fuck. I hope it wouldn't come to that. If Race and Karsen clashed, it would be a bloodbath. "You have to understand where I'm coming from."

Race nodded and wiped his mouth with a checkered napkin. "I do. That's why I'm leery to have you so close to everything I hold dear. It gives my sister-in-law an unfair advantage. Not to mention, Benny will pick whichever side you choose. Never thought that bastard would care about anyone but himself, but he's very particular where you're concerned."

I never viewed myself as particularly special in Benny's eyes, but Race wasn't the first person to point out that Benny would have my back if shit went south.

"Goddamn." I smacked a hand on the table in frustration. "Can't you just work out your issues in family therapy like normal relatives? Do you need to participate in a mafia gang war instead of, I dunno, maybe having a civil conversation about the history between you two? You're so similar; I don't understand how you can't see it." I was frustrated enough to let my thoughts and tongue escape me. Fortunately, Race seemed amused by the outburst.

"You and I are tigers, Campbell. We fight with teeth and claws. We use brute strength and any other weapon at hand. Karsen is a dragon. Dragons don't do resolution. They burn everything to the ground in the blink of an eye. They do destruction. Our family dynamics are too complicated for a mere conversation to fix. However, I like your outlook. Loyalty to loved ones is the most important thing you can bring to the table in this world." He must've decided he had said enough because he finished his lunch and sucked down the milkshake without saying another word. When he was done, he paid the bill and gave me a grin that looked like it was pulled off the cover of a magazine. It still sent a chill down my spine. "I'll see you around, Campbell. Enjoy the rest of your vacation."

He ordered one of his men to take me back to the hotel. Once his oppressive presence was gone, I managed to eat the rest of my sandwich and even grabbed my own milkshake to-go. The ride back to San Francisco was silent, and I couldn't stop thinking about the irony that I had tried so hard to leave Nowhere behind, and now I might be neighbors with the one city that might be even more dangerous. Bad things. Bad people. Bad choices. They were like a magnet that kept pulling me in a direction I didn't want to go.

I didn't bother to thank Race's thug when he dropped me off at the hotel. I was a little rattled. I took a minute to calm down before heading back to the room. It was a good thing I did because Daire was waiting for me and looked like she was ready to jump out of her skin.

"Cable McCaffery called me!" She shoved her phone in my face and practically jumped up and down. "He told me he wants to meet tomorrow." She took a deep breath, and I could see unfiltered joy glittering in her eyes. "He liked my portfolio, Campbell. He liked it so much that he didn't even ask why it didn't have my last name on it. He didn't even ask for it during the call. I can't believe this is happening."

She was vibrating with excitement.

"Congratulations, Princess." I was happy for her but couldn't get Race's question out of my mind. What was I going to do if she decided to move here? Was I willing to follow her even though it was close to a place I absolutely didn't want to be?

It scared me.

Daire looked at the to-go cup in my hand. "Did you go out? I thought you hated the crowds and were done people-ing for a while?"

I shrugged and tossed the empty cup in the trash. "I grabbed a quick lunch in an out-of-the-way spot. Where did your friend go? That was a quick visit."

"She has a group project due for school. One of the girls on her team didn't do their portion of the presentation, so Aston rushed back to make sure it got done before tomorrow. She's always been serious about her grades. It's one of the many things she and Ry have in common."

"Why is she doing someone else's work?" That wasn't a proper solution to the problem.

Daire huffed an annoyed sound. "She's a bit of a pushover. She was very sheltered by her parents because she was sick when she was a baby. Then she dated my brother forever, and he looked out for her, and I'm her best friend." She gave me a knowing look. "She avoids conflict; I actively look for it. She'd rather do the work herself than fight with someone to get it done."

I plopped down on the bed, stretched my arms out on the mattress, and gazed at the ceiling.

"You two sound very different." But it was clear the girls cared deeply for one another.

"We are. That's why we stayed friends for so long. It was interesting. And because we both love my brother." She laid on the bed beside me and put her head on my arm. "I was going to suggest grabbing something to eat to celebrate getting my foot in the door." She poked at my stomach with a finger and threw one of her long legs across mine like a horny octopus. "How about we stay in and celebrate instead? I feel like staying in bed and getting room service after we're too tired to move might be more in line with your idea of a vacation."

I curled my arm around her neck and pulled her closer to kiss her forehead.

"I need to take a shower. The place I went wasn't very clean." It was actually fine, I just felt dirty after my meeting with Race, and I really didn't want any of the filth that came from The Point to touch her. "Want to join me?"

She nodded eagerly and helped me to my feet. As I watched her walk to the fancy marble and gold-plated bathroom, it hit me dead center of my heart that I would follow this girl anywhere.

Race was right. As long as I liked her, I was willing to do whatever it took to keep her safe and make sure she was happy.

That felt closer to love than like—not that I had any experience with either.

TWENTY-ONE

chapter

Daire

Cable's shop was a lot different from my dad's. The whole vibe and aesthetic was more modern and new school, emphasizing tiki and surf culture. It made sense, considering Cable was an avid surfer. Also, his shop was one single business. He didn't branch out into a franchise the way my father and his business partners did when the original Marked Men shop took off. Cable only accepted custom work and did zero walk-ins. He had a big attitude, like my dad, but Cable was nearly a decade younger. Some would say he hadn't earned the right to be so arrogant, but his success proved that notion wrong. And it wasn't only him. The small handful of artists who worked with him were all booked out for a minimum of six months. It was harder to get an appointment with Cable than it was to get into the Met Gala.

He'd only accepted a total of three apprentices in the span of his entire career. Two of them were from overseas, and none were women. But they all went on to open remarkably successful shops of their own and had nothing but good things to say about the opportunity to learn under Cable.

I still couldn't believe he wanted to talk to me after he saw my portfolio. It felt like winning the lottery, especially because I was an artist, but not a tattoo artist. I'd never put ink on real skin before. My dad was very against it. He didn't want me to spend my twenties covered in shitty tattoos or making my friends look like sketchbooks. He always told me there was time to learn to do everything correctly. That was his gift to me. I didn't know if my lack of real-life experience would be a deal breaker, but I hoped I could convince Cable to take me on with my overwhelming passion and determination. This was the first thing, after Campbell, that I was doing for myself and would fight for.

I was acting like an over-excited puppy when we arrived at the shop. Campbell kept petting my hair to calm me down. He offered to drop me off and wait at a nearby coffee shop, but I asked him to come in for moral support until I met Cable. Plus, Campbell was heavily tattooed, and I wasn't. Having him with me gave me the credibility I lacked since I refused to use my last name to get in the door.

When we walked in the door, a bell jingled, and immediately the sounds and smells that I knew intimately from growing up in the Marked Men and Saints of Denver set me at ease. A stunning African American woman with dreads at the front desk gave us a welcoming smile, and I could see how her eyes tagged that impressive moth on Campbell's neck.

"How can I help you today? Do you have an appointment?" She was polite, but I could tell she was used to turning away people who walked in hoping to pick a design off the wall.

It simply wasn't that kind of tattoo shop.

I tried to calm my shaky nerves and forced a return smile. "I have a meeting with Cable. I'm Daire."

The woman scrolled through a program on the tablet in front of her and nodded. "I see you on his schedule. I can take you back." She looked at Campbell. "He usually only allows one person at a time in his station, though. He's a fussy one."

Campbell chuckled and took a step back. "I'll wait for her outside. No problem."

The woman waved a hand toward a doorway and pointed to a neon sign that said *Lounge Lizards*. "We have a waiting area. You can hang out in there until she's done if you want. Cable has another appointment in half an hour. He's a stickler for punctuality, so she'll be done by then."

Campbell nodded and gave my hand one last squeeze of encouragement. He disappeared into the lounge while I followed the woman to a private room. That was another big difference between Cable's shop and my dad's. My father worked in a big, open space where everyone mingled together because he worked with his best friends from childhood. Cable's station and preference seemed to be much more withdrawn.

Now that I thought about it, this was the type of shop where Campbell would be more comfortable. He was also particular and preferred being isolated, able to control every detail.

When I entered the room, a very tall man stood to greet me. He looked like a surfer. His blond hair was sun-bleached, his skin was very tan, he was wearing old school Vans, and I could tell some of the older tattoos on his hands and arms had faded from the sun. He didn't smile or stick out a hand to shake; he pushed a rolling chair in my direction and pointed to the long desk where he had been seated.

"All right, Daire No-Last-Name, tell me why you want me to teach you how to tattoo." His voice was smooth and mellow, and I caught the faintest trace of a southern drawl.

"I want you to teach me how to tattoo because I already know how to create art with every medium other than skin. I need someone who does more than put ink on flesh. I need an artist who tattoos, not a tattoo artist just also happens to know how to draw." It sounded convoluted, but it made sense in my head. Cable was the opposite of my dad. I wanted to cover all bases when I went into this as a career. I wanted to learn the business forward and back. I needed a mentor to guide me, so when I went back to work under my father, I could show him I had a solid foundation built. I wanted him to know I would do the Archer name proud. "I believe you can teach me what other tattoo artists can't."

"I don't take an apprentice very often. I'm not patient. I'm not kind. I don't tolerate anyone phoning it in."

I nodded. "I understand."

"Why did you send me your portfolio with only your first name?"

I shrugged, then remembered I was trying to impress him. I sat up straight and met his probing gaze. His eyes were dark brown, but nowhere near as fathomless as Campbell's. "I hoped it'd be good enough that you would want to find out who sent it without knowing if I was a man or a woman. I wanted to see how far my talent would get me, not my last name."

His gold eyebrows lifted, and there was finally a trace of interest on his face. "You think your name will carry any weight with me?"

"If you agree to take me on as an apprentice, we'll both find out." I don't know where the confidence came from, but I suddenly felt like Cable's bark was worse than his bite.

"Do you have any tattoos of your own?" His gaze slid over me, but not in a disrespectful way.

"Not currently. I'm impulsive by nature. I don't want to give my first one away and have it mean nothing down the road. Art means more to me than that." In fact, I attached more importance to getting my first tattoo than the first time I'd had sex. "I'll get my first one when I have the perfect design."

He chuckled and raised his eyebrows again. "Do you think you get free tattoos as a perk when you apprentice under me?"

I couldn't hold back an eye roll. "I don't think that at all. Trust me...I have someone else in mind for my first." My father might literally murder me if I let someone else put ink on my skin before he did. I would never hear the end of it, and it could very well be the end of me if I did.

Cable chuckled again. "Interesting." He propped a hip on the desk and crossed his arms over his chest. He had a very intricate spider tattooed on the back of one of his hands. It reminded me a lot of the moth on Campbell's neck. "You showed up quickly when I contacted you. Are you local to the Bay Area?"

"No. I'm in town to see a friend and look at colleges. I applied to a bunch of different art schools. But I won't commit to one until my apprenticeship is locked down." I winged my eyebrows up to match his expression. "I was planning on coming to the shop and begging to see you. I was determined to plead my case in person before I head home, so I'm grateful you called me. It saved me some serious embarrassment."

He chuckled again and pushed a tablet in my direction; pictures of different tattoos were on it. "I almost wish I'd waited to call. It's been a minute since we had someone show up at the door and beg to see me." He pointed at all the pictures and said, "Pick the best one and tell me why it's the best."

I wasn't ready for a pop quiz, so I caught my breath and took a second to collect my thoughts before starting to scroll through all the images. I could tell some were his, but most weren't. They ranged in styles and sizes, and none of them were bad. None of them were the best, either.

I knew Cable was capable of so much more, and some of this stuff looked like what my dad put out when he was in his twenties and dating my mom. I stared at the pictures for over ten minutes, the timer in my mind rapidly counting down before his next appointment. Finally, I pushed the tablet back in his direction and climbed to my feet.

"Wait here a second." I opened the door and dashed to the lounge where Campbell was waiting. He looked surprised to see me, and before he could ask how the meeting went, I pulled him back into the private studio and stood him in front of a bewildered Cable McCaffery. "This is the best tattoo." I pointed to the moth on Campbell's throat. "The line work is near perfect. The shading is unbelievable. The placement is exact. It looks like it's alive when he breathes right. The ink is in the skin, so the lines aren't blown out, yet it hasn't faded at all. It's a moth, but whomever did the design understood the symbolism means more than that. This is art on skin. This is the kind of work I want to do."

Campbell looked confused but didn't say anything as Cable stared at him.

"Who did your tattoo?" Cable sounded amused.

"Uh...a guy named Milo in Kansas City. He's done most of my work."

Cable nodded, gestured to the door, and indicated Campbell could leave. "Show and tell is over. I'll send her out in a minute." Campbell gave me a look but left obediently. Once we were alone in the studio, Cable let out a low whistle. "Impressive. You're right; that is the best tattoo of the bunch I showed you." He shook his head and uncrossed his arms so he could move to the computer on the desk. "The guy who taught me how to tattoo is named Emilio. He opened a shop in Kansas City about five years ago." I must've looked lost because he elaborated. "He goes by Milo."

I blinked and put a hand to my chest to keep my heart from jumping out. "Your mentor did Campbell's tattoo?" What were the odds?

"Can't say for sure, but I would bet my surfboard on it. I know his work inside and out. I don't know what you will do once you start handling a machine, but I'm curious. Which doesn't happen a lot. I'm not ready to take you on officially, but I'm intrigued enough to see what you're capable of. I won't offer to mentor you just yet, but I will agree to a three-week trial period to see how well we mesh. You have to start next week." There was a cold glint in his eye that told me this was the only opportunity he would give me, so I better take it and prove myself.

I was so stunned that I nodded and agreed before thinking about the fact I was *not* ready to stay in California beyond this week.

"Yes! I'd love that. I can't wait." How did I swing this when he didn't know my last name?

My astonishment was short-lived when he held out a hand and asked to see my driver's license. "We've got to get some paperwork before you can work in the shop."

I was hesitant, but eventually handed over my ID.. I saw the recognition as soon as he saw my last name.

He tossed his head back and laughed out loud. I got the impression it wasn't something he did very often. "You're fucking kidding me. Tell me you are not Rule Archer's daughter."

I shrugged and tried not to fidget nervously. "I can tell you that...but it would be a lie."

"No wonder you didn't want to put your name on your portfolio. You knew I'd call your old man and ask him why the hell his kid was asking me to teach her something he knows better than anyone." He shook his head. "I've met your dad at a couple different conventions. I also married a very pretty doctor who is outrageously out of my league. Interestingly, he and I have that in common. We've always gotten along and respected each other's work. He's a much better tattoo artist than I am."

"I didn't want to get an apprenticeship because of my dad. He started tattooing as a kid because he thought it was cool. He didn't lean into the artistic side until much later in life. Eventually, I'll work under him and take over the franchise when he retires. Before I do either of those things, I want to learn as much as possible. I want to learn from an artist who decided to make their art into tattoos, because that's what I want to do." I blew out a breath and gave him a serious look. "I don't even want him to know what I'm doing out here in California until you make it official."

That was a showdown I wanted to avoid as long as possible.

Cable snorted and handed me a pile of paperwork to bring when I returned the following week.

"As I said, it will be interesting to see how this plays out. Let's see you get through week one, Archer. Not many do."

I thanked him profusely, told him how excited I was, and practically bounced back to Campbell. He was at the front desk talking to the woman with the dreads. It seemed like she was asking where he was from, and when he replied Nowhere, she thought he was joking. Luckily, I pulled him away before the conversation turned awkward when she realized he was serious. I also thanked her for her time and threw myself into Campbell's arms once we were on the sidewalk.

"Oh, my God. Holy shit. I can't believe he agreed to let me learn from him without knowing who my dad was." I grabbed Campbell's cheeks between my hands and squished his handsome face into a pucker to kiss him. "Thank goodness I dragged you with me. I don't know what I would've done if you weren't here. You're my lucky charm, Campbell."

"Think that's the first time anyone has ever said I'm lucky. Usually, I hear that I'm a curse. When did he tell you that you could start?"

I paused in the middle of peppering excited kisses all over his face and neck. I dropped my arms and felt my euphoria at accomplishing the impossible start to wane.

"Fuck me." I shoved a hand through my hair and looked at him with wide eyes. "He wants me to come in next week to start a three-week trial. I agreed so fast; I didn't think about logistics."

Campbell frowned at the shop. "Go back in and tell him you need more time. You can't be here for three weeks without any warning."

I shook my head and pulled him away from the window that overlooked the sidewalk. I didn't want Cable or his staff to see us arguing. "I'll figure it out."

He snorted and looked at me like I lost my mind. "How? You couldn't afford a plane ticket earlier this month. Now you need a place to stay for a month. Not to mention that you only packed for a week. You jumped into this blind, Daire. It's going to backfire on you. Especially if you don't tell your folks what's going on."

I stiffened and pulled away from the hand he rested on my shoulder. "I'll stay with Aston. I'm going to make this work, Campbell. I thought you would support me, not play devil's advocate."

He swore and gave me a dirty look. "I got on a plane for the first time. I went to the pier and saw stinky sea lions. I ate terrible clam chowder. I support you. But I know you have a bad habit of getting in over your head. Sometimes you need to stop and think." He sighed. "You don't know anything about this place or the surrounding area. You might be jumping into the middle of an extremely dangerous situation and not even know it. There are real devils close by you need to guard against."

I spun around and scowled at him. I hated when he spoke in such a vague, ominous way. "Be happy for me, or tell me what you're trying to say without all the doom and gloom. If you don't think I should stay here, I need a real reason."

"I think you need more time, that's all."

I understood his concern and couldn't argue that he had several valid points. However, I would not let this opportunity slip through my fingers. I was determined to make it work. I would prove I could accomplish something on my own. After all, Remy bounced around all over the country with no plan or money, and things worked out fine for her in the end.

"I don't have time." I hooked my arm through his and leaned my head on his shoulder. "I have an opportunity. One that might very well be life-changing. It's no different than when you had the chance to come to Colorado. It was a chance you had to take. I don't want to fight with you. Let's enjoy the rest of our trip and pretend you aren't pissed as hell."

We would be separated soon, and the last thing I wanted was for him to head back home while we were at odds. I needed to know he was still on my team when everyone in Denver freaked out that I wouldn't be returning immediately. And once my family learned what I was up to, oof, I was going to need to prepare myself for battle.

I don't know if Campbell agreed with my plan to ignore the elephant in the room, but he let me drag him back to the hotel, and he didn't complain when I used my favorite method of distraction on him.

chapter
TWENTY-TWO

Campbell

D aire didn't want to fight. She wanted to fuck.

I knew she was trying to divert my attention. It wasn't the proper way to deal with conflict, but it was a lot more fun than arguing with one another.

I couldn't tell her the reason I didn't want her to stay in San Francisco for a month on her own was because of Race's thinly veiled warning from the other day. He had no reason to go after Daire. But if he really wanted me to steer clear of his territory, making sure she wasn't safe while we were separated was an excellent plan. If Daire didn't choose to stay in San Francisco, I would have no reason to plant roots so close to Race's kingdom.

Daire's fingers smoothed over my forehead as she tried to ease the frown etched onto my face. Her thumb traced my eyebrow on one side as she tilted her head to stare at me.

"That's a mean face you're making, considering the circumstances." Her gaze drifted across my chest, and down my abs, to the point where we were joined.

My hands were braced on either side of her hips, where she was propped up against the bathroom sink. She said we needed to brush our teeth after the aforementioned bad clam chowder, and one thing led to another while we were in the bathroom. I wasn't even scowling at her. I was looking at my reflection in the mirror over her shoulder. I tried to unknot my brows and pulled her closer. Her heat surrounded me, and her body quivered accordingly.

"Sorry. It isn't directed at you." I lowered my head to nuzzle her cheek.

One of her hands curled around my neck as she pulled me closer. "It can be. You're allowed to be mad at me. I can take it." She moved her lips so that she could whisper in my ear, "You can fuck me like you hate me. It might be fun to see the difference."

I didn't hate her. I couldn't hate her. Even when I wanted to. However, I was annoyed by her impulsive instincts and irritated by my own fear.

But I could definitely fuck her like I was mad at her.

I pulled out and took a step back, which made Daire gasp in surprise. Her eyes sparked with delight when I lifted her off the sink and turned her around, so we were both looking into the mirror.

She watched carefully as I stepped close to her, my cock riding the valley between her ass cheeks. I pressed her close to the edge of the vanity and forced her to lift a knee up on top of it. She was displayed wantonly and erotically before her nervous and hungry eyes. I wrapped one hand in her hair and the other snaked across her torso. I closed my fingers over her throat and tightened until her eyes widened in alarm. I bent my hips a little, so she was forced forward, and I dragged my cock down her body until the tip touched her wet entrance. Since she was already soft and pliant, I shoved back into her body and tightened my hold on her.

I pulled her head back by her hair and used my mouth to caress her ear. Her back stiffened against my chest at the rough handling, but she didn't ask me to stop. I bit her ear and moved my teeth to the side of her neck, fully intending to leave a mark right above my fingers. It had been a long time since I wanted to vent my anger. And there had never been a person in my life who told me they could take it when I was mad.

Daire was either incredibly brave or incredibly stupid. She was probably a mix of both when it came down to it.

Brave to take me on. Stupid to provoke me.

I let go of her hair and moved my palm to her breast. I held the soft skin and rolled my thumb over her puckered nipple. She released a shaky breath in response and whimpered when I pushed into her moist heat with more force than necessary.

Her expression in the mirror was torn between pleasure and pain. Yet, she still didn't ask me to stop. She reached out and put a hand against the glass in front of us to brace herself and watched me in the reflection. Her pale eyebrows lifted in a silent challenge.

Do your worst.

I swore violently against the soft curve of her neck and started to pound into her like a man possessed.

I let her taste my anger.

I let her feel my frustration.

I fed her my repressed fear.

I pushed her forward and pulled my eyes away from her penetrating gaze so I could mindlessly seek pleasure.

Daire made a strangled sound, and I realized how tightly my fingers were clamped around her throat. Maybe it was good that she wasn't going home for three weeks. Her parents already wanted her to stay away from me. They would lose it if she showed up looking like she's been strangled.

I let go of her neck and moved that hand between her splayed legs. I could feel how wet and stretched she was to accommodate my nearly violent thrusts. When I reached down to stroke her clit, I felt the way her pussy clenched and quivered around the point where we were joined. My dick felt harder than it had ever been in my life when my fingers bumped against it.

Daire put a hand over mine and pressed my fingers harder against her most sensitive place. The forward action jerked my gaze back to hers in the glass, and I was stunned to see all the hesitation fade away. She was enjoying the hard hands and rough handling. Her green eyes were lit from within, and her teeth were clamped down on her bottom lip so deeply it looked like it might bleed. Her nipples were tight, pink beads, and her chest was flushed a rosy red. Her long hair snaked down my chest, the ends barely tickling the base of my cock where it was buried inside of her.

I tugged on her clit and her nipple at the same time and watched as she came apart in my hands. Her eyes drifted closed. She moaned my name. Her entire body shuddered, and her hands curled into mine. I felt her come where our hands were overlapped. She fell forward, catching her weight on her hands, as she watched me furiously chase my completion while she panted and tried to catch her breath. I grabbed her hips with enough force to leave marks and pushed her raised leg farther up on the vanity so we both had a clear view of my cock hammering into her.

I'd had enough sex in my life that I didn't think much could surprise me.

I was wrong.

Daire always surprised me. What she wanted, what she could handle, how she reacted, how she felt, and how she understood me knocked me for a loop. I didn't have to hide the darkest parts of myself from her.

After I came, I rested my forehead against her spine and tried to catch my breath. We both made a sound when I pulled out of her, and I turned her around to face me. When I kissed her, I realized in everything that had just happened, I hadn't kissed her once.

The oversight made me feel ashamed until Daire took my hand and pulled me toward the shower. She didn't seem to mind the absence of romance.

When our eyes met, some of my dismay must've shown because she laughed and patted my cheek as she cranked the water on. While she climbed in, I took the condom off and tried to right my rioting thoughts.

"I was right; it was fun. Don't worry about me so much, Campbell. I'm fragile, but I won't break."

I shoved my wet hair off my face and stared down at her. "I'm not mad at you. I'm mad at myself." And the world where I was raised. Why did everyone have to be a victim or a survivor? A villain or a victor? "It should be fine for you to stay here for another month. I'm the reason it might be dangerous. It has nothing to do with you. I'm annoyed I put you in this situation. I'm mad that my life remains fucked no matter how hard I try to unfuck it. Even more so now that you're in the center of it."

She turned around, and the water cascaded over her skin and hair like a lover's touch. She blinked spiky lashes at me and asked, "Does this concern have something to do with where you went when you disappeared yesterday?" I gave her a questioning look and reached up to push her clinging hair from her face. She snorted and lifted her fingers to trace the wet tattoos on my chest. "I might not know you inside and out, but I know you well enough to know you wouldn't wander off just for a milkshake. You were extra tense when you got back. It reminded me of when we were on the farm. Like you're always alert and on the defense."

I sighed and pulled her to my chest in a wet, steamy embrace. "Remember when I told you there was another place like Nowhere called The Point?" I felt her nod. "It's not too far from here. It's way closer than I would like if you're considering staying here long term."

She wrapped her arms around my waist and looked up at me with questioning eyes. "A place can't hurt me if I stay away from it."

"The place isn't dangerous, but the people are. Karsen's brother-in-law is the end-all-be-all of The Point. He asked to see me when he found out I was in California. He doesn't love the idea of me being so close to his borders since I'm loyal to Karsen and Booker. He sees me as a threat. I'm worried he might come after you to keep me away. I don't want any part of this type of life to touch you, Daire."

"Talk about family drama. It makes what's going at home with me and my folks seem silly and childish." She sighed and pulled out of my arms to turn off the water. "Too late to keep what touches you from touching me. I feel it every time you put your hands on me because it's your life, Campbell. I knew that from the moment we headed to the farm. I walked into your life with my eyes wide open. You can call me a princess all you want, as long as you realize that's not what I really am. I'm not afraid of your world, and I'm not afraid of you."

I followed her into the bathroom and wrapped a towel around my waist. "You're both brave and stupid."

She glared at me as she wrapped her hair on top of her head. "I think there are nicer things you could say about me after we just had incredible sex."

"There are, but I can't think of them at the moment. I'm too busy picturing you at the bottom of the ocean with a bullet hole between your eyes."

It was graphic and ugly, but that is exactly why I was worried about her staying here without me.

"You know, bad things happen to people, even without ties to a criminal underground." Daire sat on the edge of the bed and watched me with serious eyes. "Ry got hurt because I was careless. He almost died. Remy had a rough moment as a teenager. She almost died. My Uncle Rome got shot because of a stupid bar fight. He almost died. My Uncle Remy passed away before I was born because of a terrible accident. Even if you were here to watch over me, and even if I picked somewhere far, far away from The Point, bad things might happen. My mom tried to swaddle me in bubble wrap and realized it wouldn't work. The same goes for you. There are things you won't be able to protect me or anyone else from. That's just life. We can't be afraid to live it just because we might get hurt."

Was I afraid to live my life? Maybe. I was afraid to start living it right because the only way I knew was how to live was wrong. I never had expectations because I didn't want to be disappointed.

I raised an eyebrow and bent over to pull my pants on. "You started therapy, and now you sound like a whole new person."

She stuck out a long leg and gave me a kick. "It's not therapy. It's spending time with you and seeing things in a new light." She narrowed her eyes. "Or, rather, trying to see things in the dark."

I grunted and almost fell over from the force of her kick. "No one has ever accused me of being enlightening before."

"You're too hard on yourself. You've overcome a lot. You love your family with every piece of yourself. You're fair when you pass judgment and can admit when you're wrong. Is your past murkier than most? Yes. But that doesn't mean your future can't be bright if you let it."

I tossed one of my t-shirts in her direction and pushed my wet hair off my forehead. "Where is the sad, sullen girl I was stuck with in my SUV for days on end?"

Her outlook had done a complete turn-around, and now she was full of sunshine and roses. Her optimism was startling but effective at dulling the razor-sharp points gouging my heart.

"She's still here. All sides of me want all sides of you, Campbell. We're a good fit." She pulled on the shirt and moved to shake out her wet hair. "Now that you know I can handle what you throw at me, sit down and tell me how I stay off the scary-man-who-might-want-me-dead's radar. I'm staying for the apprenticeship and will do my best to prove to Cable that I can be great. I may end up in the Bay Area longer than three weeks. Teach me how to survive when you're not here."

I exhaled and tried to get a grip on my inner turmoil. "I really wish I didn't find your stubbornness so sexy."

She wiggled her eyebrows at me in a playful manner. "But you do find it sexy."

"I do." I adored how she refused to bend for anyone, even when it would be so much easier for her. "I also like you alive. So, listen closely..."

If Race really came after her, there wasn't much hope of survival, but I could do my best to teach her how to navigate the underworld.

The truth was, she might be better suited to the dark and dangerous pitfalls than I ever was.

TWENTY-THREE
chapter

Daire

"Are you sure you don't mind stopping by to check on her?"

Aston's voice was stressed. She asked me the same question five times in the short period we'd been on the phone. I looked at the line of cool Victorian houses that lined San Francisco's famous hills. I had to walk up two of those crazy hills to finally reach the home of the girl in Aston's class. She was the wayward group project member who hadn't finished her portion of the assignment. According to Aston, the girl hadn't answered her phone all weekend or showed up to class for the presentation. She was worried. Once Aston mentioned the girl lived in San Francisco and commuted for class, offering to check on her was the least I could do. Aston was letting me crash in her tiny dorm room until I figured out a better option. The missing group member, a girl named Noble, lived a short distance from the tattoo shop, so it was easy enough to stop by on the way to my first day of work once I was in the city. The commute was killer. I needed to find a place closer to my internship sooner than later.

"I wouldn't have offered if it was a hassle, Aston." My best girl really was too much of a pushover. She needed me around to be the bad guy for her. "I'm in front of the house right now. It's huge. Seems like a pretty big place for a college student."

I jogged up the short flight of stairs to the front door and rang the bell. It was high-tech with a motion sensor and camera. I peered into the camera lens and waved.

"Noble's family has money. I think the house is something she inherited. I'm not sure. She's friendly but doesn't talk much about herself. I don't know her well, but it's not normal for her to slack off when it comes to schoolwork. This project is a huge part of our grade. No way she'd miss it."

"No one is answering the door." I took a step back and looked at the cool house. I frowned when I noticed a broken window that looked like it led to the basement. I lifted a fist to knock on the door and spoke at the recording device. "Hi, Noble. I'm Daire Archer. I'm friends with Aston Wheeler, your classmate. She's worried about you since you've missed class and won't answer your phone. She asked me to make sure everything was all right since your house is on my way to work."

I looked at the broken window again and told Aston, "There's a broken basement window. Who knows how long it's been there."

"I'm going to call the police and request a welfare check." Aston was clearly getting worked up.

"Maybe she went out of town with a boyfriend. Or maybe she's just not feeling well." I wanted to reassure my friend, but something in my gut told me something was wrong here. The first thing Campbell told me to pay attention to if I wanted to stay alive was my natural instincts. Humans were surprisingly good at sensing a predator when they knew they might be prey.

Just as I raised my hand to knock again, the speaker function of the doorbell switched on, and a man's voice crackled through. "Sorry. The homeowner isn't here at the moment. I'm the landlord. I'm doing some maintenance while she's away." It was obvious the person was trying to disguise their voice, and every hackle I had rose when I realized he couldn't be the landlord if Aston's friend owned the house.

"Thank you. Do you know when she'll be back? I need to see Noble to reassure my friend she's okay." I hung up on Aston and sent her a quick text telling her to call the police. She immediately called me back, but I sent her to voicemail.

"Umm... I'm not sure of her schedule. But she'll probably be gone a few more days. I'm sure she'll contact you when she's able. If you don't mind, I need to get back to work."

I forced a smile and tucked my phone into my purse, pretending I was satisfied with his answers and would be on my way.

"No problem. Thanks for your help." I jogged down the stairs and walked down the sidewalk until I was sure I was out of the range of the camera.

I called Aston back once I was out of sight, and she yelled at me to get away from the house.

"I think someone has your friend trapped inside." I squinted at the home and wondered if I could shimmy through the broken window without slicing myself to bits. "I think she needs help."

"Daire, don't do anything stupid! I called the police. They'll be there any minute."

"What if she doesn't have a minute? Now that the man knows someone is looking for her, he might do something worse than keeping her locked in the house." I started to creep back to the house and turned into a minuscule alley next to the driveway to avoid being seen. "I have a bad feeling."

"You are so reckless! Why put yourself in danger unnecessarily? Wasn't the accident with Ry enough of a warning that you need to be more careful?!"

I paused at her harsh words. I knew she was worried and stressed out, but that was a wound that hurt.

I sighed. "Someone just told me that I'm brave and stupid."

That someone very reluctantly got on a plane yesterday afternoon and headed back to Denver. The way Campbell hated flying was so endearing. It made me like him even more. I wished his flight had been delayed so I could send him into the house instead. I doubted that whatever danger awaited me would be a threat to him.

"That's not a compliment, Daire."

I giggled a bit hysterically, "But it was." Campbell appreciated those things about me.

I *was* brave and stupid. I was reckless and impulsive. I tended to jump before I knew how far out on a limb I might be. I thought those qualities made me unworthy of my family's unending love and forgiveness, but I was starting to see that they made me who I was. They loved me *because* of my rash and reckless behavior, not despite it. I wasn't a bad Archer; I was a brave and foolish one. And probably always would be. I was an Archer who took a little bit more work than most. I didn't have to apologize for being me. The girl who never looked before she leaped was just as worthy of good things and good people as someone as cautious and careful like Aston. We simply needed different types of love. My love needed understanding and patience to deal with my bullshit. Hers needed to protection and a sense of security.

Waldo wasn't as hidden as I thought. He was staring back at me in the mirror, waiting for me to accept and love him.

"If I don't call you back in ten minutes, worry. I'll call you as soon as I find your friend or if I see the cops. I know you don't understand why I have to help, and that's okay. You love me anyway." If I'd gone missing and someone showed up at my door to a situation like this, I would hope they wouldn't walk away. I couldn't ignore my gut when it told me to get involved.

"Daire! Daire, don't do whatever it is you're going to do! Your brother will kill me if you get hurt. And that guy you're with, I don't even want to imagine what he's going to be like if something happens to you. He's scary."

"I know he is. It's hot." I hung up the phone as she sputtered in outrage. I crouched down and scooted along the bottom edge of the house until I reached the broken window. This was a very nice row of expensive houses. The cops were bound to show up soon, so I wasn't overly worried about the neighbors mistaking me for a burglar. They couldn't be very observant if no one had noticed Aston's friend had been missing for several days.

When I reached the window, I bent down to peer into the basement. There was glass on the floor and footprints on the top of the washer and dryer where someone had clearly landed. There was also a big, suspicious stain on the concrete floor. I couldn't tell if it was blood, but my imagination was running wild. I silently hoped Aston's classmate had a terrible bout of diarrhea and was just stuck in the bathroom.

When I shimmied through the window, the glass caught on the hem of my jeans, and sliced my ankle. I swore under my breath as it beaded with blood and started to sting.

Stealthy, I was not.

I used the washer and dryer to hop down and looked around. It was too dark to see anything, and the space was eerily quiet. I clutched my purse like it was a lifeline. I wondered if Campbell was keeping an eye on my GPS tag. If so, he must be wondering what the hell I was doing.

I was wondering the same thing when I started to tiptoe toward the stairs leading to the rest of the house. As I was about to take my first step, I noticed something move under the staircase. Then I heard footsteps overhead that sounded as if they were getting closer.

I inched around the bare wooden stairs and choked back a gasp when I saw the prone figure of a young woman peeking out from underneath some haphazardly thrown boxes. She wasn't moving, but when I reached her and cleared the debris out of the way, I could see her chest rise and fall. The top of her shirt was covered in blood, and so was her long, dark hair. She was scarily still but still alive.

I looked up at the stairs and stilled when I heard the door open. The girl moaned and started to shift in pain. I reached out a hand to keep her in place and was met with unfocused blue eyes.

"Noble. Just tell me where the keys to the safety deposit box are. Your grandfather never intended for any of those stocks to be handed down to you and your mother. This will be so much easier on you if you hand them over. I promise to leave you alone once I get what I want."

The girl on the ground froze, and I could see her trying to get her foggy thoughts in line. She kept looking at me in confusion, so I held my finger to my lips and motioned for her to stay quiet. I moved farther out of sight and tried to see how badly she was injured. I mouthed that the police were coming, and she dipped her chin in response.

The top step creaked.

"I didn't want to hurt you. It's a shame you have friends that notice when you miss class. I had to throw you into the basement when that girl knocked on the door. I thought your head was too hard to crack. Stubborn girl. I'll have to get the blood out of the floor when I get the deed to this house that's rightfully mine. Now tell me where the key is!"

The man raised his voice, and his footsteps hurried down the stairs. The girl's eyes looked panicked, but I patted her shoulder and tried to keep her calm.

Before the man reached the bottom of the stairs, I pulled out one of the many self-defense devices Campbell had given me before he returned home. The last few days had been less like a vacation and more like boot camp. My purse was an arsenal, and I planned to use everything at my disposal.

I dug out a smoke bomb canister and pulled the pin. Not only did the metal rolling across the ground distract the man on the stairs, but the fog that started to fill the room obscured his view. I helped the dark-haired girl to her feet, and we both limped toward the broken window. There was no way we were getting up the stairs, not with Noble barely able to stand. I heard the man scrambling and coughing as the smoke enveloped him.

Once we reached the washer and dryer, I urged Noble to climb and practically shoved her out the window while yelling, "The police will be here any second. Don't look back."

Then, my ponytail was yanked from behind. I yelped and blinked hard against the pain as the smoke got in my eyes.

"Nosey bitch."

I felt an arm wrap around my neck and start to squeeze. Noble hesitated at the shattered window. I couldn't yell at her to leave because my air was being stifled, but I needed her to go find help.

I stomped down hard on the man's instep, and it bought me enough slack to suck in a breath as Noble did her best to scurry out the window. She wasn't moving very well because of the knock on her head.

The smoke had filled the basement, making it hard to see anything. I went limp in the man's hold, just like Campbell taught me. He lost his balance when he scrambled to catch my weight, and we both tumbled to the ground. When we fell, my purse tipped over and various weapons fell out. There was Mace, a Taser, brass knuckles, a switchblade, another smoke bomb, a personal alarm, and even a retractable baton. Campbell wanted me to carry a firearm, but that was where I drew the line.

I didn't know how to use a gun, and I was more than likely going to hurt myself instead of someone else if I had one. However, my current situation made me rethink that decision. Maybe I needed him to teach me how to use one in the future.

The first thing I reached was the personal alarm. I pressed the button and the basement filled with an ear-piercing shriek. It was so loud it was disorienting.

The man screamed and slapped his hands over his ears. I darted toward the broken window, and I could see that the police had arrived outside.

I tried to yell for help, but I choked on the smoke. I shook my head to get my thoughts in order and hoisted myself on the dryer. I reached out the window to wave, but the motion was interrupted when my ankle was caught in a tight grip.

"Who are you to fuck up my plans?" The man pulled me backward, dragging my hand across the jagged edge of the glass. I screamed at the top of my lungs when I felt my skin rip away, and my entire hand and wrist started to bleed. It burned like fire.

Something slammed into the back of my head, and the edges of my vision went foggy. The smoke was starting to dissipate, and I got my first look at the man who was about to bash my brains in with a shovel.

Surprisingly, he didn't look like a degenerate, or someone who was ready to commit murder. The man was dressed in khakis and a polo shirt. He looked ready for a round of golf, aside from the blood covering his clothes.

I twisted out of the way, and the shovel glanced off the cement way too close to the side of my head.

My hand was screaming in agony. I held it close to my chest and desperately kicked my foot toward the man's most vulnerable spot. I must've gotten lucky because he shrieked even louder than the alarm and dropped the shovel. Fortunately, just as it hit the ground, two police officers filled the doorway at the top of the stairs. Their weapons were drawn, and they yelled that no one should move.

I flopped on my back and gasped for breath. Blood dripped down my arm, and I smelled its metallic notes all around me.

I was worried about the damage to my hand, especially with the trial apprenticeship starting today. However, I was far more concerned about what I would tell my family and Campbell when they found out I was injured. I really was putting them through the wringer lately.

"We need a paramedic down here! We've got someone injured."

"She's an intruder! She broke in! This is my house!" The man screamed hysterically while the police put him in cuffs and hauled him toward the stairs. It sounded like one of them was reading him his rights.

"We've got the homeowner on the way to the hospital. She said you broke in and have been holding her captive for three days. You're looking at several serious offenses, regardless of whether you are her relative."

This nut job was related to her? Was the universe trying to show me what *real* family problems looked like?

We were perfect compared to so many others.

I groaned and squeezed my eyes closed as someone suddenly touched my arm. The person smelled medicinal and had a light touch—exactly like my mom.

I really wished she were here. I was hurt and alone. This haphazard rescue attempt was another one of my ideas that needed a bit more thought before I acted on it. While I'd gained a lot of self-awareness over the last few months, there was clearly more room for growth. I was slowly learning to accept the entirety of who I was, I still needed to take a minute and think about the consequences of my actions, regardless of how well intended they may be. I'd yet to determine if not being afraid of what the outcome of my actions was a good or bad thing? I did, however, know I wasn't going to live my life worried that I was worthless every time I made a mistake. When my father told me there was no such thing as a bad Archer, I believed him.

I moaned and tried not to look at my shredded hand.

"It hurts." My voice was raspy from screaming for help and inhaling the smoke.

The paramedic had a kind voice when she quietly told me, "I know, sweetie. You did a number on your hand. It was very brave and outrageously stupid for you to try and rescue that girl before the police arrived."

I could only offer a weak smile and say, "I know. That's just who I am." A girl that would always be daring.

TWENTY-FOUR
chapter

Campbell

"Do I want to know how you managed to get this piece of shit out of jail?"

I looked at Benny out of the corner of my eye. He was rolling the sleeves of his black Thom Browne shirt up to his elbows and taking off his stupidly expensive watch. Anyone who knew Benny would know that he only took off the watch when things were about to get bloody.

Benny chuckled and looked at the man tied to a metal chair in front of us. We were standing in an empty shipping container on the docks of The Point. I'd never been here before, but Benny walked around like he owned the place. It wasn't that different from dropping a problem off at the farm, but it somehow felt more sinister. Maybe it was the fact that I now owed Race a favor for allowing me to take care of the dirtbag who hurt Daire on his turf. Race relented when I told him that the girl Daire had rescued had ties to his best friend, Shane Baxter. Noble's father had worked for Bax at his garage-slash-chop shop for many years, even Noble's family came into an ungodly amount of money. I was curious to know if Benny had taken it upon himself to get involved in Noble's issue on my behalf, or if Race called him in as a favor for a friend of a friend.

It was hard to tell Benny's motivations at any given time, and I was learning just how far Race's reach went.

"He was out on bail. He's a rich white guy with an expensive lawyer and a family with political ties. They weren't going to keep him locked up. You know the system only works for some, not all."

The man on the chair tried to scream, but he had a dirty, oil-stained rag shoved into his mouth. He was looking at Benny like he might find an ally because of his expensive clothes and slicked-back hair. He seemed to think Benny was the least dangerous of us. Considering what this asshole had done to Daire, it might be accurate for once.

I was absolutely going to make sure he suffered the way Daire had. Even now, the only reason I was in the shipping container instead of the hospital was because she was currently in *another* surgery to reconstruct her hand. I left her family to watch over her while I went to take care of the person who put her in the hospital in the first place.

I didn't say anything to the very worried Archers, but her brother was bright. His look when I slipped out of the waiting room spoke volumes. He couldn't and wouldn't be capable of the sort of things I was, but he wanted that man to pay just as much as I did.

I realized Race was right.

If had people I cared about, as long as there was someone I loved, I was always going to be a threat. You didn't get to hurt my girl and go unchecked.

"What do you want to do with him? Drop him in the Bay?" Benny chuckled when the man started to gag behind the rag in his mouth.

I lifted an eyebrow and looked at his hands tied to the metal chair. "That feels too easy. I think we pull his fingernails out one by one and peel all the skin off his hands, so he has an idea of what Daire is going through."

Benny chuckled and clapped a hand on my shoulder. "I taught you well, kid." He flipped open a butterfly knife so seamlessly it was obvious he had a ton of practice. "You take the right side; I'll take the left."

I palmed the switchblade I'd just bought for Daire and pressed the button to extend the razor-sharp blade. The stark flood lights highlighted my reflection on the surface of the well-loved weapon.

I looked scary. Because I was scary.

There was no hint of mercy on my face. I hadn't planned to be this guy infinitely, but I understood there was no way to completely get rid of him. He was a necessary part of me. As long as there were bad people who wanted to harm those I cared about, I was going to be the guy who did bad things for reasons I felt were right. The difference was, now I wasn't going to feel as guilty about my actions. I was going to feel justified.

"You thought you could bully your cousin into handing over her inheritance because she was finally living alone. You didn't dare harass her when she lived at home because you knew her dad would end you." Benny clicked his tongue in disapproval. "I hate cowardly men the most. And I hate rich men who feel entitled to take things from others. It makes me angry."

The man in the chair screamed and threw his body from side to side as Benny maneuvered the knife under one of his fingernails. Things hadn't even gotten intense yet, and he already looked like he was going to pass out or choke on his own vomit.

I crouched down in front of him, so we were eye to eye. His face was covered in snot, and his eyes were glassy from a combination of tears and pain.

"I don't care that you're rich or a bully. I care that you put your hands on my girl. She's an artist. If you destroyed the function of her hand, you fucked up her whole future. To me, it only seems fair that your future is equally as fucked." Meaning he wouldn't have one.

His final days would be spent in this shipping container regardless of if it was on land or lost at sea. He was never going to see the light of day again. He just didn't know that...yet.

Benny grabbed another finger, and the man thrashed back and forth like a fish on a hook. I could hear him choking, and it only took one more finger before he pissed his pants.

Benny made a disgusted face and looked at the captured man once more. "You obviously didn't live with dignity. Shouldn't you try to die with some?" He took the oily rag out of the man's mouth while I went to work on his other hand.

I used a lot less precision and finesse than Benny had.

I wanted the motherfucker to suffer.

"Who are you? You'll never get away with this. Do you know who I am? Do you know who my family is? Fuck you!"

Benny hummed and reached out to smack the guy's cheek. He howled as he lost the fingernail on his pinkie finger. He turned to yell at me, but Benny jerked his head back to face him.

"I don't know you. And I don't know your family. But I do know those two girls you hurt. Neither of them deserved what you did to them. Especially Daire. She was just trying to help someone out."

"Nosey bitch. No one asked her to get involved." He screamed when the tip of my knife dug into his knuckle, peeling back muscle and flesh. I could see the white of his bone poking through the slice.

"She's a good girl. Likes to help, which means she finds trouble easily. None of that means she deserves to be lying in a hospital bed, her hand stitched together like Frankenstein's monster, just because you're a greedy asshole." Benny nodded as I drove the tip of the switchblade through the back of the man's hand until it touched the metal of the chair. Once the knife was fully inserted, I twisted it back and forth, shredding tendons and veins like he'd trashed Daire's hand.

Even if the man managed to get free, his hands would be useless when we were done with him.

"You can't just kidnap someone off the street and torture them. This is America; there are laws!"

"Let me get this straight," Benny stood to his full height and ran the blade of his weapon across the man's cheek, leaving a bloody red line in its wake. "You can kidnap Noble. Lock her up and threaten her because you felt entitled to what she has, and the law doesn't apply to you? But now that you're the one in danger, you're suddenly a legal expert and law-abiding citizen? Gotta love the logic the rich use." Benny waved a hand around the rusted, dank shipping container. "This isn't America. This is The Point. And the laws here do not favor weak, pathetic men like you."

Then Benny cut his ear off, and the man couldn't speak anymore. He passed out before he could see the irreparable damage done to his hands.

Once he was mauled to my satisfaction, I tossed the switchblade aside and looked over at Benny, who looked like he was enjoying himself a bit more than necessary.

When he caught my inquisitive look, he shrugged and wiped the blade off on his pants. "It's been a long time since I was able to get back to my roots. You'll see once you settle down. The part of you that wants payback and thrives on street justice gets restless occasionally. It's best not to ignore it." He pointed to the door of the shipping container. "There aren't any feral pigs in The Point. Finishing this off and cleaning up the mess takes a little more work than it does at the farm. Go clean up and get back to the hospital, back to your girl. I got it from here. I promise he won't be a problem for anyone else."

I looked at the blood on my hands and the pool on the ground under the captive man. This was a life I thought I could leave behind, but it seemed bound to follow me. I guess all I could do was make peace with it.

"Did you show up here to help me or because you were itching to get your hands dirty?" I stepped back as Benny kicked the man onto his back. The metal reverberated when the chair slammed on the base of the container.

"A little bit of both." He gave me a serious look and said, "Mostly, I knew you would go after this guy regardless of whether Race gave the okay. You're a tough kid, Campbell. You know a lot, and your survival instincts are unmatched, but there are some enemies it takes work to win against. Race is one of them."

"So, you're here in case he decides to kill me."

He chuckled and gave me a wink. "Something like that. For what it's worth, I think he won't start shit with you to avoid going to war with Karsen. But he's an unpredictable bastard. It's always better to be prepared for the worst around him."

"I'll keep that in mind." I opened the shipping container and stepped back into the real world. As soon as the fading sun hit me, I felt like I was walking into a different life. I was a different man. I was instantly able to shed the skin of the killer Benny raised and transform back into the man Daire liked.

I went to the rundown motel on the outskirts of The Point where I'd been staying. The kid who ran it had candy-colored hair and didn't blink when I showed up covered in blood with murder in my eyes. Daire's family offered me a room in the hotel near the hospital, but I needed to come and go without too many eyes on me while I took care of business. Plus, Daire was supposed to be released in a few days, and her family was taking her back to Denver for a follow-up with a hand specialist and physical therapy.

Her apprenticeship was on hold indefinitely, and the cat was out of the bag. She had to come clean when she asked her dad to explain to Cable why she never made it in for her first day. Cable had also suffered a terrible hand injury when he was younger, so he was unbelievably understanding. He promised Daire, and her dad, the invitation for the three-week trial was open after she healed. He told her to practice drawing with her left hand, just in case. Despite everything, she seemed determined to pursue school and training in San Francisco. She'd even managed to befriend Noble Sanders since they were on the same floor of the hospital.

Daire was truly remarkable and shockingly resilient.

When I returned to the hospital, Daire's mom and dad were in the room with her, and her brother was waiting in the visitor's area.

He gave me a once-over when I sat beside him but said nothing. There was no need to discuss what took place in that shipping container. That part of my life had nothing to do with the Archers, and I wanted to keep it that way.

"How is she?" I kept my voice calm even though I didn't feel that way inside.

"Still out of it from the painkillers. She kept saying that she understood why I pushed her out of the way of that car and took the hit instead of her. No matter how upset my mom is, Daire insists she would risk her neck again if she felt it was the right thing to do. My mom is going to have a heart attack."

"Daire has a big heart, and she's brave as hell. That's a troublesome combination."

Ry sighed and closed his eyes as he rested his head on the wall behind us. "It is troublesome. I watched out for her for as long as I could; now it's up to you. You've got to protect her from herself because you're the one she picked. You're the one she's going to listen to from here on out." He grunted and turned his head to look at me. "I didn't understand what she saw in you until she got hurt. Even though you weren't here to keep her safe, she has full confidence that whomever hurt her will never be able to hurt anyone again. She's always had a bit of a vicious streak."

"I like her when she's vicious, and I like her when she's kind. I like all the different sides of her."

"That's how I know she really wants to be with you. She's shown you more than her fake princess persona." Ry sighed again. "I can't say I think you and I will ever be friends, Campbell, but I hope we can respect each other. And I'd like to know a little bit more about your past if you're ever comfortable enough to share it."

As Daire's parents entered the room, I stood up and told her brother, "You nearly lost your life to save your sister. You've always had my respect, Archer." As for my past, that was better left unsaid for now. Maybe if Daire and I ever got married and had kids, I would feel comfortable telling Ry who I'd been. It wasn't like they could kick me out of the family at that point.

"Daire is asking for you." Her mom gave me a look and grabbed her husband's hand. "She's not making much sense at the moment, and the painkillers are more than likely gonna knock her out, so be quick."

I still had a long way to go if I wanted to win over her mom. On the other hand, her father gave me a look similar to her brother's. They didn't want to ask questions that might lead to problems, but they understood I wouldn't let anyone hurt Daire and walk away unscathed. It was similar to the way I trusted Vernon and Harlen to do whatever needed to be done to keep my siblings safe and happy.

Daire looked small and fragile in the hospital bed when I entered the room. Her right arm was wrapped up like a mummy from shoulder to fingertips, and her left hand was crowded with tubes and wires. Her eyes were glassy when they landed on me, but a faint smile touched her pale and bloodless lips.

"Hey, Princess. You're looking a little rough these days." I sat beside the bed and placed her left hand over mine. She was very cold and weak.

"I don't feel like a princess. I feel like a pincushion."

Her right hand was currently held together with pins and screws and metal rods. She was close to being bionic, and it wasn't clear if she would need more operations in the future.

I rubbed my thumb along hers and let out a deep breath. She was safe, that was all that mattered.

I noticed her eyes tear up and her bottom lip tremble. I leaned closer and brushed my knuckles against her soft cheek. Her skin felt like ice.

"I'm really scared, Campbell. What if I can't use my hand at all in the future? What am I going to do?" She sniffed loudly as the tears tripped over her bottom lashes. "I never got the chance to add some color to you."

I caught her tears on my fingertips and quietly assured her, "You can be scared. I'll be strong for you like you were when I thought Delta was missing. And I'm not going anywhere. You have plenty of time to add color to my life. Whatever the future holds, we'll figure it out together. One day at a time, remember. Right now, just focus on getting better."

I knew she was going to crash eventually. Once the reality of her actions sank in and the hard truth was left to deal with, she would be overwhelmed. Just like she'd been after the previous accident. She was already riddled with cracks. It was a wonder she didn't shatter into a million pieces upon impact.

She sniffed again, and her blurry eyes locked on my face. She used her left hand to briefly touch my cheek and whispered, "What if I don't like you anymore, Campbell?"

I stiffened for a second before I remembered she was more than likely talking nonsense because of the heavy-duty drugs. "That's okay. I like you enough to make up for it."

She sighed sleepily, and her watery eyes drifted closed. "That's nice, but that's not what I meant."

I leaned over the edge of the bed to kiss her forehead. She was always so lively and animated. I hated seeing her so still and sickly. It made me wish I had stayed behind with Benny and taken care of the clean-up myself. "What do you mean?"

"I don't like you anymore because I love you. Thank you for taking care of that awful man for me, even if it was my own fault I got hurt."

I touched my forehead to hers and lightly squeezed her fingers. "I don't love that you keep getting injured, but I do love that you aren't afraid to stick your neck out to help someone in danger. I love all the things that make you *you*, Daire."

"That's nice. I'm sleepy." She yawned and shifted uncomfortably on the hospital bed.

I laughed at myself and sat back to watch her drift off.

Of course, the one time in my life I was honest with someone about my feelings and told them I was in love with them, they passed out right after. It was oddly fitting.

"It is nice."

To love and be loved might be the best feeling in the world. And I knew as a guy who came from Nowhere, I was extremely lucky to have the opportunity to experience love because all I knew before Daire was hate.

I still hadn't found Waldo, but I had found the girl who loved me and my dark side.

She was priceless and irreplaceable.

I would do whatever it took to keep her safe and make sure she was happy. I would be whomever she needed me to be. And God help anyone who tried to get between us.

Race told me no one could rule forever, and he was right. Maybe the best way to keep Daire out of trouble was to promote her from princess to queen. She would look good with a broken kingdom at her feet.

EPILOGUE

Six months later
Campbell

~ *Come find me!*

That was the text message waiting for me as soon as I exited the plane in San Francisco.

Daire was supposed to meet me and take me to where she was living, but she was nowhere to be seen. She'd been in the Bay Area for the last three months and was getting ready to start school. We hadn't seen each other since I helped her pack up and move all her belongings from Denver to San Francisco. Her hand had still been a mess, so she could barely lift anything.

Against her mother's and the hand specialists' advice, Daire was determined to start school. She said she needed the challenge and the opportunity to see how much she could do with her injured hand while relying on her left hand. As always, she was stubborn, so no one was going to stop her. That daring, and reckless streak that always led her to trouble was alive and well. Sometimes it felt like she hadn't learned anything through all the tough life lessons she'd experienced lately. It could be frustrating since I worried about her. But when I remembered how mean she was to herself, and how badly she beat herself up over the same type of behavior in the past, watching her embrace herself, faults and all, it was a relief. I was going to be there to watch her back.

So, who cared how much trouble she decided to cause? I planned to take care of her no matter how hot the water she waded in ended up being. She wouldn't be Daire Archer, or the woman I fell for, if she wasn't a handful. There was a sense of security in knowing there weren't many who could walk in my shoes and take on the challenge that was loving a woman like Daire. You had to be tough if you were going to be with a girl who lived up to her name, both first and last, in every sense of the word.

In true Daire fashion, she was thriving in her new environment and making great strides in her recovery. Maybe it was not having her mom micromanaging her, or the fact she was alone and could focus on herself. Whatever the reason, she was healing quickly and had an optimistic outlook on the future. Even if her decision to focus on herself often left those loved her feeling left in the cold, there was no denying, her choices often worked out in her favor. Sometimes I envied her absolute fearlessness. I was impressed by her ability to put herself first when she needed to. It was a skill I needed to learn from her.

The message was cryptic but not concerning. I knew Daire had moved in with Noble as soon as she came back to California, and since school hadn't started yet, she could only be at the Victorian house or the tattoo shop.

Even though she couldn't start her apprenticeship yet, Cable offered to teach Daire how he adjusted to continue making art after he destroyed his dominant hand. He became her mentor, and even treated her like part of his crew now that she was there all the time. He was nicer and more sympathetic to her once she showed him that she wasn't going to let the horrific injury slow her down. She was certain Cable checked in with her dad daily to let him know what she was up to, but it didn't bother her as long as he continued to take her under his wing. He even had his wife, who was a doctor, keep an eye on how Daire's hand was healing, which went above and beyond.

While I could use the process of elimination to track her down, I went the easy route and pulled up the GPS tracking app attached to the tag she carried with her still. I was surprised to see she wasn't in either of the places I assumed, and instead seemed to be waiting for me at Golden Gate Park.

It was one of the few spots in the area I liked. The view was amazing, and the sound of the water was soothing. The park was a spot we frequented several times during the visit when I moved her in. I would've come to see her more often, but my stupid fear of flying and Hyde's increasingly busy schedule made it difficult. My boss seemed to work out of town more than at home. He'd already offered to extend my contract for another year, but I declined. It was a sweet gig, one I was sad to see go, but I had other priorities now. Once my time with him and Hollyn was up, I was going to spend some time with my siblings, then relocate to be closer to Daire.

I learned I could do the long-distance thing, if need be, but I didn't want to.

I wanted to be with her, especially since it seemed like she inched closer and closer to the edge of The Point every time I turned around.

So far, Race was laying low. But I owed him a favor he could collect at any time, which made me incredibly nervous. The situation felt like a powder keg ready to blow. When it did, I didn't want Daire in the blast range on her own.

I picked up the rental car, tossed my stuff in the back seat, and made my way down the coast to the park. It took a while with traffic, but the little blinking light never moved, indicating she was still waiting. I found a spot to park, paid a small fortune to leave the car, then walked along the winding path until I reached a point where both the beach and the bridge were visible. Daire was sitting on an outcropping of rocks with a tablet braced on her lap. She seemed to be drawing something, but occasionally would lift her head and look around as if searching for something... or someone.

It was me.

She was looking for me. And I made sure she could find me. It was a promise I planned to keep as long as we were together.

Her long hair blew out behind her like a veil, and her cheeks and nose were sunburned pink. Her eyes glittered when she caught sight of me, and she clamored to her feet. I hadn't seen her look this at ease or carefree since I met her. She'd really come into her own as the princess of chaos.

She held the tablet to her chest with her injured hand and threw the other around my neck to pull me down for a kiss. It was a warm welcome, and I could feel she missed me as badly as I missed her with every brush of her lips and glide of her tongue. We broke apart when some nearby teenagers started clapping and whistling. Daire laughed and pulled me over to the spot where she'd been drawing.

"I'm so happy you're here. I missed you." Daire's voice was soft and sweet, but her gaze was hot, and the way she kept licking her lips made my dick remember exactly how long it'd been since I was inside of her.

"I missed you too." I pushed her tangled hair away from her flushed face. She was still the prettiest girl I had ever laid eyes on, but that barely scratched the surface of all the things I loved about her. "It's hot out here. Why didn't you meet me at the airport?" I selfishly wanted to see her as quickly as possible.

She tucked her head under my chin and wrapped her free arm around my waist. "Because I've been working on a present I want to give you, and I wasn't done yet. It gets so frustrating trying to do something with my left hand that was so simple with my right. I kept messing it up, so I came out here to calm down. I was suddenly inspired and decided not to give up or get mad at myself for struggling to do something that is really hard. I was worried I wouldn't finish it in time if I left."

I chuckled and put an arm around her shoulders to hold her closer. "You don't have to give me anything. I get to have you, and that's more than enough."

She snorted against the base of my throat, but I felt her hands tighten at the back of my shirt. "You're very hard to handle when you decide to be sweet." She stepped back and gave me a bright look and a wide smile. "All the birthdays you missed, all the Christmases that went ignored; I know they don't mean anything to you, but I hate that you had all those good memories stolen from you. I wanted to give you something to make up for everything you lost. I've been working on it since I got out of the hospital. Some days, it was the only thing keeping me going during therapy. Both types."

She was doing physical therapy for her hand mobility and seeing someone for her panic disorder and depression. She was putting a whole lot of work into herself, so I could only do the same. The difference was that she was trying to become a better person, and I'd yet to decide if I wanted to be better or worse. Being the biggest threat still seemed like it was my best option.

Daire flipped the tablet around and showed me. On the screen was the name 'Archer.' Not surprising, since she took so much pride in her family. It was a delicate design, with fine lines and gothic filigree. Dark blues and purples were woven throughout, making it colorful but still dark. It was a stunning design, and it was impressive that she pulled it off with her non-dominant hand.

"What do you think?" She sounded hopeful; I was glad I didn't have to lie to her.

"It looks great, Daire. Is that the first tattoo you've designed entirely with your left hand?"

She nodded, and her eyes shone mischievously. "It is. It's also my gift to you."

I blinked and looked at her in confusion. Did she want me to get her name tattooed on me? Didn't she know that was a total jinx to a relationship? She was more familiar with tattoo culture than I was, and this seemed so out of character for her. I'd hoped she was simply showing me a design she was proud of, not asking for this level of commitment.

"Uh... Daire." I needed a minute to think of a response that wouldn't hurt her feelings.

She laughed at my obvious hesitation and tapped the screen. "Not the tattoo. The name. It's my most precious thing, and I want to share it with you, Campbell. You don't have a real name, but you can use mine. I'd be honored if you would take it."

I grabbed the tablet from her and stared at the drawing, which was so much more than that. I'd never legally changed my name because it didn't matter to me, but the idea of adding hers to mine to be a complete person felt oddly right.

"What does your family think of this?" I lifted my eyebrows in question, because while her brother and I may have found some common ground, her parents still weren't my biggest fans.

She shrugged. "They don't understand because they don't know about Nowhere. I told my mom you would have to take my last name if we ever got married anyway. They'll come around. Ry honestly seemed impressed I came up with the idea on my own. He called it a grand gesture. If this makes you uncomfortable, if you think it's too much, it can wait until you're ready. I just wanted to give you something no one else could. I wanted to give you something that shows you how much you mean to me and proves that I'm not going anywhere. No matter what."

I grabbed her chin and lifted her head to meet my kiss. This time I didn't stop even when the other tourists around us started to make noise. I wished she had waited until we were at her new home to offer me the most thoughtful thing anyone ever had because I wanted to take her to bed. Now! Not for a distraction or to vent my anger, but for a celebration and to show her my appreciation.

When I pulled back, I was hard, and we were both panting.

"We should go before we embarrass ourselves." She laughed and hooked her arm through my elbow as we made our way back to the rental car.

"Aren't you worried I might ruin your name if you give it to me?" She knew how gritty and rough my past was. And neither of us knew how down and dirty the future might be. If I took on tigers and dragons, there was bound to be blood, and her name would be stained with it.

"No. You'll take care of it like you've taken care of me. It's a strong name. It's resilient and loyal. You're part of something bigger and better than yourself when you're an Archer. It's a name that suits you if you want it, Campbell."

"I want it."

Maybe not right now because I was overwhelmed and flooded with foreign feelings. But once my heart stopped racing and my mind quit building fantasies of the future, I could rationally decide what becoming an Archer meant.

I kissed her on the side of her head and held her good hand on the way to the car. On the way to the ritzy neighborhood, she pointed out the local places she'd been visiting and told me about getting ready for school. She and Noble got along great, and I appreciated that they were both being hypervigilant after the attack. Noble's parents also made it a point to keep a close eye on the girls, which would've made me breathe easier if her father didn't have iron-clad ties to The Point.

I parked the rental in the driveway and made out with Daire for ten minutes before we got out of the car. I wanted to eat her alive even before she offered to share her name with me. Now, I wanted to imbed myself so deep inside her, she would feel me for an eternity.

I sent her inside, telling her that I needed to get my luggage. Hyde had taken three weeks off work so he could take Remy and Hollyn on a trip. That meant I packed for an extended trip and not the usual quickie. I rented the car because Daire wanted to see more of California before classes started. We were going to see the redwoods and then drive down the coast all the way to Baja. I was getting better at being on vacation as long as I was with her.

As soon as Daire disappeared into the house on the massive hill, I walked down the driveway and crossed the street to the black sports car waiting at the curb. With a heavy sigh, I opened the passenger door and slid onto the imported leather seat.

"Race."

"Campbell."

I leaned my head on the back of the seat and looked at the other man through narrowed eyes. "My plane landed not that long ago. Should I be concerned you're visiting so soon?"

Race grinned and tapped his fingers on the steering wheel. "You're a smart man, Campbell. I think you know you should always be concerned when you're in my backyard."

I grunted and crossed my arms over my chest. "I know I owe you one. If you've come to collect, just tell me what it is." Regardless of what this man might want from me, I couldn't say no. I hated feeling like a bug he could crush at any moment. Whenever I was around him, I thought more and more about what it would be like if he was afraid of me.

"This is just a friendly visit. I know Noble's parents and promised her dad I would check in periodically. I watched her grow up. But while I was waiting for you to arrive, something occurred to me, and I wanted to run it by you." He turned to look at me, and I could practically see the wheels turning in his head. "The kids who grow up in The Point have it rough. Sometimes they're protected, and sometimes they aren't. Sometimes the people doing the protecting end up being more dangerous to the child than any other threat." I knew he was talking about Booker and Karsen, but I refused to engage in that pointed topic. "You did a great job with my niece and nephew. Since it seems increasingly certain that you will move close to my city, how would you like to work for me and train a special group of men focused on keeping our kids safe? I feel it's a niche career opportunity tailored for you."

I swore and reached up to rub my scar. "If I say no, will you make it the favor I owe you?" Talk about being backed into a corner.

Race chuckled. "Maybe. Turn down the offer, and we'll go from there."

"I can't commit to anything right now. Once I make the move, we can have this conversation. I'm on vacation now, and unless you're calling in your marker, I don't want to see you or your men anywhere near me or my girl."

"Fair enough. Our fates feel intertwined, Campbell. I can't tell if that's a good or bad thing as of yet."

I couldn't tell either, but now wasn't the time to find out.

I got out of the car and walked back to the rental. I was pulling out my stuffed duffel bag and imagining all the things I could do with Daire to christen her new bed when she came flying out of the house, her eyes wild and her expression full of panic.

"We need to get to LA right now!"

I dropped the duffle bag on the ground and looked at her in confusion. LA wasn't on our list of places to see, and we weren't supposed to leave for a few days.

"What's going on?"

With her damaged hand, Daire reached for the heavy bag, and I immediately moved to intercept her. She grabbed the front of my shirt, and I could see tears well up in her neon eyes.

"Zowen was just arrested for murder."

I didn't know much about her elusive computer wiz cousin, but I did know when one Archer was in trouble, they all rode to the rescue.

Since I would be an Archer sooner rather than later, I had to get involved whether I wanted to or not.

I smoothed a hand along her hair and touched my forehead to hers. "Okay. Let's get to LA."

One thing I knew for certain, though, was that life was never boring or predictable when the Archers were involved.

Zowen and Aston's book;
Wayward Son, coming soonish...

NOTE

The first thing I'm going to tell you in this longer Author's Note is where you can find all the characters mentioned throughout this book, if you are interested in reading more about them.

~ Benny and Echo - Avenged
~ Booker and Karsen and Campbell - Respect
~ Harlen and Vernon - Goldilocks
~ Race - Better When He's Bold
~ Cable - Recovered
~ Noble - Downfall

The second thing I want to do is thank everyone who is reading this for being so patient while waiting for this book. The original release date was October of 2022. It's been over a year since my last publication, and this was the longest hiatus I've taken from writing in over a decade. I only planned on taking a break for two months, but time slipped away from me. My real life became increasingly complicated, and I convinced myself I was going to die when some serious health issues cropped up. It was a very unpleasant downward spiral.

In hindsight, I think I was dealing with a pretty textbook case of clinical depression brought on by the medication for one of those things I was sure was gonna take me out. Getting out of bed felt too hard some days; any minor inconvenience was enough to derail my emotions for days. I'm typically a self-aware human, but I guess when you're in the middle of something like that, you can't see yourself clearly, let alone the rest of the world.

I didn't die. I got puppies. And I started writing again when I was sure I would never be able to create another book in my lifetime. I'm so happy to be here and to share this book with you. And I'm eternally grateful to those who waited, and for the fact my readers are unbelievably kind and understanding.

Thankfully, I didn't get a nasty gram or email demanding to know where this book was. That would've been an added hurdle to what I was already dealing with. I don't know if I could've cleared it.

Now onto my notes about the actual book!

I had a lot of fun writing this one. I knew from the start I wanted to write a Marked Men/Point crossover when I started working on the kids' stories. And, as I mentioned at the beginning of this book, I specifically introduced Campbell at the end of *Respect* to write him as a hero (anti-hero) in the second-gen series. The more I got to know Daire in the *Forever Marked* books, the more I knew she needed a special story. She's such a cool girl and such a force to be reckoned with; I knew I needed to take her out of the comfort of Denver and put her to the test. I knew she needed someone who would challenge her, and I wanted the kids from Denver to have connections to others aside from the people they grew up with and had known all their lives. It was interesting to me to see if Daire could survive a guy like Campbell and fit into his world. And could he learn to love a girl like her? Having them bounce back and forth between his world and hers was such a great opportunity to meld my many worlds together; I couldn't pass it up.

Some readers may think I spent too much time on other characters and in other locations, and that's a valid critique. I'm aware I leaned more heavily on character connections outside of the family units in this book. However, that was the only way I stayed interested in telling this story, and I wasn't going to risk another writer's block or creative crash to give certain beloved characters more time on the page. For whatever reason, this was the only book I could write. I hope the majority has as much fun with it as I did.

Another thing I'm sure some will point out is the impossibility of all the connections and impossibility of these people knowing or interacting with one another. It is admittedly far-fetched.

When I write, be it a series or a standalone, I always see each book by how it connects to the rest of the overall world I've written. Think of the MCU, only it's the JCU! Each individual piece is part of a larger puzzle in my mind; there are only a couple of degrees of separation between the sets of characters. I also set all my books in places I've been or base the places on real locations I'm familiar with, so that narrows down the world even more. The likelihood of all these interaction points is much more probable when you see things from my perspective. As I said, I hope most folks have fun connecting the dots and running into all the familiar faces every few chapters.

And big shout out to everyone who wants to punch Race in the face by the end of the book! He's still one of the best villains in Romancelandia and never gets enough credit for being truly diabolical and awful. He's an underrated bad guy, and I hope Campbell teaches him a lesson!

Now that Daire's book is done, I plan to jump into Zowen's book quickly.

The question will follow: *how many more books will there be in this series?*

The truth is, I don't have solid plans past Zowen's book. There has been less interest in the second-gen than I hoped. For business and personal reasons, I only invest money in books that are profitable. I never say *never* on any idea, but after *Wayward Son*, I will definitely move on to something else.

And now, for the news that probably should've been my opener. If you're a long-time reader, you more than likely found me through *Rule*. If so, I'm excited to announce that my most beloved book, *Rule*, is being adapted into a movie by Voltage Pictures! It's so exciting.

I can't believe that Rule and Shaw are coming to the big screen ten years after release, sometime in 2024.

Rule will be played by Chase Stokes and Sydney Taylor will play Shaw. And my favorite part is that the film was directed by romance movie legend Nick Cassavetes. He was the man behind *The Notebook*.

If the movie does well, they plan to adapt the rest of the *Marked Men* series as a connected universe, just like the books. Again, THE JCU! I might have my own cinematic romance universe. It's special.

For all the updated movie info, you can check my website and follow the official Marked Men social media pages.

https://www.jaycrownover.com/markedmenmovie
#markedmenmovie
Instagram: @MarkedMenMovie
Twitter: @MarkedMenMovie
Facebook: @MarkedMenMovie
TikTok: @MarkedMenMovie

I hope you know how much this author appreciates you. For waiting. For reading. For reviewing. For your time. For interacting. For your encouragement and support. After ten years, I still feel incredibly lucky and grateful every day when I realize reading and writing romance is my actual job. Teenage me, who lost her mind over her first Sandra Brown book and begged her mom to buy her Nora Roberts novels, would be astonished that she made it this far and remains able to support herself by writing books in her favorite genre.

ACKNOWLEDGEMENTS

As I mentioned, I want to thank all the readers who have been waiting on this book. I know it took a lot longer than it should've. I appreciate your patience.

This time around a huge chunk of my gratitude goes to my technical team. I mean, I'm always super thankful to have them working on my books, but with this book I leaned on them all much more heavily than in the past. Writing a book is not like riding a bike. If you take time away from it, and the whole market has changed in the process, jumping back in is daunting. There is also the added head-fuckery and crippling self-doubt that comes with wondering if your readers are still going to be there after such a long break. It's rough. But all the folks behind the scenes made sure this book could hold its own and that it would shine for those who did wait for it.

Shoutout to my beta team: Pam, Sarah, Teri, Kelly, Alexandra, Cheron, and my assistant Melissa. They made sure this book came together seamlessly, which was no easy task since it combined two BIG series with many characters and settings. They also had to deal with missing paragraphs and chopped up sentences because I was writing while trying to wrangle two new puppies.

My rough drafts are always ugly, but this one was a monster. (Kind of on brand for Campbell and Daire, tbh.) I'm so grateful they offer their time and talent to help me get the best book out to my readers as possible. If you think they're always kind and sweet when they edit my hot messes, you're wrong. These ladies spare no feelings and pull no punches when something isn't working. Of course, they are my biggest cheerleaders when I get something exceptionally right as well.

And Mel gets even more thanks for riding the waves of feast or famine with me. Whether it's a huge dry spell or I have one-million tasks for her to complete in a minuscule amount of time, she takes it all in stride and matches my needs perfectly. We're coming up on close to a decade of friendship, and being co-workers, which I think is a testament to how valuable she is in both my professional and personal life.

As for the rest of my technical team, I'm sure you've noticed I always work with the same people on my self-published titles. That's because they always come through, and I believe they are worth every penny. They've helped keep my books and brand professional and consistent for over twenty-ish different titles. Hang comes through with perfect covers based of my vague wants and needs. Elaine makes sure the story flows and gets my underlying message across. She even reminds me that no one, even in romancelandia, needs a six-thousand-word sex scene...lol. We might not always see eye to eye on some of her changes, but my books have never suffered for it. Beth is the BEST copy editor (editor, in general). I wish I had her to fix up all my titles from the very start. She's taught me so much over the years. I know for a fact my technical skills now put my early writing to shame. She also lets me drag her to see K-pop with me, so even if I didn't love working with her professionally, I would love her for her friendship sacrifices. I don't think I've ever officially thanked Wander and Andrey for always being a breeze to work with when it comes to finding the perfect guy to go on the cover of my books. Wander is so talented and such a kind man. (His whole team is really great.) I know there are very few spot-on cover models, but I feel Wander always gets it close enough. And if you wonder if inflation has hit the hot boy market...woo-boy...lemme tell you, buying a picture for your cover is the same as paying a mortgage, so the image better be worth the investment, and Wander's always are.

Just...thank you to everyone who helps me keep being able to do what I do, even when it is really really fucking difficult. You're the bees' knees.

Marked Men Series:
https://www.jaycrownover.com/markedmenseries

Saints of Denver Series:
https://www.jaycrownover.com/saintsofdenver

Forever Marked Series:
https://www.jaycrownover.com/forever-marked

Welcome to the Point Series:
https://www.jaycrownover.com/welcometothepoint

Breaking Point Series:
https://www.jaycrownover.com/thebreakinpoint

Getaway Series:
https://www.jaycrownover.com/thegetawayseries

Loveless Series:
https://www.jaycrownover.com/lovelesstexas

Standalone Books:
https://www.jaycrownover.com/standalones

about the AUTHOR

Jay Crownover is the international and multiple *New York Times* and *USA Today* bestselling author of the *Marked Men* series, the *Saints of Denver* series, the *Forever Marked* series, the *Point* series, the *Breaking Point* series, the *Getaway* series, and the *Loveless, Texas* series. Her books have been translated into many different languages around the world. She is a tattooed gal with very colorful hair who happily calls Colorado home. She lives at the base of the Rockies with her awesome dogs. She can frequently be found enjoying a cold beer and taco Tuesdays. And if you haven't heard the news, Jay's first book, *Rule*, is being adapted into a movie by Voltage Pictures. It'll be out in 2024!

Below is a list of all the places you can find me:
Reader Group: Facebook.com/
groups/crownoverscrowd
Bookbub: bookbub.com/authors/jay-crownover
Website: jaycrownover.com
My store: shop.spreadshirt.com/100036557
FB page: Facebook.com/AuthorJayCrownover

Twitter: twitter.com/jaycrownover
Tiktok: tiktok.com/@jaycrownover
Instagram: instagram.com/jay.crownover
Pinterest: pinterest.com/jaycrownover
Spotify and Snapchat: Jay Crownover
Email: JayCrownover@gmail.com

Milton Keynes UK
Ingram Content Group UK Ltd.
UKHW020200230823
427286UK00016B/577